DEFENSIVE ZONE

CHICAGO THUNDER HOCKEY

JODI OLIVER

Cover Design by Kari March Designs

Photography by Wander Aguiar

Editing by Leticia's Edits

Proofread by Lori Parks and Rachel Rumble

Content Warning: on page head injury, post-traumatic amnesia, post-concussion syndrome, wrist fracture.

Author's Note

When I first created the Chicago Thunder universe, I knew I wanted it to be a queer normative world. A place where there is no homophobia or fear, especially within sports. Sadly, reality isn't as inclusive as it is within the Thunder-verse, but I can only hope that one day it *will* become a reality. That one day, athletes, team personnel and fans can be their true, authentic selves, and to live and love without fear or judgment.

Also, while I have tried to stay as true to the subject touched on in Zach's journey, not all athletes are as lucky as Zach. In order to stay within the 'low angst' vibe this series is known for, I've had to keep things more on the lighter side than what could happen.

(I've tried to write this as spoiler free as possible, but if you do need content warnings, please refer to the Copyright page.)

As always, this is a fictional universe and I have taken some creative liabilities. Enjoy!

Dedication

Becca and Rachel, this one is for you. Thank you for believing in me, when I didn't believe in myself.

Prologue

December - nine years ago

Zach

"Come on, Reid!"

A heavy sigh escapes my lips, but it's quickly followed by a smile. I'm unable to take my eyes off my best friend as he attempts to do the Cha Cha Slide in the middle of the living room. *Attempt* being the key word here, because while everyone goes left, Carter goes right. When they go back, he goes forward. It's a good thing he can read plays on the field; otherwise, his football career would be a disaster.

He lifts his hand, waving me over to join in, but I shake my head. I'm happy watching from the sidelines, where I have a quick escape route if it becomes too crowded. Don't get me wrong, I like parties. I'm in college, it's kinda mandatory to attend a frat party or ten, especially because I'm on the hockey team at one of the best Division I universities in the NCAA. Apparently, having your name on a roster makes you a *somebody* and gives you an open invitation to every party. The part I don't like is the sheer amount of people that attend these things. Throw in the fact Carter is on the football team too, and once you combine both the hockey and football teams, you have fifty plus dudes being testosterone-filled hounds.

And that's not even accounting for the other sports teams that come along and everyone who wants to be in attendance.

So, unlike Carter, who likes to be in the midst of it, I like to hover around the door or stay outside if it's fairer weather. Tonight, however, I have no escape except for my room, but I've already been told the host disappearing before midnight is frowned upon.

Yep, that's right. Tonight's New Year's Eve party is at our house.

Great.

When my roommates brought up the idea of hosting a party here, I should have nipped it in the bud there and then. Maybe I should have suggested they went for it while I got a hotel room somewhere and ate a pizza in bed in my underwear. But one look at the excitement on my best friend's face, and I crumbled like a house of cards in a light breeze.

I'll do anything for Carter Lockwood, even if it means breaking our ten-year-old New Year's ritual of watching *Return of the Jedi* at two minutes past ten so the Death Star explodes exactly as the clock strikes midnight.

If that isn't friendship, I don't know what is.

The song ends, and Carter makes his way over to me,

his smile bright and warm. There's a fine sheen of sweat on his forehead, and my fingers twitch with the urge to wipe it from his brow.

"I think I nailed that." He thumbs over his shoulder to where people are now dancing to some R&B track.

I arch a brow. "You did something all right. I wouldn't quite put it down as *nailed,* but a solid C for effort," I reply and give him a thumbs-up.

"Jeez, thanks." He laughs, batting my thumb away, then jerking his head toward the kitchen. "Come on, let's go get a drink before it all disappears."

It's still early into the night, but no doubt we'll see another wave of people turn up within the next hour. I follow him through the bodies toward where we've created a makeshift bar. The invite said to bring your own beer, but we did set up a keg and some homemade fruit punch that has more than the recommended amount of rum in it. I took one sniff of it earlier and nearly hurled from the smell.

I won't be drinking any of that, that's for sure.

Picking up two Solo cups from the stack, I fill one up with beer, and as I turn back to hand it over to Carter, Paisley sidles up to him, a sweet smile on her lips.

"I didn't know you were coming," she coos with a flutter of her lashes.

"Well, I kinda live here." Carter's tone is teasing, but he still flashes her his signature flirty smile.

Paisley is a nice girl. She's in my economics class, but I can't help but glare at her over the lip of my cup as her tiny hand slides over Carter's forearm and gives it a slight squeeze. All the girls like Carter. He's a super nice guy, funny, incredibly attractive too. I don't blame them for wanting to be the lucky one who gets to spend the night with him and kiss him at midnight.

Unlucky for me, though, is the fact I want that too.

I've never told him how I feel. How I was ten years old when I first felt something different for him. That fuzzy feeling in my chest. Something that went beyond the normal measures of friendship.

My gut twists as Paisley giggles and takes a step closer to Carter, running her hand up the center of his expansive chest. She lifts herself up on her toes and motions with her fingers for him to bend down. He wraps an arm around her waist, his thumb brushing over her hip. Dark spots cloud my vision as she whispers something in his ear. I tighten my hold on the plastic cup in my hands as anger burns my chest and squeezes my ribs tight.

He's mine! I want to snarl.

But I don't. Because friends don't do that.

Instead, I try to compose myself, taking in coarse breaths through my nose.

"I would love to, Paise, but I'm spending the night with my boy here." Carter's voice snaps me out of my envied daze as he nudges my shoulder with his fist. "Did you know we've spent every New Year's together since we were six? But maybe we can hang out another time."

"Of course. Sorry. I should've known." She tries to give him a nonchalant smile, but it doesn't reach her eyes. She walks off, and Carter turns to me, none the wiser.

He rolls his eyes adoringly, clearly unaware that once again, our friendship has inadvertently cockblocked him. Does he not realize some people think we're secretly dating because he always puts me before getting laid?

Not that I'm complaining. I'm happy being the center of Carter's world alongside football, but I just hope that he knows what he's doing. Or if he doesn't, that he at least doesn't hold it against me when realization hits him.

I want him to be happy, most of all, and if that means being with someone such as Paisley, I won't stand in his way.

"You could have gone with her if you wanted." The words are like acid on my tongue, but I swallow it down.

He wraps an arm around my shoulders and knocks our cups together, the movement causing beer to spill onto his fingers. "And leave you? I don't think so. Like I said to Paisley, we've called in the new year together for fourteen years. I'm not going to stop that now."

We haven't spent a single holiday away from each other during that time, but it's soon going to come to an end after graduation, and I'm not sure how I feel about that.

"What's going to happen when we make it to the pros? We might end up in different cities."

Carter's about to open his mouth to answer when the front door swings open, letting in a blast of cold air—which is appreciated because damn, I didn't realize how hot it's gotten in here—followed by the raucous roar of more people piling into the house.

"Here comes the wave," I murmur under my breath, watching what seems like never-ending people filtering in.

There are too many people.

I wiggle my fingers as they start to tingle, and it's the telltale sign it's time to make my escape, host rules be damned. I cast a glance at Carter, and without a word, he jerks his head toward the stairs, instantly reading my thoughts. He grabs hold of my wrist as we weave through the groups of people, and I follow him up the stairs. I'm thankful that my roommates declared the upper floors off limits, so by the time we reach the third floor where both our rooms are, it's quieter. Just the dull thump of bass and the sound of my breathing.

We make it to my room and close the door behind us. Carter sighs, running a hand through his dark hair as he falls back onto my bed, his arms slumping beside him.

"This was such a fucking bad idea. I'm sorry," he apologizes, glancing up at me with his face full of sorrow.

"Hey, there's nothing to be sorry for. I knew what I was signing up for when I agreed to it."

He lifts his head, one eyebrow arched. "Yeah, which was a surprise, by the way."

"I said yes because I knew you wanted to do it." I shrug.

"You're such an idiot, you know that? You don't have to be uncomfortable just to make me happy, because it doesn't make me happy knowing you're uncomfortable." Carter rolls his eyes, but there's no annoyance there as his lips tip up in a slow smile. Shifting on the bed, he rests his head against my pillow, then opens up his arms. "Don't just stand there, bring it in."

Smiling, I kick off my shoes, and he does the same, his shoes landing on the floor with a thunk. The mattress springs groan under my weight as I press a knee onto the bed. We're both big guys, and this bed can barely support us. Slotting my shoulder against his rib cage, I rest my head on his shoulder. He wraps his arm around me, and we just lie there in contented silence as we listen to the sounds of the party.

Some might find it weird that two guys in a platonic friendship are so affectionate to one another, but we've been this way since we were six. I was out front playing hockey, my goal situated in front of the fence, when an SUV and U-Haul van pulled up in front of the house next door. The moment he climbed out the back of the car, he spotted me. His face lit up, and he ran over, a football in his hands. He demanded I play with him and told me hockey wasn't as fun as football, but he would play with me as long as I played football with him afterward. One look at his goofy grin, and I was sucked in.

Warmth spread through my chest. Something akin to pure happiness as he told me right there and then, "You're my best friend now. No backsies!"

I wasn't a very social child. The kids at school would make small talk because of my older brother, Brody, or my dad, who was an NHL superstar at the time, but they didn't want to be *my* friends. So, I preferred my own company. It was safer that way. And when I wasn't playing hockey, I would be sitting in my room, reading comics and playing video games.

The day the Lockwoods moved in was the first day someone chose *me* as their friend.

Since then, we have done everything together. We went to the same schools and spent every night together. Weekends and vacations, we were inseparable. We even made sure we got into the same college because we didn't want to be apart.

I don't want to think about what it will be like when we graduate and head to different cities. Neither of us is naïve enough to think we'll end up playing our respective sports in the same place because life doesn't work like that, but I hope the distance won't destroy our friendship.

"Do you ever think about what life will be like when we head to the pros?" I ask, giving light to the thought running through my mind.

"Sometimes," he answers, his deep rumble vibrating against my ear. "Wherever we end up, we've got to promise to always hang out whenever we're in the same city. To spend our off-seasons together. We need to go on at least one vacation together a year. We've gotta talk every day, even if it's on FaceTime while we heat up our pre-made meals. No matter what, *we* come first. We make each other our priority."

I have no doubt I will. Carter has been my priority for most of my life, but there is this inkling of doubt that when I'm not around, the distance will become more than just geographical. When he inevitably meets someone because I'll no longer be a cockblock.

"We've still got time to watch *Return of the Jedi*," he suggests with a tilt of his head, looking down at me. "Maybe we can stick to tradition after all?"

My insides light up.

"Yeah?"

He nods, smiling lazily. "Load it up, Reid."

Leaning over, I grab the TV remote from the nightstand, load up the streaming service, and find the movie. As the intro rolls, I settle back onto the bed. Carter wraps his arm around my shoulders again, threading his fingers through the hair on my crown. Whenever we lie like this, he likes to play with my hair. A few years ago, I decided to grow it to give him more to play with, as he says it's calming for him.

And I'm not going to lie, it's calming for me, too.

Placing an arm over his stomach, I snort as he begins to recite the words on the screen in a cinematic voice. A sense of peace settles between us as we watch the movie that's been our routine for ten years, occasionally echoing the words as they're spoken on screen. I'm pretty sure we could recite the entire script off the top of our heads.

We're almost two hours into the movie when Carter sits up with a groan. I roll off him and onto my back, watching as he removes his phone from his jeans pocket, tapping the screen to light it up and check the time.

"Okay, we have ten minutes until we can time it right. Let me go get some snacks, then we can bring in the new year with a bang." He grins.

I laugh, pausing the movie as he climbs over me.

"Hurry up! The Death Star has gotta explode at midnight to count!" I call out, listening to the thunder of his feet as he runs down the stairs.

I keep an eye on the time on my phone, watching as minute after minute goes by and there's no sign of him coming back.

When there's four minutes left of our timer, I get up and head downstairs. Maybe he got caught up or there's a problem. These parties never usually go without some form of altercation. But as soon as I get to the bottom of the stairs, my stomach drops. With the bag of our favorite potato chips tucked under one arm and the other placed on the wall by her head, he's chatting with Paisley, his face bright with whatever topic he's talking about. She tips her head back and laughs, and then her dainty hand is back on his chest, and his dark, hooded eyes sparkle at the move as his head gets closer to hers, and his tongue swipes over his lips. A rush of heat floods through my body, but it's not from desire.

No, it's from jealousy—and embarrassment.

I was ten years old when I fell in love with Carter Lockwood. I didn't know what it was at first—the feeling of euphoria that would take over me whenever he was around. It was only when I got older that I realized it was love, but I kept my feelings to myself in fear of losing him. Carter would talk about girls in a way that let me know he didn't feel the same way about me, and I told myself that was okay because he was still my best friend.

Tonight, our New Year's Eve ritual came to an end. I've kept my feelings squashed down for the last decade, but I guess it's time to squash them down for good.

As the only thing exploding tonight is my heart shattering into pieces as the clock strikes midnight.

Chapter One

June – present day

Carter

Sometimes, I wish I had a special power. Be a superhero or a Jedi. I could use the Force to do something good. Like making the offensive players always fumble with the ball, allowing us the easy attack, or in this instance, keeping the puck away from the back of the Thunder's net.

I would wave my hand like Obi-Wan Kenobi and say, _This is not the net you're looking for._

But I don't have any kind of superpower, and the Force isn't with me.

My heart is in my throat as I watch my best friend on the ice, his shoulders slumped in defeat. The Chicago Thunder were so close to making the Stanley Cup Finals.

So damn close.

But Los Angeles got one up on them with a sneaky goal,

making it a 4-3 win in double overtime of game seven. Shit. Even just thinking about it rips my heart in two, and I'm not the one on the ice.

Zach lines up to shake the opposing players' hands. I know he will be congratulating them and wishing them all the best in the finals, because he's a good guy like that, but me? I'm feeling bitter, and I'm kinda hoping LA will choke in the finals. I know it's bad sportsmanship to wish bad luck on a team, but still. I really wanted to see Zach and the rest of the Thunder make it to the finals.

After missing out on the Super Bowl in February, I was hoping that I could get a different kind of win this year, even if it was in the form of my best friend's team.

The crowd claps loudly in support as the Thunder players do a final lap of the ice, holding their sticks in the air in salute, before disappearing down the tunnel, and I take that as my cue to leave.

"Thanks for keeping me company," I say to Alex. He's dating the Thunder's star forward, Blaine Olsen. I've been sitting with him and his friend Nate at every game since I arrived in Chicago a few months ago.

His blue eyes are glassy with unshed tears as he turns to me. Alex is a big hockey fan, having followed the team since when he was a kid. He met Blaine at a game back in November when Blaine spilled his beer all over him during warm-ups, and I know his emotions are high right now, not just for his boyfriend but because he's a fan too.

"I don't know why this one is hitting harder. They've lost before." His voice trembles.

"Yeah, but you're on the inside now. Just because it's not

you on the ice doesn't make you any less part of the journey."

With a shaky smile, he gives me a hug. "Make sure you look after Zach."

"I will," I promise. "Same goes for you with Blaine. I'm sure we'll see you before we go on vacation. Zach will want to get his sugar fix."

He lets out a small chuckle. He runs a bakery with his brother Jacob, and Zach has been a regular customer since they opened, feeding his sweet tooth with their delicious baked goods. "I'll make sure his favorites are ready for him."

"Thanks, he'll really appreciate it."

After saying goodbye to Alex and Nate, I head up the stairs to the concourse and make my way toward the team area.

I know Zach's going to be gutted about this loss, even if he doesn't say it outright, so I'm already trying to think of ways I can cheer him up. One positive to having his season end earlier than we'd hoped is the fact we will be able to go on our vacation sooner than we'd planned. We've booked a beachfront villa in Hawaii with a private pool. The photos look incredible, and I've been daydreaming of surfing at dawn and all the incredible food we're going to eat.

Just having uninterrupted time with Zach is my favorite time of the year.

Hopefully I can get him feeling a little bit brighter if I can pull it off.

I make a quick stop at the family room to use their facilities, then I wait near the locker room. Leaning back against the concrete wall, I scroll through my phone as I wait for Zach to finish up his post-game cooldown then shower and change. Sometimes it takes ages for him to come out, especially if they've won. They like to have post-game singalongs, or, I should say, Elliot Olsen, the Thunder's goaltender, likes to partake in post-game singalongs, but I don't think there will be any singing today. I don't think they will want to stay in this arena any longer than necessary.

When Zach appears, my breath whooshes out of me in a rush. Dressed in a dark gray suit and crisp white button-down, he looks smart and handsome. I often tell him he could be a model if he ever gave up hockey. With his height and incredible body, plus he's got these icy blue eyes that look so piercing against his dark brown hair.

Without a word, I open my arms, and he steps into them, wrapping his around my waist. I hug him tight, trying to channel that special power I wanted so badly so I could alleviate his heavy feelings.

"Wanna go home?" I murmur into the side of his head.

It's not really my home, but Zach's apartment is like a second one for me.

He nods, and when he steps back, my chest clenches at the devastation in his eyes.

Fuck. I wish I could take it away. I would take it on myself if it meant he was free of it.

We're silent on the drive back to his apartment. I put on his favorite playlist, and he gazes aimlessly out the window. His silence doesn't worry me, though. He's always been quiet and kinda introverted. It's one of the things I love most about him. His calmness.

"What do you need?" I ask as we walk into his apartment twenty minutes later.

"I'm gonna take another shower and get changed," he says, fetching a bottle of water from the fridge. "Could we watch a movie after?"

I nod, knowing his habits like the back of my hand. It's been like this since he was twelve, when he came back from a tournament complaining that the showers at the rink made him feel dirtier than when he went in, so it became part of his post-game routine to shower again when he gets home.

"Do you want something to eat?"

"Yeah, that would be awesome. I'm starving."

"You got it." I turn around and get a saucepan from the cupboard and fill it with water to boil.

"Carter?"

"Yeah?" I reply, glancing over my shoulder.

He smiles tiredly, and his blue eyes shimmer with gratitude. "Thank you."

"Anytime." I wink. "Now go get in the shower and think about what movie we're going to watch."

With a nod, he heads into his bedroom, and I busy myself in the kitchen, making his favorite chicken and broccoli Alfredo and retrieving the glazed donut that I picked up from the bakery earlier from the fridge.

I'm plating up the pasta when he reappears, this time wearing his plaid sleep pants and a pullover hoodie. His dark hair is slicked back and still damp, and his pale skin is flushed pink from the hot water. I slide the bowl and a fork over the countertop with a smile.

"I've got a surprise for you."

His eyebrows lift in a silent question.

I grab the small plate with the donut from the counter behind me and hold it out to him. "I know I can't make you feel any better after that game, which, by the way, should have been yours. I call goaltender interference—" He snorts at that. "—but I can try to give you a little drop of dopamine in the shape of a donut."

His eyes soften as he looks from the donut to me, then rounds the counter to bring me in for a hug.

"Thank you for being here," he murmurs into the collar of my shirt.

I return his embrace and give him a squeeze.

"Always." I step back and point to his bowl of pasta with one hand and slap his ass with the other. "Now eat up. I'm going to get into something more comfortable. I swear denim is the devil for thick thighs."

He laughs and carries his food over to the couch.

After a quick change, I walk back into the living room and fall back onto the couch, letting out a satisfied groan as I sink into the cloud-like cushions, causing Zach to chuckle around a mouthful of food.

I watch as he demolishes the bowl of pasta in record time before getting up to put it in the dishwasher and returning with the donut.

Grabbing a cushion, I place it on my lap, then give it a pat. Zach eyes it for a beat before leaning back so he can lie with his head on the cushion. My hand goes to his hair on instinct, combing my fingers through the soft strands, occasionally using the pads of my fingers to massage his scalp. He lets out a relaxed hum, and a rush of pleasure runs through me.

"What movie are we watching?" I ask.

He takes a bite of his donut and looks up at me. "*Revenge of the Sith?*"

"Good choice." I load it up on the streaming app and settle back into the couch, continuing to idly run my fingers through his hair.

We've been glued at the hip since we were six years old, when my parents and I moved into the house next door to the Reids. The second I jumped out of the car, I saw him playing hockey, and I ran over, begging him to play football with me. I knew he was hesitant. I could see it in his light blue eyes that he wasn't quite sure what to do or say. I had pretty much bulldozed my way over to him and left him startled, like a deer caught in the headlights, but I plastered on my easygoing smile, and he soon gave in.

Right then, I told him we were going to be best friends.

We've done everything together. School. College. Spent every off-season together since we made it to the pros. This time I get with Zach is what I look forward to all year.

Don't get me wrong, I love my job. Getting to play in the NFL is the best job in the world. It was what I dreamed about since I was a kid and my dad took me to my first football game, but no wins ever come close to the happiness I feel when I'm with Zach. The five to six months we get to spend together keep me going. My girlfriends over the years never got it. They couldn't understand why I was so excited to spend time here in Chicago, even when he was on the road.

It's about moments like this. Chilling out, watching a movie, being close to my best friend. It's all I want in life.

I wish I could take away his disappointment. Take away every ounce of sadness he's feeling. I know it won't last forever, but I just want him to be happy, always.

Because he may not know this, but I would be lost without Zach Reid.

Chapter Two

Zach

I didn't know how badly I needed this vacation until we arrived three days ago.

The warm sun soothing the aches and pains that are a result of a tough season. The coarse sand between my toes reminding me that there's tranquility in this world when life has been hectic. The relaxing sound of ocean waves crashing against the shore lulling me into a peaceful sleep every night.

The uninterrupted time with Carter refills my soul.

Look at me, getting all poetic and shit.

When Carter suggested moving up our vacation the morning after we got knocked out of the playoffs, I could have kissed him. I didn't though, because you don't kiss your best friend. Especially the one you're secretly madly in love with, even if it is out of gratitude.

But Chicago was beginning to feel… suffocating. The

pitying looks I was getting anytime I left my apartment were becoming tiresome, and I knew I needed to get away for a while. I needed some space to lick my wounds in paradise before we head to Denver ahead of Carter's preseason training camp.

And paradise it is. This beachfront villa in Oahu is the perfect place to unwind. I have amazing views everywhere I look. Behind me is the ocean, where I went surfing this morning as the sun came up. Palm trees sway in the light breeze on either side of the sun lounger I'm currently lazing on. But it's the view in front of me that has the happy atoms bouncing inside my body.

Carter's lounging on an inflatable pool float, his beer wedged into the cup holder. His light brown skin glistens under the sun as it catches the water droplets that are nestled in the grooves of his sculpted chest and abs.

I haven't been able to take my eyes off him. I've had a prime view from this shaded sun lounger next to the pool, watching him swim and now sunbathe. You won't see me sunbathing though, no matter how many times he tries to convince me. I've spent far too many hours sitting in a tattoo chair to let them fade from sun exposure.

"I could live here," he announces, breaking the comfortable silence.

"Yeah?"

"Yeah! What else could I possibly want in life? The weather is amazing. This pool is awesome. I've got a beer, and there's fresh mangoes growing in the trees right over there." He points them out, then tilts his head toward me and grins. "And I've got my best friend. Like I said, what more could I want?"

His declaration stings a little. Not because it isn't true. I know without a doubt he's one hundred percent genuine when he says it, but because I know what more *I* would want.

Him.

Yeah, I have him in my life. A best friend, a confidant. But I don't *have* him—not wholly.

The crush I told myself I would get over back in college? Consider it quadrupled. It seems the years we've been apart have only caused it to grow. I'm reminded of that saying, *Distance makes the heart grow fonder.* Well, I'm very *fond* of Carter Lockwood. So much so that I've moaned his name while hooking up with another dude on more than one occasion. I felt like a complete asshole afterward. It wasn't my finest moment, but I suppose neither is having a crush on my best friend for nearly two decades.

"When we retire—"

I balk, my eyes widening behind my sunglasses, and I hold up my hand to stop him.

"Whoa, hang on! We're not even thirty yet, and you're retiring us? Do you want to jinx us and end up on IR next season?" I ask, referring to the injured reserve list. He knows we don't talk about the R-word before it's time.

"No, you jackass." He snickers, splashing me with water. "In many, *many* years to come. When we've hung up our skates and cleats, I think we should buy a house out here, and then we could come out here as often as we wanted." He sits up slightly, and those delicious abs of his tighten, making my mouth water. "We could even move here."

I swallow a few times then clear my throat. "Yeah, that sounds like a good idea."

He grins before finishing off his beer, and that sting in my chest returns. I know he isn't doing this intentionally. I know he doesn't mean to hurt me, because he doesn't know how I feel about him.

I've never told him. I never will. But like I always do, I entertain it, because that's just what I do. It's almost like I enjoy torturing myself.

Because in years to come, he's going to have a wife and kids, and I don't want to be a third wheel, watching the love of my life live his with someone else.

The next few days pass by with sun-induced naps, dips in the ocean, working out with Carter before indulging in delicious food, and exploring this beautiful island. The hike we're currently on is tough. It's humid and muddy. We weave our way through overgrown greenery, some of it so sharp that I'm glad I read the reviews before we left and opted to wear pants. My legs would be scratched within an inch of their lives if I was wearing shorts.

"Fuck!" Carter hisses. He slaps the branch away and gives it the middle finger before rubbing his arm where it scratched him. "I'm going to look like I've been in a brawl with a cheetah by the time we get back."

I snort. "Or a vicious kitten."

He flips me off over his shoulder and continues up the path. I snicker, following close behind. We stop as we make our way up the trail to take photos and drink some water when we reach certain vantage points that offer beautiful views. With it being so hot today, the last thing either of us needs is to suffer from dehydration.

Sweat drips down my back from the exertion, causing my sleeveless T-shirt to stick to my skin.

"I feel like I'm going to melt."

"Me too. I think my balls are stuck to my thigh." Carter laughs, tugging on the crotch of his hiking pants.

I suppress a groan. I really don't need to be thinking about his balls being all hot and sweaty right now. I'd do anything to nuzzle against his sac. I was already having a hard time with how good he looked in those pants. I nearly dropped to my knees and burst into tears when he turned the corner this morning and I saw how they emphasized his incredible ass and thighs.

Ugh. My cock gives an appreciative throb at the memory. Now is *not* the time to be boning up.

Think about anything else. Anything except his ass or his balls.

It should be illegal for someone to look so fucking hot. I've jerked off at least twice a day while we've been here. Seeing him practically naked, in only his short swim shorts, for nearly the entirety of the trip has made my dick be in a constant semi-hard state.

"There should be a pool up here that you're allowed to swim in. I'm definitely going for a dip when we get there," he says, completely unaware of the salacious thoughts in my brain.

When we reach another flat area, I stop and dump my backpack on the ground so I can take off my shirt. It's practically dripping with sweat. I wring it out before using it to wipe my chest and my lower back. I don't want to put my damp shirt in my bag, so I tie it to the straps, then turn to

Carter. He's peeled off his own shirt and his chest glistens with sweat. My tongue feels too big for my mouth as I ogle him behind the safety of my sunglasses.

"Can you put some sunscreen on my back?" I croak out.

He nods and retrieves the sunscreen from his bag and pours a generous amount into his palm. He runs his hands all over my back and arms in circular motions, and it takes every ounce of strength in me not to purr like a damn cat under his touch.

I'm more than capable of doing my chest and arms, but it doesn't stop him from squirting more into his hand and stepping around to do my front, grinning like an idiot as he puts some on my nose with his finger.

"You're such a dork." I laugh, rubbing it in with my hand.

"Don't want your nose burning like that time in Mexico. I'm pretty sure planes could have seen your red beacon of a nose from the sky."

"Yeah, fuck you very much." I scowl. "Someone didn't think to cover my face when I fell asleep in the hammock."

"Hey! That someone covered your body with a towel! I saved your tattoos."

"You could've saved my face too," I grumble.

He laughs and gives my nipple a flick once he's finished rubbing in the sunscreen. If I wasn't sweating like a beast right now, the move would have gone straight to my dick.

I'm about to ask him if he wants me to put any sunscreen on him when he speaks.

"Come on, let's find that pool," he says, throwing the bottle into his bag.

I let out a sigh of relief. It's not that I don't enjoy putting sunscreen on him, it's the fact I enjoy being able to run my hands over his smooth skin a little too much.

We continue on our hike, making sure to stop for regular water breaks to stay hydrated and to take more photos.

"I think we're close," I announce as I hear the sound of rushing water.

My speed picks up in excitement of cooling off in the pool. I'm already calculating whether to lose my pants or go in fully dressed. Swimming in pants won't be ideal, but it's so hot, they will dry quickly. But in my haste, I don't notice the rocks leading to the waterfall are slippery, and I lose my balance.

"Fuck!"

My arms flail as I try to stay upright. I startle as Carter's arms wrap around me tightly. The move prevents me from falling, but I end up turning around in his arms. My bare chest is pressed up against Carter's equally naked one. His hands grip my waist above the hem of my pants. My nipples brush against his as our chests heave with our panting breaths, and my dick doesn't fail to notice. Heat races down my spine, and I take a steady step back, needing to create some distance between us before he feels the evidence of my arousal.

I'm thankful he can't see my eyes behind my sunglasses because I'm sure what he would see would ruin our friendship.

I want to kiss him. Devour him with my mouth before stripping out of our clothes and seeing just how close we could get while naked in the pool.

"You've gotta be careful. I don't want to be explaining to Coach Harris why you broke your leg on vacation," Carter scolds, dumping his bag to the side and unbuttoning his pants.

I stand there for a moment, completely dumbfounded. My head is a mess from nearly falling and the weight of Carter's sweaty body pressed up against mine. The feel of being skin to skin. My cock throbs in my briefs as image after image floods my brain like a reel of us sweaty and naked in bed.

"You coming?" he asks, eyeing me curiously from the edge of the water.

My head jerks in his direction, snapping me out of the daze. He takes tentative steps into the pool, making sure he doesn't make the mistake I nearly did. He stripped down to his boxer briefs and kept his sneakers on. We both packed an extra pair of shoes and change of clothes in our bags for the trek back down.

"Y-yeah," I rasp.

I put my bag on the ground next to his and take a drink of water, giving myself some time to let my dick deflate. I run through stats and practice drills in my mind, and remind myself of the time I threw up doing bag skates and once it calms down, I take off my pants and place them neatly over our backpacks.

This time, when I step onto the rocks, I take it slow and steady. Carter is right—Coach Harris would have my head if I injured myself during the off-season.

When I'm in up to my stomach and the water reaches my belly button, I let out a shuddering breath. It's cold and refreshing and exactly what I—and my cock—needed to cool down.

I walk further in, then push off the ground and swim

over to where Carter is. He's floating on his back, arms out wide as he peers up toward the top of the waterfall. We learned a few years ago not to stand under them, no matter how tall they are, after he got hit with a falling log and cut his shoulder.

I shift to float on my back next to him, but he lunges, grabbing hold of my shoulders and dunking me under the water. I'm coughing and spluttering when I resurface.

"You just couldn't help yourself, could you?" I glare, wiping the water from my eyes.

He grins, and when he opens his mouth, I get my revenge. I dunk him under, then wrap my arms and legs around his neck and body. Our laughter bounces off the surrounding trees as we tussle, trying to get one up on the other.

Eventually, we swim to a shallower end where we can stand, the water coming up to mid-chest. I just stand there, allowing it to soothe my heated skin as I take in the stunning surroundings.

"I'm really glad I get to experience all this with you." Carter's voice is soft, almost vulnerable.

"Me too." Glancing over at him, I smile softly as an ache blooms in my chest. "There's no one else I would want to share these memories with."

Even if memories are all I'm ever going to have.

Chapter Three

Carter

Our time in Hawaii is coming to an end, and I'm not quite ready to go back to reality. These past two weeks have been a dream. There's just something about being here that I find so…peaceful. I wasn't kidding when I mentioned buying a house here when we retire. We try and visit different places each summer, but somehow, we always end up coming here. I guess in a way, in my mind at least, it's ours.

I never want to leave, but reality always comes calling.

Just not tonight, as we're going for dinner at one of our favorite steak restaurants and then going to a beachfront bar for drinks.

I adjust my watch as I wait for Zach by the front door. The location of this villa is perfect, as we're close enough to walk to the shops, bars and restaurants but far enough away that we're not in the mix of it all and we have the privacy we crave.

When Zach rounds the corner, my breath hitches slightly. Dressed in all black, the sleeves of his lightweight linen button-down are rolled up to mid-forearm, allowing his tattoos to play peekaboo. The buttons are open to the top of his abs, showing off his wide, sculpted torso, earned through dedication and hard work in the gym. His shorts fit his thick muscular thighs like a second skin, and the tattoos on his legs add a pop of color to his otherwise dark outfit.

"Damn." I let out a low whistle and fan myself with my hand. "You looking to hook up or something?"

The second the words leave my mouth, something goes weird in my chest. And not a good weird.

Huh, what's that about?

He laughs quietly. His long, shoulder-length dark hair falls around his face as he ducks his chin. I fucking love when he wears his hair down. I don't know what it is about his hair that I love so much. He has this almost Viking-esque vibe with day-old stubble lining his jaw, and the whole dark ensemble he's got going on makes his light blue eyes so striking.

My best friend is an absolute snack.

He doesn't answer though, and I'm not sure why that bothers me. It's kind of been an unspoken rule that we don't hook up with others while we're on vacation. This time is meant to be strictly ours. Two weeks of uninterrupted Carter and Zach time.

And to be honest, I don't want to share him with anyone else. I'm not ashamed to admit I'm selfish when it comes to spending time with Zach. I want to be the sole focus of his attention, and I will fight dirty if someone tries to get in the way of that.

"Ready?" he asks.

His scent fills my nose as he leans in and picks up the keys from the side table, and I can't help but take a deep inhale. He smells so fucking good. Like sandalwood, amber and cardamom. All rich and decadent, making him even more irresistible.

Ugh, get with it, Lockwood.

I can't be thinking things like this. He's my best friend.

With a smile, I nod. "As ever."

I open the door, letting him walk through before I slap my palm against his firm ass cheek. And on the entire walk to the restaurant, I try to squash this unfamiliar feeling bubbling in my chest.

A few hours later, we're people-watching while sipping on drinks in our favorite bar. I'm floating in that happy space where my stomach is satisfied from delicious food, and I've got the gentle buzz from the cold beer in my hands. The light breeze from the beach only adds to that relaxed vibe.

"She's hot." Zach's voice is quiet, but loud enough I can hear him over the music pumping throughout the bar.

Subtly looking over my shoulder, I lock eyes with the brunette sitting at the bar, watching us with keen interest. Throughout dinner, I couldn't get the idea of Zach hooking up out of my brain, and when he kept pointing out beautiful women, it only intensified. Is he trying to hint at something? Does he want me to find someone so he won't feel guilty about sneaking off with someone himself?

When I turn back to face him, I'm unable to read the

expression on his face. He brings his beer to his lips, takes a swig, then watches me with a thoughtful look.

I wish I could read his mind right now.

"You should get her number," he suggests.

"Are you trying to get rid of me?" I blurt out, letting those intrusive thoughts win.

He lets out a choked sound, then covers it with a small laugh. "No, but she's eating you up with her eyes. I wouldn't hold it against you if you wanted to go there."

My cock would love to go there, because, let's face it, she's hot as hell. But my head and my heart want to just chill with him, as we haven't got long left.

Plus, I can use my hand for a bit longer. My cock will understand.

But I don't have time to argue the point because movement in my peripheral catches my attention, and the brunette hottie from the bar sidles up next to me.

"Hey," she says with a smile. Holding a glass of white wine in her hand, she motions to the seat next to me. "Is this seat taken?"

Mentally shaking myself, I flash my most charming smile. "No, it's all yours."

She introduces herself as Raegan, and in a weird happenstance, she's from Denver. The three of us chat about our time on the island, and life back home. Although I plan on shutting down any advances, something settles in me when she engages with Zach, showing him equal interest. She isn't flirting with him as she is with me, but I appreciate her making an effort with him. Women I've dated often ignore the fact that we come as a package deal.

Because while not in the traditional sense, he's my other

half, and I would rather be single than date someone who doesn't respect that.

"I'm going to get us some drinks," Zach announces, scraping his chair back as he stands.

I look up at him, trying to find a glimpse of how he's feeling on his face, but just like earlier, those blue eyes are unreadable.

My gaze follows him to the bar, noting how the other patrons watch him as he goes. He's captivating, that's for sure, with his six-foot-six frame and muscular physique. His dominating presence draws you in, but it's his gentle calmness that hooks you.

Your friendship is unnatural.

Those were the words my last ex-girlfriend spat at me when we broke up, and it wasn't the first time I heard something along those lines either.

But how can you explain to someone you're in a relationship with that your soulmate is someone else?

"So, where in Denver do you live?"

My attention is drawn back to Raegan. She's eyeing me curiously, like I'm a puzzle she's trying to figure out.

You might be here for a while, honey.

"I've lived in Cherry Hills Village since I moved to Denver seven years ago."

Her eyes widen slightly in surprise, and I'm wondering if she even follows football. I only moved there because most of my teammates live there. "Wow, there's some beautiful homes there."

I give her a clipped nod and give myself another mental shake. I'm being rude, and that's not like me. I may be feeling completely out of sorts tonight, but it's not fair to take it out on this nice woman.

"So, what do you do?" I ask, picking up my beer.

She begins to tell me about her work and how she's here for a conference, and no matter how hard I try to pay attention, her voice ends up being tuned out as my eyes latch on to a man and woman sidling up next to Zach at the bar. Neither of them is doing anything to disguise how they are eating him up with their eyes. Zach's never hidden his bisexuality from me, and I wouldn't want him to. But tonight, my usual complacency has been replaced with something unfamiliar. That same weird sensation that I felt earlier. An emotion I've never experienced before with Zach when it comes to potential sexual partners.

Jealousy.

The man places a hand high on Zach's thigh, and my jaw actually pops from how hard I'm clenching it.

I want to go over there and swipe his hand off his leg. Bile burns my throat as the territorial feeling brews even stronger in my chest, and it's sending me off-kilter.

Who the fuck does he think he is touching him like that? Zach is *mine*, goddamnit. We're on this vacation together. To spend time together. Which I know is fucking contradictory as hell considering I'm sitting here with Raegan.

Fuck. Raegan. I completely zoned out again.

"Carter?" Her voice filters through the rage bubbling in my ears.

My head snaps to face her. There's a crease between her perfectly shaped brows. She's fucking stunning, and the frown on her face looks out of place.

"Where did you go? I just called your name like five times."

"Sorry, I spaced out."

Understatement of the century.

She gives me a pointed look, calling me out on my bullshit without having to say the words. Her eyes flick to Zach as she asks, "How close are you two?"

"He's been my best friend since we were six years old."

She hums but doesn't say anything. She takes a dainty sip of her wine, and I try to take a subtle glance over my shoulder. The couple are still with Zach, flirting up a storm. Zach angled his body toward them invitingly, spreading his legs so one bare knee is next to hers where she's sitting on the stool, and the guy is able to stand between them as well. He's interested. Really interested. The couple couldn't make it any more obvious that they want Zach to be the tasty filling in their bedroom sandwich, and I fucking hate that I want to go over there and ruin it all for him.

The sound of an empty glass clinking against the tabletop snaps my attention back. Raegan gives me a sad smile, collecting her purse and hooking it on her shoulder.

"I think I'm going to call it a night."

I open my mouth to argue, but I can't. I have nothing to say to defend my behavior. I've been lousy company. She seems like a really nice woman, and here I am, wanting to stomp my foot on the floor in a childish tantrum over my best friend flirting with someone—or should I say *someones* —else.

Scrunching up my nose slightly, I offer her what I can only hope is an apologetic smile. "I'm sorry, my mind is elsewhere tonight. Maybe we could get together back in Denver? Dinner maybe? My treat."

"Sure, that would be nice. You can make it up to me back in the city."

We exchange numbers and promise to see each other. She leans over and presses a kiss to my cheek. "See you around, Carter."

She waves her fingers at Zach as she passes. He waves his hand in return, then shoots me a concerned look. I shake my head, picking up my drink and downing what's left of it before standing up. I'm not going to ruin his night. I'll head back to the house, maybe watch a movie, and question why I'm feeling so fucking… out of sorts.

"I'm going to take off," I tell Zach once I reach the bar, thumbing over my shoulder toward the exit.

"I'll come with you." Zach goes to stand without hesitation, but I place my hand on his shoulder, pushing him back down.

"No, no. You stay." I look at the couple. Damn, they are both really hot. She's got long blonde hair tied up in a high ponytail. Petite, great tits, and a tiny waist. He's hot too, with classically handsome features. I wouldn't be surprised if I'd seen them both on a billboard, making some plain-as-fuck underwear look irresistible. "Enjoy your night."

But to my surprise, Zach shakes off my hand and stands up.

"It was really nice to meet you both," he says to the couple.

"Likewise," she purrs, placing her small hand on his forearm and giving it a gentle squeeze.

"If you're ever in Nashville, give us a call." Hot Guy

smiles, slipping a card into Zach's palm. "It would be really good to hang out sometime."

Yeah, I'll bet.

My jaw snaps shut as I glare at where his hand lingers on Zach's for a moment longer than necessary.

"Have a nice night." I force a tight smile and head out of the restaurant without checking if Zach's following. Why am I so agitated over this? The only reason he was talking to them was because I was chatting with Raegan.

Fuck, I'm such a shit friend. Cockblocking him because I'm getting a little jealous.

I don't realize how far ahead I've walked until I hear Zach calling from behind as he jogs to catch up with me.

"Carter, wait up."

I slow my steps and run a hand through my hair, letting out a shaky exhale. There's concern etched into Zach's features as he studies me.

"What happened back there? I thought you and Raegan were getting along well?"

I have no idea…

"Headache." I hate how easily the lie slips out. "We agreed to see each other when we're back in Denver."

Zach frowns. "Are you not feeling well?"

"Eh, not so much. Maybe I had too much sun today. I probably didn't drink enough water, and then the drinks…" I wave my hand in the air. It's a load of bullshit, but I can't tell him the real reason because I don't know. I don't know why I wanted to rip that dude's hand off. I don't know why I had a ball of jealousy in my stomach.

I just *don't know.*

"Let's get you back. I'll make you a drink with some electrolytes."

We're silent on the walk back to the villa. Zach keeps shooting me concerned glances. I hate that I've ruined his night. I hate that I've lied to him about feeling unwell. I hate that I'm feeling like this, all jealous and territorial.

I'm confused.

Tired.

Frustrated.

This wasn't the first time I have gotten jealous over others receiving Zach's attention, but it's the first time jealousy has entered the equation when it comes to sex.

And I don't know what to do about that.

Chapter Four

July

Zach

Carter's training camp started a week ago, and we've settled into our usual routine. He trains every day at the team facility, while I train at his home gym, then I prep us food before hanging out for the rest of the day. Denver has become my home away from home over the years, and usually I feel just as content here as I do in my apartment back in Chicago, but this year is different.

This time, I'm tense and uncomfortable.

Not long after we got back from Hawaii, Carter went on a date with Raegan. I had to pretend like I was excited for him. Hell, I was the one who urged him to talk to her when we were at that bar. But joke's on me because now they're officially *dating*, and every day I wake up and come downstairs to see her wearing nothing but his T-shirt and a satisfied smile, drinking her coffee out of *my* cup, the fracture in my heart grows bigger and bigger.

With my workout finished, I take my coffee outside and sit on one of the couches that surround a fire pit. Carter is due back any minute, and the typical excitement I would feel about his return isn't there. It's now replaced with a feeling of dread, and it's not something I've ever felt toward him.

It's not even about Raegan. She's great. She's exactly the type of woman I'd imagine him settling down with, but each time I see them caught up in a moment, it only makes the ache in my chest deepen.

And when I overheard them the other night talking about the future, something told me this might be it—Raegan might be the one who will give him the family and the two point five kids. The fact she's put up with me being here for so long has been the big difference compared to his previous girlfriends.

Carter has always fallen hard and fast, but I think this time it might be the real deal. He even said as much last week when he looked at me with bright eyes and said the five words that tore my heart in two. "I think she's the one."

But while Carter might think he's got it all, all I can hear is the timer ticking down to the end of *us* as we know it.

My phone vibrates against the cushion, snapping my brain from the negative space it had drifted off to. My teammate Elliot's name flashes on the screen and instantly lifts my spirits. If there's one person who can cheer me up, it's Elliot. Aside from Carter, Elliot's one of my closest friends.

I swipe my finger to answer and lift it to my face.

"Zach!" he hoots the second the call connects, and his face appears. "I'm so happy you answered. Dude, I've missed you. I was at the park earlier playing Pokémon Go, and I was just sitting there deciding where to grab some lunch. I couldn't decide if I wanted a pasta salad or a sandwich, and then it just hit me that you're not gonna be here for my birthday party tonight, and I was just like, *dude,* that's not acceptable! So, what have I gotta do to make you come home already?"

His words come out in a rush, then he lets out a gasping breath before sticking his bottom lip out in a comical pout. I can't stop the laugh that bubbles in my throat at his put-out expression. Elliot is one of a kind. He has the ability to make you laugh without even trying.

It's been playing on my mind that it's the twins' birthday today. I don't usually get to celebrate with them as it coincides with when I'm here in Denver, but this year, Blaine's boyfriend Alex is hosting a party for them, and guilt has been churning in my gut about missing out.

Would Carter miss me if I left earlier? Maybe, but probably not as much as he would if he didn't have Raegan.

Images rush through my mind of what they could get up to if I wasn't here. If I wasn't that awkward third wheel that clings to Carter like a limpet.

Ugh. The thought makes me want to scream.

"I can't promise anything, but I'll see what I can do," I say to Elliot.

His face lights up at my response.

"Anyway, tell me what Pokémon you caught."

He fills me in on the game we play together. Halfway through, he tells me about how he looked after Blaine and Alex's dog Ernie and took him to the beach, then all the bracelets he made with our teammate, Jackson's, daughter Isabela the other day.

His mouth slams shut mid-sentence. His head tilts to the side like a curious dog, green eyes assessing me through the camera. "You okay?"

The question startles me. *Shit*, did I let my mask slip? I'm usually so good at hiding my feelings. Burying them deep down.

"Yeah, I'm okay."

He furrows his brows. "You're quieter than normal, which is ironic because you're normally quiet, but you're like, the quietest of quiet. Is quietest a word?"

I snort. "Yes, it's a real word."

"Awesome, I'm gonna use that in Scrabble." He grins, then the frown reappears. "You know you can talk to me, right? I might reply at 3 a.m. or in my head, but I'm always here for you."

Squeezing my eyes closed for a brief moment, I send a silent thank-you to the universe for bringing this eccentric guy into my life. He really is the greatest friend.

"I'm good, and thank you, it means a lot. Same goes to you."

"Always! You're my best Zach."

"I'm your only Zach."

"Exactly!"

I smother my laughter with my hand. Elliot distracts me a bit longer, telling me some of the things Alex has organized for the party, and when we hang up, I'm feeling lighter than I did earlier.

But the feeling doesn't last long. The sound of laughter coming from inside catches my attention, and my stomach twists.

Reluctantly, I stand and pick up my empty cup before heading in. Raegan's sitting on the kitchen counter, her arms wrapped around Carter's head as he nuzzles into her neck, causing her to giggle. The throbbing ache in my chest steals my breath, and the blood pounding in my head causes my ears to ring.

"Sorry," I mutter, quickly dashing around the island to put my mug in the sink.

Carter lifts his head and flashes me an easy smile. "Sorry, didn't see you there."

Clearly.

Ah, fuck. Look at me getting all snarky.

I give him a tight-lipped smile and motion to the stairs. "I'm going to take a nap." I don't give him time to reply, turning on my heels and practically running up the stairs.

By the time I reach the top step, the ache in my chest is palpable.

I can't do this anymore. I can't watch him fall in love with someone else again. Someone who isn't me. I can't keep doing this to myself. This endless loop of torture.

I *can't.*

It's time for me to go.

Closing the door behind me, I take my suitcase from the closet and throw it onto the bed. I start tossing everything inside, not caring to fold anything or make sure it's neat. My original flight back to Chicago isn't for another six weeks, but I know I can't be here any longer. I need to go now.

For the first time in nine years, I'm going to break the pact we made when we were lying on my bed on New Year's Eve in our sophomore year. The pact where we promised to spend every summer together. But younger us were naïve. It wasn't feasible long-term. The childhood dream we had of being together until we were old and gray, living in houses next to each other, was just that.

A dream.

I'm grateful I've had this time with him, but now it's time to move on. For good.

Once everything is packed, I sit on the edge of the bed and look up the next flights out to O'Hare. There's one leaving in two hours. I know Carter isn't going to let me go without a fight, but Elliot's words filter back to me, reminding me that I have the perfect excuse. I'll land in time to make it to the party at Blaine's apartment. I book it before I can second-guess and talk myself out of it.

I need to do this. I need to be selfish and put myself first. If not for my heart, then for us. I don't want to cut him from my life, but I don't know if having my heart continuously broken will get to the point where I become resentful. Make me start acting out of character.

I check my room and en suite again, making sure I've packed everything, then order a rideshare to the airport. I know I'll have to sit around, but I can't stay in this house any longer.

Heading downstairs, suitcase in hand, I rehearse what I'm going to tell him in my mind. I'm going back to Chicago for the twins' birthday. I need to act as normal as possible to avoid any suspicions. But the moment I reach the bottom of the stairs and see the confusion flooding Carter's expression, the words disappear from my brain. He jumps up from the couch where he's sitting with Raegan like his ass is on fire and walks over to where I've stopped by the door. His gaze jumps from me to my suitcase, those dark brows furrowing deeper and deeper as each second passes.

"Zach…" There's a note of caution in his tone. "What's going on? What happened?"

"Nothing's happened. I decided to head back to Chicago."

"But… why? Your flight isn't for another six weeks."

My eyes lock with Raegan's over his shoulder. Her bottom lip is tugged between her teeth, and there's pity in her eyes.

She knows. How could she not?

She's caught me on several occasions watching Carter. When I allowed my shield to drop and the love I have for him was so prominent, I couldn't hide it.

When I bring my attention back to Carter, I'm not prepared for the heartbreak I see. His brown eyes glisten with unshed tears. Fuck. I don't know if I can do this. I don't know if I'm strong enough to walk away.

I think she's the one.

The memory of his words hits me square in the chest. I raise my hand, rubbing over the center of my chest, trying to ease away the ache.

"I… I don't want to be in the way, plus it's the twins' birthday today and Alex is throwing them a party tonight. Elliot called me earlier, practically begging me to go." I shrug, hoping it comes across as relaxed, but my entire body is tense. "You know I can't say no to him. So, I figured, why not go back early?"

Carter's Adam's apple bobs as he swallows hard. His voice cracks as he says, "But I don't want you to go."

I wince.

He'll get over it. Raegan will distract him with her witty charm and infectious laughter, and he will soon forget about how I left earlier than normal. He'll be so wrapped up in this new relationship and training camp, it'll fill the void he would have felt before.

But me? I'll be working on getting over these feelings once and for all.

I've been in love with Carter Lockwood for nearly two decades, and I don't think my heart can cope any longer.

Today marks the day I take a step back to protect myself. To learn how I can be the friend he needs, the one who can support him without the constant heartache.

"You won't even notice I'm gone." I squeeze his shoulder and force a smile.

"What if I speak with Coach about reducing my training time? We can go hiking. We can try out that new burger place we keep talking about." His voice gets higher and higher with each word, panic laced in his tone.

"You know that's not an option." I shake my head softly. "I just need to go home."

Home is wherever the other one is, you got it?

His words from when we graduated college come barreling back at full force. And from the distraught expression on his face, he's remembering them too.

His mouth opens and closes a few times, like he's trying to argue but can't think of the words to say. After a minute, he takes a step forward and engulfs me in his arms so tightly, it knocks the breath from my lungs. I wrap my arms around him, returning his hug as Raegan watches us from her spot on the couch.

"I'm sorry," she mouths, remorse lining her brows.

I squeeze my eyes closed and return Carter's hug. When he finally lets go and takes a step back, his eyes are shimmering wet, tears clinging to his dark lashes. I fucking hate that I've upset him.

"I won't get to see you until November." His voice shakes.

"I know." I rub the back of my neck. "At least we had Hawaii, and these last few weeks."

His tongue peeks out, licking over his trembling bottom lip. "I don't want you to go, Reid," he says again.

A sigh shudders out of me just as my phone vibrates in my pocket, letting me know my rideshare is outside. Carter looks at the door, then back to me.

"I could've taken you to the airport." This time his voice breaks and a tear spills down his cheek.

Instead of answering, I bring him in for another hug and kiss the side of his head. "See you in a few months."

When I step back, I look over to Raegan. "Look after him, yeah?"

"Of course." She darts around the couch and wraps her slender arms around my waist. "Take care of yourself."

With a lump thick in my throat, I pick up my luggage and head to the door. I know he'll be hurting right now, but it's for the best. For both of us. If he's serious that Raegan might be the one, then it's unfair for me to be invading on their time together. He'll understand. Eventually.

Glancing over my shoulder, I manage a small smile as I say goodbye, then close the door behind me. The moment the door clicks shut, my heart shatters in my chest, and I finally allow the tears to come to the surface.

It's for the best, I remind myself, but my heart doesn't feel too sure.

Chapter Five

October

Carter

"You've got this," I mumble under my breath as Zach successfully intercepts the puck from Minnesota's forward.

It's only preseason, but my nerves are still shot to shit for him. They are playing really well in these exhibition games. The new guys have gelled in perfectly, and the lines Coach Harris has put together are looking strong. Elliot is rock solid in the crease, too. He's had an incredible start to the season, getting three shutouts in the first four games they've played so far, and I know the media are eating up the team's early success. But again, it *is* only preseason, and a lot can happen between now and the end of regular season.

It doesn't stop me from hoping that this is the Thunder's year to bring the cup back to Chicago, especially after getting so close to the finals last time.

"Carter, we need to talk," Raegan announces, rounding the couch and taking a seat on the other end of it.

We've been dating since Zach and I returned from Hawaii a few months ago. She's a great woman. Incredibly intelligent, insanely beautiful, and she actually gives a shit about my best friend.

She's everything I thought I wanted, but the last few months have been… difficult. Since that day Zach left to go back to Chicago, there's been an underlying tension between us. Things haven't been as easy as they once were. It's like we're trying to force two puzzle pieces together, regardless of the fact they clearly aren't a match.

Those four words, along with the resigned tone of her voice, tell me that maybe she's also feeling that things aren't as good as they were before.

My eyes bounce between her and the TV as Zach jumps over the boards for his next shift.

"Sure, what's up?" I ask.

She takes in a deep, steadying breath before she begins to speak. "Look, Carter… I think you're a great guy, and these last few months have been great, but I think we're on two different paths. Which, don't get me wrong, isn't a bad thing, but it would be bad for us to stay together when I don't think we're right for each—"

My attention snags to the TV as one of Minnesota's defensemen slams Zach hard into the boards, despite not even having possession of the puck. "Fuck! Where's the boarding call, ref? It's fucking preseason, why so aggressive?"

"Carter," she repeats, her voice stern. "I need you to listen to me, please."

Shit. She was in the middle of telling me something.

I turn to face her again, and this time my gaze lands on where her overnight bag sits on the cushion beside her.

Frowning, I ask, "I'm sorry. What were you saying?"

She sighs. "I think we should break up."

My mouth drops open, eyes widening in surprise. Well, okay, I wasn't expecting that.

"Oh."

"It's been on my mind for quite some time now, and I don't think we're each other's endgame. I don't want to be the one who stands in the way of you finding happiness, and I don't think you would want that for me either."

"No, of course not. I want you to be happy, Raegan, and I'm sorry that I've made you feel that way," I say, genuinely apologetic.

She shakes her head, a small, sad smile playing on his lips. "It's nothing you've done, Carter. Sometimes we meet people, and it's amazing in that honeymoon phase, but once the newness wears off, it just... doesn't work, and that's okay."

I get what she's saying. I'm not the same guy she met. It's as if the day Zach left, he took a part of me with him. I know he went earlier to spend time with the Olsen twins on their birthday, and I don't blame him when I hadn't exactly been the most available friend, splitting my attention between him and Raegan and training camp starting again.

I hadn't experienced heartbreak before, but I'm pretty sure the ache that's been present in my chest ever since has been from my heart breaking in two when the door closed behind him.

"So, this is it?"

"Yeah, it is." She nods, running her palms down the front of her jeans.

I should be sadder about this, right? I should be fighting for her. Telling her to stay and promising we can make it work, but… I can't. Everything she said was true, and it would be unfair of me to ask her to stay when I'm nowhere near feeling the same level of panic as I did when Zach said he was leaving.

I guess this is just another failed relationship to add to my endless list of failed relationships. At least this time, it hasn't ended with my and Zach's friendship being thrown in my face as the main cause.

Standing up, I hold my arms out for a hug. She steps into them, wrapping her arms around my waist.

"We can still be friends, right?" I ask.

"Yeah, we can still be friends." She tilts her head up to me and smiles. "But will you promise me something?"

"Yeah, of course. Anything."

"Keep an open mind. I think you're going to find what you're looking for, but you've been looking in the wrong places. Also, I think it's going to look different from how you're expecting it to look… So, just… keep an open mind. An open heart."

Despite being confused by her vagueness, I nod, not wanting to poke at an already sore wound by making her elaborate. "I can do that."

We say goodbye, and I watch from the window as her car disappears down the road. I hope she meant it when she said we can remain friends. She's fun and we did have a good time. It would be a shame to fully end our friendship just because I'm shit at being a boyfriend.

Sighing, I sit back down on the couch and watch the rest of the game, counting down the minutes until I can call Zach and hear his voice. There's only three weeks to go until we head to Chicago for our away game, and we should have at least an hour together between my game ending and him needing to be at the arena for his game that night.

I've been clinging onto that hour like a life raft, and it couldn't come soon enough, especially now.

The Thunder win 4-1, putting an end to Elliot's shutout stint. It's going to be a few hours at least until Zach's free to talk, so I busy myself by cooking dinner, scrolling through my phone and watching the recap before firing over a text.

CARTER

Great game! That D should've gotten a penalty for boarding for that hit. Totally uncalled for. Call me when you're out!

I take a shower and make myself dinner, and by the time I make it back onto the couch, nearly two hours have passed. I purposely left my phone down here so I couldn't keep sneaking glimpses. My chest suddenly tightens when I see the message was read thirty minutes ago and there's no reply.

It's okay, don't overthink it.

He's probably still in press. They don't always know if Colleen is going to pick them to do post-game press. But what if he isn't doing press and he's out celebrating the win at Gino's, the local sports bar where they hang out? It hadn't stopped him from calling me before, but after the last three games, he hasn't answered. He just sent a text saying he was busy, and he would call me the following morning, but even when he did, he didn't sound like *my* Zach.

I'm not the kind of guy who overthinks things. I'm usually the kind who goes with the flow, but right now, anxiety is creeping up my throat as panic sets in. I don't think I can wait until morning to talk to him. I need to talk to him now.

Without a second thought, I hit Call. It rings out and goes straight to voicemail, so I hang up. I chew on my bottom lip as I debate what to do. Do I call him again? But what if he is in press and I'm going to look needy and desperate?

"You're being irrational, Lockwood," I murmur to myself. "He's probably busy." Tingles rush down my arms and into my hands, my fingers going numb, and I nearly drop my phone when it vibrates in my hand.

ZACH

Just at Gino's. I'll call you tomorrow when I'm back from breakfast with Elliot.

You good?

Anger bubbles in my veins. I love the guy, but fuck, I hate that Elliot gets to monopolize his time. It seems he's always with Zach recently. Sure, I had Raegan until a few hours ago, but it seems like he's getting Zach all the time, and I'm being left with the scraps.

That's not fair.

Ugh. I know I'm being a jackass. I'm glad Zach has Elliot to keep him company when I can't be there. I'm being selfish because my pride is wounded from the breakup.

Sighing, I begin to type. This isn't something I wanted to talk about over text, but I'm unable to think clearly.

CARTER

Raegan broke up with me tonight.

ZACH

Oh shit, I'm sorry.

CARTER

She said we were on different paths and we're not each other's endgame.

I don't know what that means.

ZACH

I'm not sure either. But even so, I'm sorry.

CARTER

Can you call me before you head for breakfast? Or when you get home tonight?

I just need my best friend.

ZACH

I'll see what the time is when I get back. I don't know what these guys have planned tonight but I'll let you know if it's not too late.

CARTER

Okay. One positive is it's only 3 weeks until I'm in Chicago!

Get thinking about where to take me. I'm ready for some good Chicagoan food.

And one of your hugs.

ZACH

Can't wait.

CARTER

I miss you so hard.

ZACH

Miss you too.

CARTER

Go celebrate, you've deserved it.

Rubbing over the center of my chest, I dig my fingers in to try and relieve the ache in my chest. I should be heartbroken over the fact that my girlfriend dumped me—the woman I thought could be the one—but the ache is stemming from someone different.

It's coming purely from the man who's currently drinking beers in Chicago with his teammates.

The man who has been my favorite person since I was six years old.

And if I wasn't already confused by Raegan's words earlier, I'm definitely confused now.

Chapter Six

November

Carter

This day can't get any worse.

Keeping my gaze lowered, I head back to the visiting locker room, shoulders slumped in defeat. I don't know what happened out there. It was like my hands were covered in butter. Every tackle I made was a fail, and I couldn't have sacked the quarterback if my life depended on it. I botched every play. Tripped over thin air.

I played like a fucking embarrassment.

Throwing myself into the seat in front of my designated stall, I toss my gloves against the wood paneling a little harder than necessary and let out a heavy sigh.

Fuck. This game was shit.

For the last seven years, I've always been voted within the top 5 defensive ends in the NFL. There were some guys who didn't like coming up against me because I didn't hold back. Off the field, I'm laid-back and happy-go-lucky as they come, but when I'm out there, when I get into position, it's like my vision turns red. I have one target in my sights, and I'm a hungry bear until I get it.

This season, however? I couldn't have stopped the opposing team if they had stood dead still and slapped me in the face.

Like I said, I'm an embarrassment, and there's only one thing that will make this day any better.

Zach Reid.

Stretching as far as my pads will allow, I retrieve my phone from my bag and swipe my finger across the screen to unlock it. I wonder where he'll take me today. It's been four months since I've seen him, and I've been counting down the days. We don't get to see each other much during the season, especially because the NFL and NHL seasons overlap until January, but we always meet up whenever we're in each other's city, and Zach always takes me to grab some food before I catch my flight back to Denver. Last time, we hit up this incredible pizza place that was worth breaking my strict in-season diet.

But the rush of dopamine I typically get when I see his name on my phone doesn't come. No matter how long I stare at the text message on the screen, it doesn't change. There's no *Just kidding!* follow-up text.

> **ZACH**
>
> I'm sorry, I can't make it today. Maybe next time?

. . .

An unpleasant ache that has become all too familiar recently blooms in my chest. There won't be a next time. I'm only playing in Chicago once this season—the next time we face them will be at home—and when Zach is in Denver, I'll be away in Pittsburgh. This was the only chance we were going to get to see each other until January at the earliest, because I doubt we're going to get a spot in the wild card round, and he'll be on a road trip during my bye week.

We made a pact, goddamnit.

Nine years ago, when we were lying on his bed in college on New Year's Eve, we promised we would always see each other whenever we were in the same place. We might have been nothing but two punk-ass twenty-year-olds with big dreams of making it to the pros, but we weren't naïve enough to think the odds would be on our side and we would land on teams in the same city. Being apart for the first time since we met was tough; throw in the fact that we were now states apart, not even in the same time zone, and it's been hell. But we always got through it by sticking to the pact.

Until now, and this is the second time he's broken it. I forgave him in the summer when he went back to Chicago six weeks earlier than planned. But now…

My fingers are flying over the screen, typing out a reply before I can think it through. A mix of desperation and frustration bubbles away inside me, causing me to not think clearly.

CARTER

What? Why? What's so important you can't see me for 20 minutes before I have to leave for my flight?

ZACH

I'm seeing the trainer about my shoulder before the game tonight. I'm sorry.

Jaw clenching, I let out a frustrated groan. Now I feel like a dick because I know his shoulder has been bothering him since last season, but still, he *knew* I was coming. He knew this was the only game I have in Chicago all season. I sent him my schedule the second it came through. Hell, I sent it to him before I even had a chance to read through it myself.

Why does it feel like he's avoiding me?

I scroll through our message thread. It's a sea of blue bubbles. A one-sided conversation. His responses have become shorter, less frequent over the last few months.

I don't know what has happened to cause this... distance between us, but I don't like it. Not one bit.

I miss my best friend. I miss him to the point it's causing me physical pain.

Rubbing the aching spot over my chest with my palm, I close my eyes and take a deep, steadying breath. There's no point in getting angry because there's nothing I can do about it, but it doesn't stop me from being disappointed. I've been looking forward to seeing him for months.

The football season hasn't gone as well as I'd hoped. I genuinely thought this was going to be our year. Our time to shine and bounce back after our Super Bowl loss last year.

Instead, I have reporters questioning whether being awarded Defensive Player of the Year last season has become a curse because I'm having the worst season of my professional career.

Knowing that I was going to be seeing Zach today has kept my chin up. It has kept me from spiraling into a cloud of negativity, especially now, given we just had our asses kicked by Chicago on the field.

But now the cloud is looming, darker than before, and I don't know what to do.

"Not seeing your boy today?" Walker asks as he sits down in the stall next to mine to lace up his shoes. He's a defensive tackle on my D-line and probably one of the guys I'm closest to on the team.

I haven't even begun to get undressed, not feeling the usual urgency or eagerness to get out of here.

"No." I shake my head. "He's got a session with the trainer."

Walker winces. "Shit, man. Bad timing."

Bad timing, indeed.

Or purposefully bad timing.

No, that's unfair. I don't think Zach would intentionally avoid me like this. He's quiet and introverted and so damn intelligent. Nerdy, too, but I think that's what makes him so endearing. The guy could recite the entire script of *Return of the Jedi* by the time he was ten, and I made it my mission to learn it so I could impress him like he constantly did me.

Throughout my life, his opinion was the only one that mattered. I've never cared for the press or the so-called fans who comment on whatever slice of life I decided to share on my social media. I've never cared about what anyone else thought. Only Zach.

Because Zach Reid has been my buoy for the majority of my life, keeping me afloat, and now I'm lost, drowning without him.

Heaving a sigh, I muster up the energy to get undressed and head into the showers. My movements feel sluggish, like that stupid text has sucked every ounce of energy out of me. By the time I'm dressed in sweatpants and a team-branded hoodie, I shove my feet into my sneakers and make sure all my belongings are in my duffel bag. I've been in this game long enough that I've learned to double-check my stall before I go. I've left way too many things in visiting locker rooms over the years.

I thank the equipment team as they load our gear onto the specialized container units, then make my way out of the arena to the bus that's waiting to take us to the airport. Normally, I would be rushing through my post-game routine, eager to get out so Zach could pick me up so we could do our thing before he dropped me off at the airport.

But there's no reason for me to rush today.

Fuck, I can't keep torturing myself like this.

I run an agitated hand through my hair. I don't know what to do with myself. As I take the steps up into the bus, I'm greeted with surprised expressions.

Palmer's, another defensive tackle on my D-line, eyebrows rise to his hairline, jaw dropping open. "Holy shiiit. What have you done with Carter Lockwood? He doesn't ride the bus with us in Chicago."

I want to flip him the bird, but I don't have the energy. I just grunt in response, glaring down at my shoes as I head further in and take a seat, quickly pulling my noise-canceling headphones out of my bag. A clear sign for nobody to bother me.

Selecting an upbeat, pop playlist, hoping it will boost my mood, I scroll through our message thread again, then close the app to go on Instagram. I bring up Zach's profile and click on the stories, just like I've done a thousand times since last night. I go through each of the slides and pause on the photo of him and his teammate Elliot at Gino's. Elliot has his arm wrapped around Zach's shoulders, both of them with a beer in hand. Zach's hair is tied up off his face in a bun, and my hands itch to take it down. I love his hair. It's so long and silky, I find it relaxing to run my fingers through it.

My ex-girlfriends always thought it was weird how I would be so openly affectionate with him. I love him, he's my best friend—why wouldn't I show my affection? I always wanted to be near him, touching him, even if only our knees connected. His presence has always brought me peace, but it's his smile in this particular photo that makes my stomach twist uncomfortably. It's like a sucker punch to the gut.

He hasn't smiled at me like that in so long. Probably since the summer, come to think about it. When we were in Oahu on our vacation.

Our video calls haven't been as regular, either, and whenever we've spoken, it's like there's this… something… between us. I don't know, some kind of awkwardness.

Ugh. I'm probably overthinking this. I've been doing a lot of this recently, too, which isn't like me.

When we board the team plane that will take us back to Denver, I stow my bag in the overhead bin and drop into my usual seat by the window and press Call on Zach's name. He might not want to see me, but I'm not going to allow this… whatever it is, to come between us. I'm not going to be the one to break routine. Not being able to see him has already put me on edge. Going hours without hearing his voice might just break me.

I suck in a breath when the phone connects and instantly relax at the sound of his familiar voice.

"Hey," he says.

"Hey." I clear my throat, then let out a strained laugh. "I… It's weird, I kinda don't know what to do with myself not being able to see you." I pick at a loose thread on my sweatpants. "I feel like I haven't seen you in years, and I'm kinda going out of my mind."

I'm expecting laughter or a joke about how I saw his face on FaceTime only the other day, but none of that comes. There's silence, and after a beat, nausea sets in.

"Yeah, I'm sorry. It was the only time Joe could see me, and I need to get myself strapped up for the game tonight. I just got out of the ice bath."

"No, no, I understand." *I wanted to see you. I* needed *to see you.* "How do you feel about facing Ottawa tonight?"

"Eh, I'm not too concerned. We're prepared. They won't shake us."

I chuckle nervously under my breath. Ottawa has been known to try and ruffle feathers, trying to get under the players' skin, but the Thunder boys have been cool as cucumbers this season. They have the lowest penalty minutes served. Even Blaine Olsen has managed to keep his visits to the penalty box to a minimum, which is a record in itself.

"Will you call me later after your game?"

Another long pause. "I'll try, depends what time we get out."

"I'll be awake." I hate how the panic is evident in my voice.

He sighs. "If I can't call you tonight, I'll call you in the morning."

Fuck. Why is it so difficult? It's never been like this before. We always had so much to say to each other, often getting into trouble because we didn't want to hang up and say goodbye even as the plane was about to take off.

"I better go," he announces, and I have to fight the urge to beg him to stay on the phone a little longer.

"Okay." I swallow the lump in my throat. "I'm on the plane now. I hope you have a good game."

"Thanks." Another pause. "Have a safe flight."

"Thanks."

The line goes dead. My stomach twists and curls as I drop my phone into my lap and close my eyes, hitting my head back against the seat.

Between my career being at its lowest and my best friend drifting away, I don't know who I am anymore.

It feels like my world is falling apart, and I don't know what to do to make it right.

Chapter Seven

December

Zach

If someone asked me if there's a city I love playing in other than Chicago, I would have to say Vancouver. The energy here is magnetic. Elliot played here three seasons ago, and if you thought they would hate him for moving to a different team, you would be wrong.

Vancouver still loves Elliot Olsen, which makes every visit enjoyable.

More so tonight, as we hit the ice for the start of the third period, and we're currently in the lead, 3-1. I take my position near the blue line as Ethan lines up for the face-off. The ref drops the puck into play, and Ethan slaps it to Blaine, who passes to Jackson. Vancouver must have received a pep talk during intermission as they are hungry for another goal to try and close the gap.

Kendrick and I stay close to the blue line, ready to block any advances. Luckily, the puck remains in the offensive zone, and when there's a stop in play, I skate to the bench for a line change. I squirt some water into my mouth before squirting it down the back of my jersey to cool down my heated skin.

We're on a mini-Canadian road trip. Tomorrow morning we'll head to Edmonton, where we've got a day off before our game the following day. Then it's back-to-back games in Edmonton and Winnipeg before we head home. Normally, I'm eager to get back, but this time I've been grateful for this four-day road trip, as it's given me the distraction I needed.

Carter's not having a good time right now. With Raegan breaking up with him a couple of months ago, the unfortunate football season he's having, and the fact that I couldn't see him when he visited Chicago, it's taking every ounce of willpower not to give in and fall back on old habits because I hate that he's hurting.

But I have to push all thoughts to the back of my mind when I take to the ice again. Vancouver's forwards are all up in Elliot's space, but he's keeping it cool. Kendrick and I make ourselves as big as possible, deflecting and battling tight in the corners. We're exhausting them, but when one of the wingers steals the puck from Blaine, I'm watching it with eagle eyes.

"Wanna go, Reid?" Eklund taunts, shoving me with his shoulder. "When you gonna fight me?"

"You know I don't fight," I mutter without tearing my eyes off the puck.

"Shame. You are a big guy, it would be fun, no? Your brother always likes to fight me."

I ignore him. This isn't the first time someone tries to provoke me. Eklund is a big bruiser of a D-man. He's known for his taunts, and he's been trying to get me to fight with him since we first played against each other years ago. But he's shit out of luck because, despite my size, I'm not one who drops the gloves. That's more my brother Brody's specialty.

I tune out the Swede's taunts and focus on helping Elliot, who's currently trying to protect the net with everything he's got, dashing from side to side, creating rebounds that Vancouver snaps up easily. There are players surrounding him, limiting his ability to move with ease. The puck lands on their left winger's stick, and I have to make a split-second decision. I dive in front of the net, blocking the shot, and the puck bounces off my shin pad.

Fuck, I'm going to feel that later, but it's the price to pay to stop them from scoring a goal.

Thankfully, the rebound lands on Jackson's stick, and he skates off into the offensive zone.

"Fuckin' hell!" Elliot shouts as I jump back onto my skates with a wince.

"You good?" I ask.

"Yeah." He nods, his eyes hyperfocused on the action further down the ice. "That was crazy busy. I was like, ahh, get away from me!"

Heading toward the blue line, I groan under my breath at the dull pain rushing up my leg. It's not the first time I've jumped in front of the puck, and it definitely won't be the last. As a defenseman, it's my job to do everything I can to defend the net, and that means using my body as a shield when necessary.

I motion with my glove for a line change. There's only three minutes left; the boys can cope without me.

"Great job." Coach Harris slaps me on the shoulder, and I thank him with a quick nod as I squirt water into my mouth.

The third period goes scoreless, so when the buzzer sounds, we win the game 3-1.

After we have our mini post-game celebration in the locker room, we shower, do press, and head back to the hotel. As we're not traveling to Edmonton until the morning, it gives us the night to relax and enjoy our win. There's a sports bar not far from our hotel where we planned to get food, so once we've changed out of our suits, we make the short walk.

"I am starving," Jonathan Peyton announces as we take over one side of the restaurant.

"You're always starving," Kendrick replies with a chuckle.

"What can I say?" Peyton lifts his T-shirt to show off his abs. "It's a hungry job to look this good."

Elliot lifts up his own T-shirt to his chin, flashing his bare chest. "Mine are better."

"Elliot, put your nipples away and sit down," Ethan grumbles, sounding like a tired dad. He spent the entire walk from the hotel stopping Elliot from stepping out into the road because he was too busy talking to pay attention to where he was going.

With an exasperated sigh, Elliot does as he's told and the noise in the restaurant increases as we all sit down and start talking. We order, and soon the table is filled with food. I chat with Jackson on my left and Ethan on my right as we dig in.

"Didn't Carter play today?" Ethan asks, motioning to the TV mounted on the top of the bar showing highlights from Carter's game earlier today against New York.

My eyes are glued to the screen as Carter gets into position, and when the ball is in play, he gets past the blockers easily, but as he goes to tackle New York's quarterback, he dodges Carter so gracefully, like he's a fucking ballerina. Carter falls to the ground, and before he can get up, the quarterback throws the ball down the field to his receiver. Denver's defense is scattered all over the place, pretty much handing New York the touchdown.

I can't do anything except watch as my best friend makes his way off the field, his head dropping in defeat. Subtitles appear on the screen, catching my attention, as one of the commentators says, "I think we can all agree that Carter Lockwood won't be receiving the award for Defensive Player of the Year again this year. What a terrible season he's having."

My stomach drops. Terrible is the understatement of the year. It's his worst season to date.

No matter how much it feels like being punched in the gut repeatedly with an iron fist, I need to stay strong.

He'll overcome this. He's an incredible player. This season is just a fluke. When August comes around, this poor performance season will be a distant memory, and he'll go back to owning the gridiron.

My attention snags to my phone as it vibrates against the wooden table, Carter's name flashing on the screen. A few months ago, I would have answered the second it started ringing without hesitation, regardless of being out with the guys. We would text nonstop, morning, noon, and night, but since I left Denver at the end of July, I've kept my promise to myself.

It's hard. Really fucking hard. But with time, I know I'll be able to be the friend he deserves without my feelings getting involved and fucking everything up.

I'm sure he's noticed the distance between us, too. Our text thread has become almost one-sided. Our daily phone calls have become weekly, and I can't remember the last time we spoke on FaceTime. I'm running out of excuses, though, and I know I'm going to have to face the music soon enough, especially when Carter's season ends next month and he makes his way to Chicago, like he's always done.

"Are you going to get that?" Jackson asks, motioning to my phone with his bottle of beer.

I shake my head. "I'll call him back later."

The table drops into silence. I ignore the shocked expressions on my teammates' faces as I watch it ring out and then watch the missed call notification pop up. It's been hard to break habits of a lifetime. To keep strong and avoid falling back into that pattern. Even when he texted the other month and told me Raegan had dumped him, I had to squash down my instincts to go running back, not to give in and open myself up to fall back into the routine I've been putting myself through for years. But I managed to stay strong. I didn't give in. I gave him support while also protecting myself.

I don't know how long I can do this for, though. It's

breaking me, and it's almost like I'm grieving for someone who is still very much present in my life.

I guess I'm grieving the fucked-up notion I've held on to for so long that one day he might love me back.

Unable to look at my phone anymore, I slip it into my pocket and pick up my beer.

Out of sight, out of mind, right?

Well, kinda.

It might be out of sight, but Carter is never out of my mind.

"Is there trouble in bromancadise?" Peyton asks.

I eye Peyton over the bottle. "What?"

"Bromance paradise. Bromancadise." Peyton rolls his eyes. "Duh."

Elliot snorts mockingly and echoes, "Duh."

"No, there's no trouble. I'm out with you guys, so I'll call him back later," I say and take a sip of my beer, hoping it's the end of the conversation, but that hope is quickly squashed.

"Well, fuck me. Who would've thought we'd see the day when Blaine swapped places with Zach to be the one glued to his phone?" Peyton snickers, throwing his thumb over to where Blaine has been typing away on his phone since we left the arena.

Without lifting his head, Blaine flips him off and resumes texting. This isn't new. Blaine popped the question to Alex a few weeks ago and has become even more smitten, if it was even possible. Gone are his playboy ways, and he's so disgustingly in love with Alex, it's almost nauseating.

But I'm happy for him.

Even if I am a little jealous.

"Don't be jealous, Peyton. Just because you're single as a Pringle doesn't mean we're all going to be lonely like you," Blaine retorts. "You should count yourself lucky that I'm sitting here. I could be jerking off on a video call with my fiancé right now."

Elliot slaps his hands over his ears and sings, "La la la!"

"Look what you've done! Now you've upset your brother." Peyton playfully scowls over the table at Blaine.

Elliot slaps his hands on the table, causing his full beer to slosh over the rim of his glass. "It's bad enough I see your balls hanging out when I walk into your apartment. I don't wanna know when you're jerking off."

Blaine throws his hand up in protest. "It's *my* apartment! I can walk around with my balls out whenever I want."

I pinch the bridge of my nose, chuckling under my breath. Peyton sits back with a smirk, amusement dancing in his eyes now that he's riled up the twins.

"You're going to be married into this one day, you know?" Peyton wags his finger between the twins while addressing Ethan. "Absolute chaos. You're never gonna know what the meaning of peace is ever again."

Ethan simply watches on unfazed as he sips on his beer in silence.

"As long as I have Jacob, bring on the chaos," he replies, lifting his shoulder in a carefree shrug.

My phone vibrates again in my pocket, and a sigh escapes me as I see Carter's name and the numerous texts.

CARTER
Can we talk? Please?

How's your leg? Can't believe you threw yourself in front of it like that.

I know you're probably out celebrating with the guys. You deserve it btw. That game was killer.

I just need you.

Zach, please.

I just need ten minutes.

"Is everything okay between you two?" Jackson asks quietly, jutting his chin at my phone as he leans in close.

Ethan and Jacob are the only ones who truly know about my feelings for Carter. I'm sure the others have their suspicions because it's not like I actively try to hide it around them. We're together so often, it would be hard to wear the shield constantly.

But also… we *are* together often. We're like family. And last summer, when we found out how much Ethan had been hiding behind a wall for the sake of wanting to be strong for us, we all felt a little hurt that he thought he couldn't confide in us.

Isn't what I'm doing just as bad? I know these guys will be there for me. They will help me carry this heavy weight and stop me from falling back into age-old routines.

"Sort of," I say truthfully. "I've taken a step back, so to speak. I…" I trail off, wondering how much to reveal.

Jackson was traded to the Thunder last season from Buffalo. He had recently gone through a divorce and put in a trade request to be closer to his parents, who live in a village north of downtown Chicago, so they could help out with his two young kids, Ryan and Isabela. Sometimes, when guys who have families join the team, they don't connect as much off the ice, which is understandable, but Jackson was different. He showed interest in getting to know us from day one. Invited us over for dinners and barbecues and even offered up his lake house in Michigan whenever we wanted.

He's good people.

I scoff. "How much time do you have?"

"As much time as you need."

I quickly glance around the table. Everyone else is engaged in conversation or preoccupied with their phones. Running a hand through my hair, I tell him everything. From when we were kids to that day in Denver when I left with a broken heart, to how I'm trying—and failing—to get over him.

"Damn, I'm sorry. That sounds really tough."

"It is. I don't want him to think he's done something wrong, because he hasn't. But we couldn't keep going on like we were. *I* couldn't keep going on like we were, but I'm pretty sure he knows something's up, and I don't know what to do about it."

Jackson flashes me a sympathetic smile. "Will he be heading to Chicago when his season ends next month?"

"Yeah, more than likely."

"I think you need to talk to him. It'll be unfair on both of you to spend those six or so months treading on eggshells around each other. You've just gotta rip the Band-Aid off. Expose the wound; only then will it be able to heal."

"I think I'm just afraid. I don't want to lose him."

"I don't think you'll lose him, but you can't keep going this way. It's clear that both of you are struggling with this shift in your dynamic, so being honest is the best way forward."

Before I can respond, my phone begins to vibrate in my hand, and Carter's name flashes on the screen.

"I better answer this."

Jackson gives me a reassuring nod and squeezes my shoulder. "It'll be okay, I'm sure of it."

Pushing my chair back, I answer and head toward the door.

"Hey, everything okay?"

"Hey. Fuck, I'm really happy to hear your voice," Carter says, his tone relieved. I hear the rustling of bedsheets, and my mind conjures up images of him lying in bed. Is he naked? He usually sleeps naked.

Stop thinking about him being naked.

His voice is quiet when he speaks again. "I wish you were here. Today fucking sucked, and all I keep thinking about is how much I want to cuddle up with you on the couch while we watch a Star Wars movie so I can forget how much I fucking suck at football."

Squeezing my eyes closed, I lick over my dry lips. "I'm really sorry about how your season is shaping up. You know this isn't a reflection on you, right? It's a fluke season. Ignore all the bullshit and see these last few weeks through. Next season it'll be better, I'm sure of it."

He sighs. "I know, it's just hard when everywhere I look, I see people saying how shit I am."

"You are *not* shit."

"I am. Argh!" he groans, then lets out a pained sigh. "Anyway, enough about me. You do know you're not supposed to stop pucks with your body. Elliot's the one with the pads, let him stop them with his."

"All part of the job, dude." I chuckle. "I will protect that net with everything I have, even if it comes with bruises."

"You're crazy, Reid." He laughs. "Tell me how your Canadian road trip is going so far."

I fill him in on our plans and how we're feeling going up against Edmonton and Winnipeg. But nothing could prepare me for the pain that hits me in my chest when he says, "I miss you."

Oh, fuck.

Stay strong. Don't give in.

Scrunching up my face, I rub over the center of my chest, trying to ease the pain from my heart breaking. "I miss you too."

It's not a lie. I miss him like crazy. I've had to stop myself multiple times from texting him back straight away or not evading his calls. I've had to fight against everything I've known since I was six years old to resist the gravity that has always pulled me toward Carter.

Jackson's right. When Carter comes to Chicago next month, I need to tell him, because I don't know whether I can survive going on like this any longer.

"I'll let you go. I…" He trails off, sounding so defeated. "I can't wait for this season to be over so I can see you again. I think it's been the longest five months of my life."

Swallowing the lump in my throat, I say, "Carter?"

"Yeah?"

I run a hand through my hair and stare at my reflection

in the window. "I know you're feeling like shit now, but I promise it'll work out. You're an amazing player, and you're an amazing person. It'll be okay."

"Thanks, that means a lot. Love you, man." I can hear the smile in his voice.

"I love you, too."

More than you'll ever know.

Chapter Eight

January

Carter

"I'll let you know if I need you for anything," Hayden, my agent, says. "Enjoy your time off in Chicago. Oh, and Carter?"

"Yeah?"

"Keep your chin up, all right? I know it feels like shit right now, but this season wasn't a reflection of your talent. I wouldn't stress too much because even if they do let you go early—not that I think they will—there's teams waiting to snap you up."

Even though I'm not able to see his expression, I can tell by the sound of his voice he's got a reassuring smile on his face.

When the NFL season ended for us, I mentioned to Hayden how I wouldn't be surprised if Denver traded me. I have one year left on my contract and no no-trade clauses. It's a business at the end of the day, and I didn't perform to the standard that was expected of me. But Hayden, being the great guy he is, has managed to reassure me that even if it does happen, it won't be the end of the world.

"Thanks, I'll do my best."

And I mean it. Hayden Cassidy has been my agent for four years now, and I trust the man explicitly. If he tells me not to stress, then I'll do my best not to stress. I like him because he doesn't bullshit me, compared to my last agent, who screwed me over a few times. Being a retired athlete himself makes him more relatable.

Plus, he works with Zach and a few of the Thunder guys, which helped seal the deal for me.

"You know where I am if you need me."

We hang up, and I collect my bags from baggage claim and make my way out into arrivals. The sky matches my gray and gloomy mood as I step out of O'Hare and head to the waiting rideshare I requested.

I stayed in Denver for the mandatory debrief meetings and farewell dinners for guys who aren't staying next season, but after two days, my house began to feel like it was closing in on me, and I hopped on the first flight out this morning.

I haven't told Zach I'd be flying in today, and for the entire flight, I thought I was going to be sick. I don't know why I feel so fucking nervous. I've never once felt nervous around Zach. We've always had this easy, open, and honest relationship, creating this safe space to be vulnerable about our fears and feelings. But as I glance down at my phone and see my texts are still unanswered, I'm wondering if that safe space has been broken.

Something has changed between us. Our bond has been fractured, and we're standing on separate islands. I can see him, and I can hear him, but I can't reach him. He's drifting away from me, and I don't know what to do to close the gap.

And I really hope he isn't going to be mad that I'm just turning up unannounced.

My knee bounces as we head toward downtown. My gut twists and turns with anxiety as my mind runs at a hundred miles an hour. Could he have met someone and the reason he's been distant is because he's been preoccupied? I mean, maybe? But we've always been so open with one another. He wouldn't hide something like that from me. A wave of jealousy burns my insides, and I bite down on the inside of my cheek until I can taste copper, and I pick at the skin around my nails.

Get yourself together, man.

No, he wouldn't keep secrets from me.

"I'm sorry about your season," the driver says, eyeing me in his rearview mirror.

"Oh, uh, thanks."

"I hate to say this, as I'm a Chicago fan and all, but you deserve better. I hope you can find a team who gives you that. We would be lucky to have you on our defensive line."

I want to argue that I don't deserve better. That I was the reason for our piss-poor excuse of a season, but I don't. This pity party of one needs to take its departure because it's done now and there's nothing I can do to change it.

"Thank you. I appreciate it," I manage to force out.

Luckily, he drops it, switching the subject to how snow is expected any minute now. I'm grateful for the brief reprieve for my anxious brain, but it returns like a freight train when he pulls up outside Zach's apartment building.

"All the best next season." He smiles as he takes my luggage from the trunk.

"Thanks, man. Have a great day."

I make a mental note to give him a generous tip once I get inside and make a beeline for the doors just as snow begins to fall. Zach has a game tonight, so hopefully it doesn't get too heavy.

"Mr. Lockwood, I wasn't expecting to see you today."

My head snaps up to see the doorman, Steve, stepping around the front desk and taking my luggage from me. "Is this a surprise visit for Mr. Reid?"

I clear my throat and offer a shaky smile. "Uh, yeah, it is."

"Great. Let me get the elevator for you." He heads to the elevator bank to press the button. Knowing Zach hasn't removed me from his approved list settles something inside me.

That must mean something, right?

I thank Steve as the elevator doors open, and once I'm inside, I press the button for the sixty-ninth floor. The doors close, and I close my eyes, taking a deep inhale through my nose.

Maybe I'm overthinking this. Maybe it's just been a wave of shit luck and I'm being overly sensitive because my football season has been so fucked up.

When I reach his apartment door, I raise my hand and rap my knuckles against the wood. Minutes go by with no sign of Zach, so I knock again and try not to let my nerves take over again. This time, I hear the sound of footsteps on the other side of the door before it opens. Zach stands there shirtless, in just a pair of sleep pants and pillow creases on the side of his face.

Fuck, I've probably interrupted his pregame nap.

"Shit, I'm sorry. Did I wake you?"

He shakes his head and yawns, rubbing his eyes with the heel of his palm. "It's fine, I needed to wake up anyway. What… What are you doing here?"

I furrow my brows. "Uh, it's my off-season, Zach. Where else did you think I would be?"

Alarm bells start blaring in my mind as he shrugs his huge shoulders and steps aside without a word. What the hell is going on right now?

Tugging my luggage behind me, I head into his apartment, kicking off my shoes and leaving my bags by the door. He disappears for a minute, then reappears, pulling a T-shirt on. Him being shirtless around me has never been a problem, and the simple act of him putting a shirt on now has my palms sweating with anxiety.

"Want a drink?" he asks, opening the fridge.

I open my mouth, brows furrowed in confusion. Since when does he ask me that? His apartment is like my second home. We don't bother with pleasantries because what's mine is his and vice versa. We make ourselves at home.

My heart rate kicks up a notch. I need to tell him how I feel, how it feels like we're drifting apart. The longer I leave it, the longer it's going to play on my mind, and I can't carry on like this.

"Zach, what's going on right now?"

His eyes widen slightly, clearly not expecting me to ask that. "What do you mean?"

"You leaving early during the summer. The bailing out of our video calls. The inconsistent texts, the constant excuses whenever I want to speak to you. Tell me if I'm taking this the wrong way, but it feels a hell of a lot like you're avoiding me, and I don't know what the fuck I've done wrong."

I'm now trembling with nerves and anger. The back of my eyes burns with tears as I watch his face morph through various emotions.

Guilt.

Regret.

Sadness.

He lets out a long, heavy sigh and runs a hand through his hair. "You're not taking it the wrong way. I haven't handled this very well at all. I thought it was for the best, but it's clearly hurting both of us."

"What was for the best? What could possibly be the reason why you felt like the best course of action was to distance yourself from me?" My voice gets higher the more panicked I become. "Because from where I'm standing, I've spent the last six months wondering what the fuck I did to make my best friend not want to speak to me. We had a pact, Zach. *Always* speak to each other, *always* make time for each other, and you threw that away without any—"

"It's because I'm fucking in love with you!" he shouts, cutting me off.

I can't do anything except stand there, completely startled. I've never heard Zach raise his voice in all the time I've known him. We've never fought. Even when career pressure is bad or we disagree on something, we've never argued.

Zach is the calmness in the eye of the storm that is me.

He rubs his face with his hand and lets out a defeated sigh.

My brows furrow in confusion. "Yeah, so? I love you too."

His expression turns pained, and that's when it clicks.

He's in love with me. As in *in love* with me. Not the *friend* kind of love or *bro* love.

Love love.

"I… uh…"

I don't know what to say. I'm at a complete loss for words. It's been me and him for so long—more than twenty years of being each other's constant. But now that I think about it—how did I not see it?

Now that it's staring me in the face, it's clear as day. Memories flick through my mind like a reel. The way he would always retreat whenever I started dating. The lost look in his eyes whenever I spoke about them. The way he left Denver just days after I told him that I thought Raegan might be the one.

I'm such a fucking idiot.

"Zach…" I trail off, an apology on the tip of my tongue, but he holds up his hand to stop me.

"I don't need an apology because you have nothing to apologize for. You didn't know because I didn't see the point in telling you. It was something I needed to deal with on my own."

I open my mouth to speak, but nothing comes out. Blood pulses in my ears as my heart races even more, beating like a wild bird caged in my chest.

Fuck, Carter, say something.

"Are we going to be okay?" I hate the panic in my voice.

It's taking all of my strength not to cry right now. Not to throw myself at his feet and apologize for all the pain I've inadvertently put him through.

And I'm unprepared for the way my heart cracks when he shrugs.

"Maybe? Probably? I just need time, Carter. It sounds crazy because I've never *had* you, but I have to mourn you. Let go of my feelings for you and move on, so I can be the friend you deserve."

"You are the friend I deserve!" I bellow, raising my arms.

He shakes his head. "Friends are not secretly in love with their friends for nearly twenty years. I've loved you since I was ten years old, Carter. I thought I could stomp it down. Ignore it so we could carry on, but I *can't.*" His eyes become glassy with unshed tears. "I can't do it, Carter. I still need time, so I think it's best if you go."

There's a lump the size of a football lodged thick in my throat. I'm unable to breathe. The pain in my chest tears right through me.

I shake my head in denial, and he lets out a frustrated sound.

"Carter, please don't make this any harder than it already is."

"What if I don't want to go? You're my best friend, Zach. We've spent all of our free time together for so long."

Despite the anger burning in my veins, it's not him I'm mad at.

He's the most important person in my life. I can't lose him.

"That's the thing, Carter. Every time we're together, my attention is solely focused on you. I couldn't wait to spend time with you, but over the years, that time wasn't just ours anymore. I had to share you with whichever woman you were dating, and I had to watch as you fell in love with them and then watch when they would break your heart. I don't want to do that anymore. I don't want to feel jealous. And all those women were nice people; they didn't deserve the feelings I held toward them." His voice cracks like glass shattering against a wall, and my heart splinters along with it. "If we're gonna be able to go back to how we used to be, I need time. *Alone.*"

Fuck. *Fuck.*

How can I deny him that? How can I possibly fight him on this when I've been unconsciously causing him pain over and over again?

I'll do it, because I would do anything for Zach. He's my person. My favorite person. He always has been. Always will be.

But why does it feel like this is the end? That we're almost saying goodbye?

I clear my throat and give a shaky nod. "Okay. I'll… I'll leave in the morning. I'm sorry."

"There's nothing to be sorry for. I should have told you how I felt before it got to this point, but I thought I could get over you."

I don't know why hearing those words feels like I've been sucker punched in the gut. But I'll take it—repeatedly—as long as it means I won't lose him.

Chapter Nine

Zach

This fucking sucks.

I don't know what I was expecting to happen when I finally got the balls to tell Carter about how I was feeling, but it certainly wasn't this.

And shouting at him, too? Fuck, that definitely wasn't how I wanted to tell him either.

I didn't want the moment I told him that I was in love with him to be in the midst of frustration and hurt, because *fuck*. Seeing the pain on Carter's face almost killed me. I don't ever want to see that look cross his handsome face ever again.

In the few hours between him arriving and me needing to leave for the arena for tonight's game, he became withdrawn. Gone was the laughing, smiling, happy-go-lucky guy I've known all my life, and in his place was a hollow shell who could barely look me in the eye.

For the first time in our lives, we were like strangers, awkwardly dancing around each other and making small talk. He sat as far away from me as possible on the couch and turned down my offer for food. Hell, when I asked if he wanted to come to the game tonight, he kept his gaze downcast and nodded with a quiet, "Yeah, okay."

I don't know why I was so surprised to see him on the other side of the door because he *always* came here after his season ended. I don't know why I questioned it. He's just been through the worst season of his career—why wouldn't he come here? Knowing Carter as well as I do, he's probably hypersensitive and came to me seeking comfort, and I went and threw my feelings in his face like a weapon and told him to leave.

I'm the worst fucking friend.

The atmosphere between us was tense and so unfamiliar that I was too chickenshit to deal with it and ended up leaving a little earlier than normal. Putting it down to the snow and catching a ride with Elliot and whatever other weak-ass excuse I could come up with because I couldn't stay there any longer. The guilt has been eating away at me ever since.

What the fuck have I done?

I didn't want to hurt him. I didn't want to break his heart, but it's exactly what I've done. And I can't help but think—have I made a colossal mistake?

Yes, you asshole.

The thing is, I don't actually want him to leave in the morning. I just assumed that was the best way to protect my heart and protect *us*, when in reality, it's done the polar opposite. I've probably blown up our friendship with my own selfish stupidity.

But maybe I can make this right. Maybe we can talk when I get home from the game later and we can have the conversation I wanted to have, rather than the one that went down.

It doesn't have to be this way.

Right?

Movement in my periphery catches my attention where I'm pedaling on the stationary bike, and I greet Jackson with a jerk of my chin as he gets on the bike next to mine. I pause my playlist and remove my earbuds.

"Hey."

"Hey, you good?" he asks, starting at a steady pace.

I let out a long exhale and shake my head. "No, not really. Carter arrived earlier. I ended up telling him how I felt."

"Oh, shit. I take it from that sigh that it didn't go very well?"

"No, it couldn't have gone worse." I tilt my head to look at him, my brows pinched. "I yelled at him and told him it was best if he left."

"You yelled at him?" Jackson's eyes widen. A moment of silence passes as he simply blinks at me, jaw slack. "You? Yelled? As in raised your voice?"

I nod, grimacing.

"Holy shit. I didn't think it was possible for you to raise your voice. Even Isabela calls you the quiet giant."

I chuckle under my breath. His daughter is adorable. Whenever she sees me, she always wants a piggyback ride, and she often paints me pictures. But he's right. It was so out of character for me to raise my voice like I did. Panic took over as my feelings came bursting through the flood gates at the sight of him, catching me off guard.

"I feel like shit about it. He was so… upset. I've never seen him like that before. Even when his ex-girlfriends broke up with him, I've never seen him as distraught as he was today."

"I'm sorry, man." Jackson's smile is sympathetic. "Do you want him to leave?"

"No, I don't, but he said he'd leave in the morning. I… I don't know what to do to make it right."

My confession is left lingering in the air as we pedal. A few of the other guys have come to do their warm-ups before we head out into the corridors to play soccer. My gaze bounces around to where Ethan's jogging on the treadmill and Peyton hops on the machine next to him. Elliot's on the floor doing his insane mobility stretches while Blaine does side lunges next to him.

"Are the kids okay?" I ask, unable to cope with the silence anymore but not wanting to talk about me.

"They're good. They enjoyed spending time with their mom while she was in town, but Isabela is back to being clingy now that her mom's gone."

Jackson has told me all about how his ex-wife is a news journalist and received a promotion that would take her outside the US. Despite them being split up, he didn't want her to turn it down, but between him being on the road and his ex-wife being away with work, he didn't want the kids being left with a nanny either. So, they agreed he would move to Chicago with Ryan and Isabela and get help from his parents, who take care of them when he's away to give them some stability, and she visits in between her work assignments.

From what he's said, they now get along better than ever.

"That's tough. Are they here tonight?"

"Yeah, but my mom will probably take them home before the second period since they have school tomorrow. Knowing Isabela, she'll get so excited and worked up during warm-ups watching Elliot she'll be asleep by the time the puck drops."

I laugh, not surprised in the slightest.

Jackson chews on the inside of his lip in thought as we slow down to stop. "Could you talk to him tonight when you get back? Just be honest and explain things, see if you can work it out," he suggests. "I know we've only known each other for a year, but I know how important this time you have together is for both of you."

Hearing him echo my earlier thoughts brings me a sense of relief. I *can* make this right, even if it means having an uncomfortable conversation and laying my heart out.

I reach over and squeeze his bicep. "Thank you. For listening to me ramble and giving me solid advice."

"Anytime, brother." He grins, slapping my shoulder. "It's time to put Carter to the back of your mind for now because we've got a game to win."

"We cannot let them get the better of us," Ethan states, pacing the locker room floor. He hasn't sat down since we trudged back here after the first period. He's like a caged lion, fists clenched at his sides, angry and ready for the attack.

Washington is sitting just below us in overall standings, and while Vancouver is a team I enjoyed playing against, Washington is one I dislike the most. They have come to fight tonight, literally, and they're not afraid to get a little dirty. Something Blaine's learned firsthand, as he's already received two penalties, and I wouldn't put it past the refs not to make them his last.

The hits are always harder. More intentional. We might be in different divisions and conferences, but we're still competition.

They want to hurt us, and they will try anything to get under our skin and make us crumble.

"If Volkov comes near me one more time, I'm going to punch him." Blaine grunts.

"That's what he wants," Peyton replies. "Don't give him the satisfaction of knowing he's getting to you. Do you think Alex will want you to go home with your pretty little face all bruised up?"

Blaine grumbles something about how it would make him feel better and how Alex will nurse him back to health anyway.

My gaze flicks to Elliot, who has been surprisingly silent the entire time. He's staring at the floor, his mouth open slightly. He's in a trance, and it seems everyone knows not to disturb him. He's been on fire tonight, stopping shot after shot, and considering he's only let in two out of twenty shots on goal, he's playing incredibly.

When we get back out onto the ice for the second period, it continues to be fast-paced and all action. We're racking up penalty minutes quicker than Coach can tell us to keep our heads in the game. Despite the words of wisdom Peyton gave Blaine not long ago, Peyton found himself watching from the penalty box after getting a double minor penalty for roughing and instigation. At least when Blaine gets his third penalty of the night for tripping, he's not alone in there.

It definitely seems the refs have it out for us tonight because they've allowed Washington to get away with almost every call.

The tension is building up on the bench too. The anger radiating off Ethan is palpable. His dark eyes are menacing while he tracks the puck as the second line fights for possession. He's dangerous when he gets this worked up, and I feel sorry for whichever player is brave enough to provoke him—I definitely wouldn't want to be on the other side of Ethan Parkes's aggression when it's unleashed.

The bench begins to vibrate as his leg starts bouncing. He's just as eager to get back out onto the ice as I am, and the second we hear the video game power-up-style chime signaling the end of Blaine's penalty, we make a quick line change to join Blaine out on the ice.

The next two minutes go scoreless, and one of Washington's wingers cross checks Peyton the second he steps out of the penalty box, and it goes uncalled by the refs. Again.

"This is such bullshit," Kendrick snaps, hitting his stick so hard on the top of the board in rage that it snaps in two.

It is, but there's nothing we can do about it except try to keep our heads cool. Judging by the smart-ass grins they're sporting on the bench, Washington is succeeding in what they wanted to achieve.

Riling us up.

I'm back on the ice in time to take possession of the puck as it goes sailing up toward the defensive zone. I'm aware that Mueller, one of Washington's defensemen, is breathing down my neck, but I know Kendrick is clear for the pass. I hit it around the back of the net, and I shift on my skates to turn, but Mueller isn't stopping. He hits me with such force, I'm lifted off the ice. He slams me hard into the boards, my head bouncing off the ledge of the boards like a pinball. A shooting pain rips up my arm from where my wrist is crushed beneath me, and the bright lights of the arena are the last thing I remember before I fall and my head hits the ice.

Suddenly, everything goes black.

Chapter Ten

Carter

Zach isn't moving. Why isn't he moving?

It's like time is standing still as the arena goes eerily silent. So silent, I can hear Elliot call Zach's name in a panicked shout as he rips off his helmet and throws his stick down onto the ice. His glove and blocker are next, and he skates over to where Zach is lying face down in the corner and drops to his knees, shielding his unmoving body.

"Hurry the fuck up!" Elliot shouts over to the bench, and chills ripple across my body.

Blaine's next to Elliot, manically waving his hand for attention. Jackson Wilde skates over to the bench, lending an arm to help the Thunder trainer, Joe, as he hurries across the ice with his medical bag. The paramedics are waiting at an open door behind the goal, ready to jump into action if needed.

Please get up, I inwardly beg.

I can tell Ethan's torn between wanting to smash his fist into Mueller's face and protecting Zach. The hit was completely unnecessary. Everyone saw that at the speed Mueller was skating, it wasn't just going to be a simple case of boarding. It was intentional. He wanted to hurt Zach.

No doubt it'll be investigated, but right now, the sole focus is on making sure Zach is okay.

Joe crouches down by Zach's head, and the rest of the boys create a shield around him, allowing enough space for him to work. Even Washington's trainer rushes over the ice with the aid of their captain.

Chills course across my skin and blood pounds in my ears the moment Ethan motions for the waiting paramedics to bring the stretcher onto the ice. I'm on my feet in an instant, but I don't move just yet. There's murmuring coming from the ice, and relief floods through me as Zach moves. He tries to push himself up but falls back down. Alex shoots me a panicked look, fear laced in those big blue eyes of his as he grabs onto my arm, giving it a squeeze. Luckily, he doesn't say a word. I don't think I will be able to hold it together if he speaks to me, but I'm grateful for his reassuring touch.

They put a C collar around his neck then carefully transfer him onto the backboard and secure him, then I'm running up the steps onto the concourse, heading toward the locker room.

Flashing my badge at security, I'm thankful they don't try to stop me because I'm not made for running. I'm two hundred and sixty-five pounds. My body is made for blocking and knocking down the opposition, not running like my life depends on it.

But right now, it does.

Because Zach *is* my life, and right now, he's hurt.

I'm vibrating with adrenaline and panic when I meet the paramedics wheeling Zach to the waiting ambulance. Joe spots me first, his face falling.

Fuck.

Resting my hands on my knees, I try to catch my breath. It's coming out in ragged pants from running. I probably need oxygen, but I don't have time.

"How's… he… looking?" I ask as I gasp for air.

"He's got a concussion, for sure. He's delirious right now, understandably as he was unconscious for around thirty seconds."

Was it only thirty seconds? It felt like the longest time of my life.

"They're going to need to do some scans to check for any bleeding around his brain. They'll also need to do an X-ray as it looks like he may have broken his wrist."

Bleeding around his brain? Fuck.

I'm no doctor, but I've seen my fair share of concussions in the years I've been playing football, and I know the longer you are unconscious, the more dangerous it is. The fact that this isn't Zach's first concussion won't work in his favor either.

"Go with him. It'll settle him seeing you," Joe says, squeezing my shoulder. "I'll come by the hospital as soon as I can."

A small voice in my head says seeing me is likely *not* going to settle him, especially with what happened earlier today, but I can't let it get the better of me. I can't let that voice of doubt win when he needs me right now.

Nodding, I let him know I'll send updates if there's any before he arrives, then I climb into the back of the ambulance. My heart splits in two at the sight of Zach. There's blood on the side of his head, his skin is ghostly pale. And while I know it's precautionary, the sight of the C-collar makes the back of my eyes burn and my chest clench.

I know we have high-risk careers, but seeing him like this just shows how dangerous these sports can be.

He lets out a pained groan, and *fuck*, I feel so fucking helpless.

Scooting up the bench slightly, I reach up to slip my hand in his and squeeze his fingers gently.

"Hey, I'm here," I say softly, not wanting to startle him. "You're going to be okay."

He lets out another groan before murmuring a confused, "Carter?"

"Yeah, it's me. Just stay still, okay? They're going to get you sorted."

"Carter…" he repeats, but this time, his voice trails off.

"Stay awake for me, Zach," the EMT says as he cuts through his jersey and the elastic of his pads to expose his arm and puts in an IV.

Zach mumbles incoherently, slurring his words.

"That's it, buddy. Keep talking."

"I can take off his skates, if that will help?" I offer. "I've watched him tie his skates since we were kids. I know how to tackle the weird way he likes to tie them."

The EMT flashes me a grateful smile. "That would be great, thanks."

Shifting around so I don't get in the way, I begin to unlace his skates and slide them off his feet as gently as I can without jostling him. I place them between my feet, and a choked laugh escapes me as I see his worn Chewbacca socks.

On his thirteenth birthday, I bought him a set of Star Wars socks with my allowance. There were three pairs in the set, and I was so fucking happy with myself at finding them. He wore the Chewbacca pair for one of his state tournaments, and they won. From then on, they became part of his superstition, and he would only wear Chewbacca socks for his games. Of course, by the time the season ended, they were worn out and covered in holes, but he wouldn't wear anything else. It brings a small smile to my face that sixteen years later, he still has the same tradition.

I'm just glad he buys a new pair at the start of each season.

I carefully slip the threadbare socks off his feet and stuff them into his skates, knowing that if anything was to happen to his socks, he would be really upset.

Once we get to the hospital, I follow close behind, not wanting to get in the way but not wanting to be too far from Zach either. I'm pleased when they take him straight through to a private room where the nurses and doctor are waiting to begin the job of taking all his hockey gear off. For some bizarre reason, people like to take photos of athletes, regardless of the fact they're in a hospital. I don't understand it.

"So bright," he groans, squinting his eyes.

"Should I turn off the light?" I ask, pointing to the light switch like an idiot.

"You can dim them." One of the nurses nods.

"Better?" I ask Zach once I've dimmed them, making sure there's enough light that the staff can keep working.

His words come out slurred. "Yeah. Why was the sun in here?"

I bite the inside of my cheek. "I dunno, but it's gone now."

They roll him slightly onto his side to remove his chest pads, and the small movement causes him to throw up.

I stand out of the way while the nurses do what they do best. Thankfully, they took off his gear before he was sick, so the equipment is clean when they put it in a bag and hand it to me. I put it in the corner of the room where I already stashed his skates. Not that he can use it again, but I don't know whether the Thunder's equipment manager, Jordan, has a process for dealing with damaged or broken equipment.

They dress him in a hospital gown as he continues to slur his words as he talks. His blue eyes are dazed, unable to focus on anything.

"The doctor will be in shortly." The nurse, whose name badge reads Beth, smiles. "You can be with him, you don't have to stay in the corner."

I let out a nervous laugh and rub the back of my neck. "Oh, okay."

Zach's face lights up in a lazy smile when I reach the top of his bed. Taking his hand in mine, I give it a gentle squeeze, relieved when he squeezes it back.

"Where am I?" he asks.

"You're in the hospital. You took a nasty hit in the second period, but you'll be okay." I can't stop myself. I lift my hand and card my fingers through the dark strands, pushing them off his face.

He closes his eyes and hums, so I do it again, hoping that it brings him a tiny bit of relief.

"Have I been here long?"

"No, ten, maybe fifteen minutes tops."

"'Kay."

It's silent apart from the beeping of the machine he's hooked up to and the noises from outside his room.

"Carter?" he rasps.

"Yeah?"

"What am I doing here?"

My heart falls.

One of my teammates had post-traumatic amnesia after he suffered a concussion two seasons ago. He couldn't remember anything up to the incident. His earliest memory happened three days prior, and it took two weeks for it to come back, but even then, there were still patches where he couldn't remember anything, including the hit that caused him to be concussed.

Closing my eyes, knowing we'll be having the same conversation for a little while, I open them and tell him again, and this time he gives my hand a small squeeze along with his slurred "'Kay."

Even though it's only been a couple of minutes, it feels like an eternity has passed when a doctor finally comes into the room with a clipboard in hand.

"Hi, I'm Dr. Bradley. Are you Mr. Reid's family?"

"Uh, hi, I'm Carter Lockwood, and, uh, no, but we live together."

She looks down at her chart, then nods. "Great. You're listed as Mr. Reid's emergency contact," she informs me.

I am? I look down at Zach's spaced-out expression, and my chest tightens. He has no idea how much this means to me. He's listed as my emergency contact too.

"We'll be taking him for a CAT scan shortly, where we'll check if there's any swelling and any potential bleeds. Afterward, we'll take him for an X-ray to assess the state of his other injuries. Depending on the results, we may need to operate, but we'll get a better idea of where we stand once we get the results of the imaging back."

"Thank you." I chew on my bottom lip, my eyes flicking to Zach as he struggles to keep his eyes open. "Will he…" I swallow. "Will he lose his memory at all?"

"He's most likely going to have some memory issues, especially short-term. It's called post-traumatic amnesia. I'm unable to determine how long it will last, though. Sometimes it's minutes, hours. Sometimes it can be days or weeks."

Fuck. Okay. Well, there's no way in hell I'm leaving in the morning, that's for sure. If Zach wants me to go back to Denver, he'll have to physically push me onto a plane because I will not leave him.

Not now. Not ever.

"I'll come find you as soon as we have more news," she says after doing a quick check of his pupils, and I step aside as people come in to take Zach for his scans.

Stepping out into the hall, I watch as his bed is wheeled down the corridor, and it's only when it disappears around a corner that I allow all the emotions of today to come to the surface.

His confession that he's in love with me. The knowledge that I've been breaking his heart over and over again. The fact he thought he was a bad friend because he had feelings for me, and the only way to fix that was to get over me.

The hit. Seeing him lying there motionless on the ice. Being wheeled off on a stretcher.

Gripping my hair, a choked sound escapes the depths of my chest as tears fill my eyes, blurring my vision.

The thing is… I don't want him to get over me. I know it's probably selfish of me to think that, but… What if this is what Raegan was talking about when she said to keep an open mind and an open heart?

Did she know?

It's not like I haven't thought about Zach in more than a platonic way, especially after the time in Hawaii when I got jealous about the couple hitting on him. There have been times since where I was jerking off and found myself thinking about him instead of Raegan. But I chalked it up to us being such close friends. To the fact that Zach is always on my mind.

I just didn't realize, it's always been him.

My mind spins as things start to make more sense. Why my relationships never worked out, and they would always bring up my friendship with Zach as if it were an issue.

It's like I'm finally *seeing* him. The blindfold is off, and he's there, clear as day, and I don't really know what to do with it all.

I don't want him to think I'm only feeling like this because I don't want to lose him after he told me how he truly felt.

I have the opportunity to make things right. A second chance. A do-over.

I slump down into the plastic seat in the waiting area and pull out my phone. I send a quick text to Ethan, letting him know what the doctor said so he can relay it to the rest of the team, then pull up a new text thread with Zach's mom, Laurie. She and Kian, Zach's father, are currently on a cruise around the Mediterranean, so they're at least seven or eight hours ahead, and the chances of them seeing it right now are slim. But I know if the roles were reversed and it was Zach in the hospital, she would text me to let me know regardless of what time it was.

CARTER

> Hey Laurie. I know it's the middle of the night there and I hope this doesn't wake you up. Zach took a nasty hit on the ice tonight. We're currently at Northwestern Hospital. He's got a concussion and potentially a broken wrist. He's having a CAT scan now, and once they've assessed his head, they will do an X-ray. I'll let you know when I hear more, but I'm here for him, Laurie. I promise you, I'm not going to leave his side.

I don't realize tears are falling down my cheeks until one splashes against my phone screen. Fuck, I've got to get myself together.

He's going to be okay.

He *has* to be okay.

Time seems to go by painfully slow. People come and go,

but I don't pay them any attention. Eventually, I close my eyes and rest my head against the wall behind me. I must doze off as I jolt out of my seat when someone touches my shoulder.

"It's okay, it's just us," Ethan says, giving my shoulder a squeeze. "Has he come out yet?"

Blinking the tiredness away, I shake my head. When I look up, the waiting room is now filled with some of the Thunder boys—Blaine, Jackson, Peyton, Kendrick—but when my eyes land on Elliot, it only takes one look at his face and I'm on my feet, bringing him into my arms. He looks like he's seen a ghost, staring at the doors that Zach disappeared behind I don't know how long ago.

"Hey, it's all right. He's going to be all right." I don't know whether I'm reassuring him or myself.

Elliott shivers. He rests his head on my shoulder, and his voice is so quiet when he says, "I was so fucking scared, Carter. He wasn't moving."

"He's strong, and you were there for him. He'll really appreciate that you were looking out for him."

There are hushed whispers around us, and when I look up, Dr. Bradley is standing by the door.

My heart plummets into my stomach when she says, "Mr. Lockwood? Would you come with me, please?"

Chapter Eleven

Zach

"There is some swelling that we will need to monitor closely," the doctor says to Carter. I think her name is Dr. Bradley, but I can't remember for sure. "His neck and spine are OK, so we've removed the C collar; however, there may be some residual pain, which we'll manage with pain relief."

I'm struggling to stay awake. The room is swimming a little, but I force my eyes to stay open because I think they're talking about me.

"We'll need to wait for the swelling to go down before we operate on the break in his wrist. We've put a splint on it for the time being."

The lights in the room are off, but when I glance down at my wrist, I can just make out the black splint. When did I break it?

"The scans showed it was a clean break, so we should be

able to operate within the next few days, and then we'll need to discuss recovery."

Oh, yeah. I had some scans, I remember now. It was kinda loud, it made my head hurt.

"I live with him, so I will be able to help with anything he needs," Carter adds quickly. "I won't be leaving his side."

Good, don't leave me, Carter.

I think I say the words aloud. I can't remember when Carter got here, but I'm glad he isn't leaving. I've really missed him.

She gives a small nod, her gaze going to the door. "Great. I would recommend limiting the number of people in his room at one time. He may be easily confused and will be highly sensitive to sounds and light, so I would suggest no more than three people at a time. It can be overwhelming, and don't be surprised if there's a level of agitation."

I want to ask who's confused, but the words don't come.

Shit, I'm so tired and my head hurts. A lot. Damn, who put my head in a vise?

"No problem, I'll make sure they understand." Carter nods.

She gives him a small smile, and when she opens the door, I groan as light floods the room. She quickly shuts it behind her, and Carter rushes over to me. He combs his fingers through my hair, pushing it off my face. My eyes close instantly, enjoying the soothing motion. I love when he does that.

"My head hurts," I murmur.

"I know. It's going to hurt for a while, but it'll be okay." His voice is so quiet, but I'm grateful.

Everything seems to make my brain hurt. Noises and lights make it feel like it's churning like a mixer.

"The boys want to see you, but they won't stay for long because you need to rest."

I open my eyes and look up at him. "Why are they here?"

"They just want to say hi and make sure you're okay. You scared them tonight."

"Heh," I snort under my breath.

"It's not funny, Zach," he chides, but his tone is light.

"Why did I scare them?"

He runs his fingers through my hair a few more times, his mouth twisting like he's trying to figure out what to say. "You took a bad hit on the ice," he says after a beat. "You were knocked unconscious, and it worried them. Especially Elliot."

I frown. "I scared Elliot?"

"Yeah, but don't worry, he'll be okay."

"Mhm," I murmur, closing my eyes again as exhaustion takes over.

"I'm gonna let them in now, so keep your eyes closed while I open the door."

I give a small nod, missing the feel of his fingers in my hair as they leave my scalp. I hear his footsteps head toward the door, followed by the soft murmur of chatter filtering into the room. I wince when light fills the space. Even with my eyes closed, it still feels like a stab in my brain.

"Hey there, big guy."

I open my eyes to see Ethan standing at the top of my bed. Next to him are Blaine and Peyton, and on the other side of the bed are Kendrick, Jackson, and Elliot. All of them have their brows pinched in concern.

"How are you feeling, dude?" Peyton smiles, squeezing my ankle under the horrible, itchy blanket.

I look to where Carter stands at the foot of the bed, chewing on his bottom lip. He looks so tired, like he hasn't slept in days.

"How long have I been here?" I ask out loud.

"A few hours," Ethan answers. "You'll probably be here for a little longer, just until your head's okay and they fix your wrist."

"Yeah, my head hurts a lot." I look down at my splinted wrist again. "I broke it. Or I think the doctor said I broke it, but my head is…" I wave my left hand in the air, trying to find the right words to describe how confused I feel right now. "I don't really know. Everything's a bit confusing."

"Fuck," Blaine mutters. "That fucker Mueller is going to pay for this."

They begin to talk quietly, then there's a female voice interrupting them. This time, she sounds annoyed.

"I know everyone is worried about Mr. Reid, but he needs rest right now, and having multiple visitors will be overstimulating. Say your goodbyes, and you can come back tomorrow."

My eyes are so heavy, I can't keep them open any longer. I'm so fucking tired and my head hurts. Maybe if I sleep for a while it will help.

"We'll come back to see you in the morning," I hear someone say. I know their voice, but it's distant, so I don't know who it is.

"'Kay," I croak.

The room goes quiet. The beeping of the machines is kinda soothing, lulling me to sleep.

When I wake up sometime later, the room is completely dark aside from the glow of the monitors I'm hooked up to. Blinking wearily, I glance around the room to see Carter sitting in the chair next to my bed. He's resting his head against his fist, watching me silently. He gives me a small smile but doesn't say a word.

Then I spot a second figure slumped on a chair in the corner. The hair sticking out from beneath a baseball cap tells me it's Elliot. He's resting his head against the back of the seat, fast asleep.

"He didn't want to leave you," Carter whispers, his hand reaching out to comb through my hair again.

Keep doing that, I want to tell him, but I can't find the energy to speak, so I hum.

"He is a little upset about the game and asked if he could stay."

"Why? What happened at the game?"

"You played Washington tonight, and Mueller took you out with a dirty hit. You were knocked unconscious and broke your wrist. Elliot was the first one to get to you, but you were unresponsive, and it upset him."

Fuck, I don't want Elliot to be upset. He's too good of a person to be upset. I don't remember anything, though. I don't remember the game. I don't remember when I got here.

One thing I do know is my head is fucking killing me.

"Carter," I rasp, gripping his hand tight. "Don't leave me. Please."

"Never." His voice cracks. "I'll never leave you; I promise."

The warmth in my chest at his promise is the last thing I remember before sleep takes me again.

Chapter Twelve

Carter

Zach was released from the hospital five days later. They operated on his wrist, and since he's been home, he's been struggling with migraines. The kind of migraines that have wiped him out for three days so far. I've tried to leave him alone so he can get some sleep, only waking him when it was time to take his medication and to make him drink some water to avoid dehydration, but other than that, he's been asleep.

I've taken it upon myself to sleep in his bed every night too, or sometimes I simply lie there with him. Running my fingers through his hair and watching him rest.

And maybe it makes me a creeper, but I love having the chance to really *look* at him. To really appreciate the handsome lines of his face. His sharp jaw that's now lined with several days' growth. It's thick and dark, and I was pleasantly surprised at how soft it was when I ran my fingers over it. His long, dark lashes cast half-moon shadows under his eyes.

And his lips? Damn, how have I never noticed how kissable they are? Soft and pink but framed by his beard, making me imagine how it would feel to kiss him. To feel them graze my skin. His bottom lip is slightly bigger than the top, and my mind's wandered on how he would react if I sucked on it.

The thought made me hard as a rock, then I felt like an asshole for getting a boner over my best friend, especially when he's fast asleep and injured.

The last few days have given me a lot of time to think, and for the first time in my life, I'm a little scared. Not scared about being with Zach in a romantic sense—or being with a man in general for the first time—but whether he will reject the idea.

Yeah, he told me he's in love with me, but if given the chance, would he *want* to see where things could go with us?

It's not like we'll need to go through the whole getting to know each other phase, but we would be learning to navigate an area that was previously grayed out.

And then there's sex.

I've loved the times I've been pegged by the women I've dated, but I know I can't compare that to having sex with a man. There were also the times I've watched porn with two guys and a chick. I often thought it was hot if the guys touched each other, but I put it down to being horny, and now I'm wondering… How could I have been so oblivious all this time?

He doesn't remember the conversation we had when I first arrived here in Chicago. He doesn't remember when I arrived either, but it's like his confession has given me a lightbulb moment, placing all the pieces that have felt scattered for so long together, but I also don't want to get too ahead of myself.

When it's time for his meds and mandatory glass of water, I peek my head through the door, and I'm surprised to see him sitting up against the headboard. His hair has come out of his bun—a bun that I managed to do haphazardly while he was delirious—and the dark strands are sticking up all over the place.

"Hey," I say quietly and step inside.

The room is dark due to his blackout curtains, but there's a small, colored night-light that he's switched on, offering a warm glow that's not as harsh as his bedside lamp. I'm unable to tear my eyes away from the soft shadows it casts onto his bare chest.

"Hey." He smiles, rubbing his face. "What time is it?"

"Just after two in the afternoon." I round his bed and place the tablets into his good hand. He throws them into his mouth before I hand over a glass of water. He finishes it in a few easy gulps and passes the empty glass back. "How's your head feeling?"

"Okay, I think? Or at least it's okay for now."

"That's good, hopefully it'll stay that way. It'll be good if you can have a few hours out of bed." I walk around to the other side of the bed and climb on to sit next to him. He shuffles down and rests his head against my shoulder, and I instantly wrap my arm around him, kissing the top of his head.

"Dude, you need a shower." I grimace.

He snickers. "I know. I smell so bad."

"Why don't you take one while your head isn't hurting? It might help."

"I don't know if I can stand up for that long without getting dizzy."

"I'll help?"

He tilts his head up to face me. "Really?"

"Yeah, of course I will." I flick his nipple. "I'll do anything for you, you know that."

I jolt when he pinches the soft skin above my hip.

"Fucker," I curse, causing him to laugh. "Okay, come on. Let's get you in the shower."

I stand up and move back to his side of the bed. We take it slow and steady, making sure he doesn't rush standing up and risk giving himself another headache. He pushes up with his good hand, but once he's on his feet, he sways slightly. I instantly reach out to grip his biceps, holding him steady as a wave of dizziness takes over.

"I'm fine," he says, but I ignore him and wrap my arm around his waist for support as we head into his en suite bathroom.

He sits down on the closed toilet seat, and I reach inside the shower, flicking on the water to warm up. Shit, he's going to need something to sit on. I'm a strong guy, but I'm not sure I'll be able to help him wash if I have to prop up his two hundred and fifty-pound weight.

"Wait here," I say, pointing my finger at him. "Don't move."

"Don't worry, I won't be going anywhere fast." He closes his eyes, his head tipping back to rest against the tiled wall behind him.

I chuckle, glad he still has some sense of humor, and go

into the kitchen to find something for him to sit on. All his chairs and stools are fabric, so they won't work. Peering my head around the door to his game room, I spot a small, plastic stool that has some books stacked on top. That should do the trick.

Moving the books to his gaming desk, I pick up the stool and carry it back into the bathroom. His eyes open at the sound of me reentering, and those dark brows furrow in confusion when he notices the stool in my hands.

"What are you doing with that?"

"You're gonna sit on it in the shower."

"But I'll ruin it."

"Then I'll buy you a new one," I argue.

I place it inside the shower, then take off all my clothes until I'm only in my boxer briefs before stepping into the shower to find the right position for the stool. Once I've got it in the right spot, I grab the towel off the hook, pat myself dry, and walk over to him. "Right, up you go."

Holding out my hands to steady him, he grabs hold of one arm, hoisting himself up. His eyes go a bit weird as he has another dizzy spell, then he seems to come to.

"What about my cast? I can't get it wet."

"Well, it's a good thing I've had some time on my hands while you've been in dreamland because I went down an internet rabbit hole and found a waterproof cast cover." I jerk my chin to where the cover is sitting on the counter.

"Of course you did." He huffs a laugh, then holds on to my shoulder as I slip the plastic sleeve on his arm.

We take slow, steady steps toward the shower, and once we're at the door, I realize he's still got his pajama pants on.

"Shit. Okay, put your hand on the wall for a sec. I gotta take off your pants."

"You could at least buy me a drink first."

I laugh, shaking my head. "Quit fooling around and get naked, Reid."

Placing his good hand on my shoulder for balance, I hook my fingers into the waistband of his plaid sleep pants and pull them down. I crouch, trying not to let my eyes linger on his soft cock hanging heavy between his thighs.

Has he ever touched himself while thinking about me? Was I on his mind while he fucked someone else?

My cock jerks in my boxers, and I curse internally. Now is not the time to be getting hard.

Carefully lifting each foot so he doesn't lose his balance, I toss his pants to the side before glancing up, meeting his gaze. He's looking down at me under hooded eyes.

The angle provides an incredible view of his physique. Thick, muscular thighs covered in colorful tattoos and dark hair. His abs so defined, I'm tempted to trace the grooves with my fingertips to see if they are as deep as they look.

"Carter?"

My head snaps up at the sound of his voice. Shit. I completely got lost in my head.

"Ready?" I ask, standing up.

Guiding him into the shower, I motion for him to take a seat on the stool and adjust the showerhead to get the right angle. Squirting some shampoo in my hand, I wash his hair first, scrubbing at his scalp. He hums, leaning into my touch as I give it a second wash. After, I take the shower gel and lather it up in my palms and begin moving my hands over his shoulders and back in circular motions.

He hums again, dipping his head so his dark hair creates a curtain around his face as it dampens.

"Tell me if you get dizzy, okay? I know sometimes the heat can make you lightheaded."

He doesn't answer, but he nods softly.

I move around to his front, gliding my hands over his sculpted chest, over his biceps, and under his arms. When I reach his stomach, I kneel between his parted legs, squirting more shower gel into my hands. My boxers are soaked right through. There's no doubt he can see the outline of my half-hard cock, but when I look up at his face, his eyes are closed. He looks exhausted. Like the last few days have really taken their toll on him.

I run my hands along his thighs, admiring the colorful tattoos lining his strong legs as they peek through the bubbles.

"Can I have some body wash?" he asks quietly, his voice barely audible over the spray of the shower.

"Yeah."

I pick up the bottle from where I tossed it on the shower floor and pour some into his hand. I'm unable to do anything but sit back on my haunches and watch as he washes between his legs, his fingers and palm coasting over his soft cock and balls and as far back as he can reach.

My cheeks heat. Showering together is strangely… intimate, but in a tender way. I'm glad I'm the one helping him. Being here for him through all of this because the thought of someone else doing it makes me insanely jealous.

I've been a terrible friend over the years. Completely oblivious to his feelings and my own, really, but I'm going to make it right.

I would do anything for Zach Reid, but I haven't realized *why* until recently.

I've been in love with him all this time. I just wasn't ready to acknowledge it.

Reaching up, I comb my fingers through his hair, tucking the wet strands behind his ears, his shuddering breath coasting over the inside of my wrists. He chews on his bottom lip, watching me so intently with those icy blue eyes. The need to kiss him is visceral. Every fiber of my being wants to lean up and take his mouth with mine. To let him know that this is us.

It will always be *us*.

"Carter…"

It's those two whispered syllables falling from his lips that make me move.

With my hands resting on his knees, I lean up and press my lips to his. They're soft and wet, and kissing him is even better than I imagined it to be. A couple of seconds go by where he doesn't move, but then he lifts his left hand and cups the side of my face before sinking into the kiss.

There's nothing frantic about it. It's tender, slow. Like we're savoring the feel of our mouths fitting together so fucking perfectly.

I tentatively swipe my tongue across the seam of his lips, not wanting to be pushy and go faster than what he's comfortable with, but I'm desperate to taste him.

A low whimper escapes me as he welcomes my tongue, and my cock throbs when his tongue meets mine. My body is tingling like a live wire, only intensifying with the gentle scrape of his beard against my skin, sending shivers from my head all the way down to my toes.

I'm kissing my best friend.

Should I be freaking out over this? I've never kissed a man before, and I'm aware I'm having some kind of monumental sexual awakening moment while my tongue is in my best friend's mouth, but all I keep thinking is… How can a kiss feel so right?

All of my previous relationships seem so miniscule now, because nothing, *nothing*, could compare to how fucking perfect this is.

How perfect Zach is.

We lose ourselves in each other, tasting and exploring each other's mouths. When the water begins to cool, he slowly pulls away just a fraction. I open my eyes, and my heart swells in my chest at the blissed-out expression on his face. Knowing *I* put it there.

"What was that for?" he asks.

"I wanted to. It's something we should've been doing all along."

His Adam's apple bobs as he swallows roughly. There's apprehension in his eyes, which I understand. I know I'm going to have some explaining to do. But I'll show him that, if he wants this, I'm all in.

"Really?"

I nod, then a full-body shiver rakes through me as the water turns cold.

"Wanna get out of here and do some more of that on the couch?"

Chapter Thirteen

Zach

We're both silent as Carter shuts off the water and we step
out of the shower. He wraps a towel around his waist before
wrapping one around me and guiding me over to the closed
toilet seat.

"Sit," he insists, his voice barely above a whisper.

Taking a seat, I chew on my bottom lip, watching as he
quietly moves around the dimly lit room. The only light is
the soft glow from behind the mirror, and the thoughtfulness
squeezes at my chest. I've been struggling with lights
recently, ever since I ended up in the hospital, and now with
the migraines as a result of the concussion. The fact Carter
is conscious of it and making sure I'm comfortable makes
me want to grab his face and kiss him again.

Because holy shit, that was one heck of a kiss.

I know my head has been all over the place recently, but
I really hope I didn't just imagine that. I've imagined what it

would be like to kiss Carter so many times. I've often wondered whether his lips were as pillowy soft as they looked and whether he tasted like the Tropical Twist gum he's always chewing on. But all the fantasies I had pale in comparison.

That kiss was *everything* and more.

And as much as I want to do it again right now, there's a lot we need to talk about first. Like where the fuck this has suddenly come from.

Carter hums as he rubs a towel over my hair, then over my shoulders, arms, and chest. He tosses it into the laundry hamper before removing the cast protector and taking my hairbrush from the countertop.

"I can do that." I reach out with my good hand, but he slaps it away and scowls playfully.

"No. Let me take care of you, damnit."

I chuckle under my breath and run my gaze over his face. There's a slight flush over his cheekbones from the shower, and his lips are pink and swollen. Long, dark lashes frame his eyes, and his brows furrow in concentration as he carefully works the brush through my hair. Maybe it's crazy considering we had our tongues in each other's mouths only a few minutes ago, but I've never felt closer to him than in this moment.

It takes someone special to step up and be a caretaker. Showing their love through actions instead of words. He's done it so effortlessly.

He uses my electric razor to shave my beard, then helps me get dressed in sweatpants and a hoodie before we head into the living room. I lie down on the couch as he lights an unscented candle in the middle of the coffee table and makes quick work of closing the drapes, basking the apartment into complete darkness except for the lone flame flickering away.

Resting my casted arm on a cushion, Carter curls into my left side, his head on my shoulder. I wrap my arm around him, softly stroking my fingers over his ribs.

"This is nice," he murmurs.

"Mm," I hum.

Today is the first day I've felt relatively normal. The throb of pain in my skull has eased to a light discomfort, and I don't feel like I'm going to throw up the second I open my eyes. Although I've slept for what feels like an eternity, I still find myself beginning to drift off because I'm so relaxed, but I blink my eyes open when his quietly spoken words stir me awake.

"You've probably got a lot of questions for me…"

"Yeah, I do." I clear my throat and try to find the right words to explain the whirlwind that's going on in my brain or where to even begin. "Why… When…"

He shifts to lean up on his elbow and a few dark curls fall onto his forehead as he looks down at me.

"I arrived in Chicago the same day you got hurt. I had been sensing there was this distance between us and couldn't figure out what I'd done wrong or what had caused it. I thought I was losing you, and we ended up in a bit of an… argument, I guess?" He fiddles with the string of my hoodie, avoiding my eyes. I hate seeing his confidence slip, but it's a conversation we need to have. When he speaks again, his voice cracks. "You yelled at me. You told me you were in love with me, and then you told me to leave because you needed time to get over me and wanted to be alone. I didn't know what to do. It was like my world shifted on its axis."

Fuck. I don't remember any of this.

The doctor said I may never be able to remember anything that happened just before or after the hit, and clearly this is one of those things. I can't believe I yelled at him. I'm usually such a calm guy. I never let anything faze me; even on the ice when other players try to rile me up, I always keep my cool.

Well, always except the time I ran away from Denver with my heart in my hands, but that doesn't count.

"I yelled at you?" I frown. "Fuck, I'm sorry."

When his eyes lock with mine again, there's pain in my favorite pair of brown eyes. Not the same kind of pain I caused when I told him I was coming back to Chicago early, but still, pain my actions caused when I thought I was doing what was best for both of us.

He shakes his head at my apology. "Yeah, but I deserved it. I didn't know how I'd made you feel all this time, and I wasn't quite sure how to handle all the emotions I was feeling. There have been a few things about myself and my feelings that haven't really made sense to me since that night I met Raegan when we were in Hawaii. Some of those feelings didn't add up until now."

Oh, wow. I don't know what I was expecting him to say, but it sure wasn't that.

All those times he reached out, wanting to talk to me, and I avoided him, made excuses not to speak to him—was he trying to tell me something? Has he been trying to work through these feelings on his own because I wasn't there for him?

Something twists in my chest. A deep-rooted ache at the thought of a confused, lonely Carter wanting nothing more than to speak to me—the person who was supposed to be his best friend—and all I did was keep pushing him away instead.

Fuck, I'm such an asshole.

Swallowing hard, I'm almost scared to ask, "And what feelings are those?"

"That I've been looking for love in the wrong place. That it's been right in front of me all this time."

My breath hitches.

Is this really happening?

This is everything I've wanted for so long. For almost two decades, all I've ever wanted was for Carter to feel the same way about me. To love me as more than a friend.

So why do I have this heavy weight of uncertainty in the pit of my stomach? I don't know if I could survive having a taste of Carter just to have him decide it isn't for him.

That *I'm* not for him.

It would completely destroy me.

"I know it all seems very sudden, but I've had a lot of time to think about things." His words come out in a nervous ramble as he twirls the hoodie string around his finger, dark brows furrowing in concern. "And I understand if you need time. I want you to know that I'm here, and I would like to see where this goes with no barriers between us, if that's what you would like too. I'm not going anywhere."

He's right about it being very sudden, but he's also right that he's had a lot of time to think about it. He's had over a week to think and reflect on the conversation I can't remember having while I've been in the hospital and knocked out in bed with a migraine.

Don't get me wrong, I trust Carter with my life, but there's still this level of... apprehension. The walls I've carefully constructed around my heart over the years remain in place, and I don't want to lower them too soon. Not until I know he's all in and that he won't freak out.

Not until I know this won't completely ruin us, because I can't risk losing him if it goes wrong.

But it doesn't mean I can't enjoy it. It just means I need to remember to make sure I go slow and ease him into this gently.

I reach up and run my hand over the back of his head, combing my fingers through the soft curls before gripping the back of his neck. I tug his head down and nip his bottom lip.

"Good, because I don't want you going anywhere."

Surprise flicks over his face as he lights up with a wide, toothy grin. "Really?"

"Yeah, really."

"Mhm," he murmurs and brushes his mouth against mine. "So, where were we?"

This time, when our lips meet, it's not soft and languid like it was in the shower. Our tongues meet with a little more urgency. His tongue explores my mouth with eager, hungry strokes.

I don't know why I expected Carter to be more hesitant, because whenever he's set his mind to something before, he's fully committed.

He moans into my mouth, fingers clutching the wet

strands of my hair as he grinds his hips against my thigh, and holy fuck, he's hard.

I made my best friend *hard*.

Am I having some kind of fever dream? Am I actually awake, or is this a crazy illusion my migraine has curated, deciding to torture me in a different way?

My cock thickens in my sweats as his teeth graze over my bottom lip, sucking it into his mouth and releasing it with a wet pop.

"Will you… Will you tell me about it?"

"About what?" I rasp, blinking him into focus.

"Having to hide it all this time. You said you've been in love with me since we were ten, but will you tell me about it? I hate that I didn't know…" His eyes widen in alarm, and he quickly adds, "Not that I blame you for not telling me, I totally get why you didn't… I just… I've been thinking about whether we could have had this sooner if I knew… I get why you left early in the summer."

My cock softens instantly. Fuck, this isn't something I wanted to talk about.

I let out a heavy exhale. "You really wanna know?"

"Yeah, I do."

"It's gonna kill the vibe."

He presses a quick, fleeting kiss against my lips. "I don't care. I hate the fact I hurt you, even if it was unintentional. I just want to know what it was like for you."

I shift underneath him, and he moves off me to sit upright. Sitting up, I lean back into the couch cushions and rub my face with my hand before letting out another sigh.

"It was New Year's Eve, and we had made a blanket fort on the living room floor in front of the TV to watch *Return of the Jedi*. When midnight hit, I remember turning to look at you, and your face was lit up from the fireworks they were setting off next door."

"I remember that night. I thought you were watching the fireworks."

I shake my head. "No, I was watching you, and I remember thinking, *Damn,* Carter is the most beautiful thing I've ever seen."

His eyes shimmer with wonderment. "You did?"

"Yeah. I felt this weird pull in my chest at the thought, and I didn't realize what it was until I was older." I brush my thumb over his cheek, before tracing the shape of his lips. "It was love, and it never went away."

He lets out a shaky breath. He has to clear his throat a few times before he speaks again. "Fuck, Zach. I don't know how you managed all this time."

"I won't lie to you, it was hard. I was so afraid of losing you, and I thought you were straight, so I didn't see the point in telling you, and as for leaving early, yeah. You and Raegan seemed to be getting on really well, and that day I just… snapped. I knew if I carried on the way I was, I was going to end up resenting her, and she didn't deserve that."

"I'm really sorry I put you through that."

I shake my head. "No, don't do that. Don't apologize for something you knew nothing about. I'm the one who's sorry for keeping it from you. Let's just make a new pact not to hide anything from each other going forward. If you're serious about this with me, then we need to tell each other everything. I know I need to be more open with how I'm feeling, and if you don't want to do something, you're unsure about it, or you're not ready, tell me."

"I will." He kisses the corner of my mouth. "Now, shut up and kiss me, Reid."

✕

I'm currently on my second day without a headache, and I'm taking that as a major win. I'm still following doctors' orders and avoiding screens, but it means I'm bored out of my mind. I'm not allowed back in the gym yet, and I can't play video games or watch TV. I can't lose hours mindlessly scrolling social media. The most exciting thing to happen was the afternoon Carter found a thousand-piece Star Wars jigsaw puzzle in Target. It kept me busy for most of the day, as having my dominant hand in a cast made things entertaining.

Who said professional hockey players are all about the high life? Give me a puzzle, and I'm a happy soul.

And as much as I love kissing Carter, there's only so much kissing we can do to fill the hours before our mouths are raw.

I miss the guys, too.

Every time they have come over, I've been asleep, and now they're on the road. Carter said they visited me in the hospital, but I don't remember. I need to see Elliot and tell him that I'm okay, let him see me with his own eyes. It kills me knowing how upset he was. Other than Carter, he's one of my best friends. His friendship means a lot to me, and I know he'll be worried.

Luckily, the team's trainer, Joe, has lined up my first appointment for when they get back, so I have a few more days until I return to the rink. I won't be allowed on the ice, but being back around my teammates will help me feel a sense of normality.

Because although I'm an introvert at the best of times and love my own space—my home space—it's beginning to feel like the walls are closing in.

"Come on," Carter says as he enters the living room with my boots in hand. "It's finally dry outside, so we're getting out of this apartment for a few hours."

He drops my boots down by my feet, then disappears back into my room, only to return moments later with my winter coat, scarf, and hat.

I raise a questioning brow and chuckle as I eye the knitted accessories curiously. "Is it snowing outside or something?"

"No." He glares. "But it's cold, and I don't want to risk you getting sick."

My heart squeezes at his words. He's taken the role of caretaker very seriously, and since our kiss in the shower, his sleepy cuddles have now been accompanied by sleepy kisses.

I'm so happy about it, I could cry.

Sliding my feet into my boots, I attempt to wrap the scarf around my neck one-handed before giving up. I toss it aside and tug on my hat. Carter rolls his eyes and gives me an adoring smile before he helps me into my coat, making sure my cast doesn't get stuck in the sleeve. I follow him toward the door as he puts on his own coat and picks up my car keys from the bowl where I keep them on the kitchen island.

"So, where are we going?" I ask as we head out into the hall.

"It's a surprise." He wiggles his eyebrows, smirking.

We ride the elevator down to the parking garage, and when he takes my hand and laces our fingers together, my heart has never felt so full.

"You know I don't like surprises," I groan.

"Tough shit, you're getting one. I thought it would be good for you to get a change of scenery, especially with the headaches finally giving you a break."

He steps in front of me and curls his other hand around the side of my neck. I lean into his warm touch.

"I thought we could get some lunch, maybe look at a shop or two. Maybe stop by the bakery."

My interest spikes up. "For donuts?"

"Yeah." He nods, a soft smile on his face. "For donuts."

Carter takes us to our favorite hole-in-the-wall Italian restaurant for lunch, and once we're full of delicious homemade pasta and more side dishes than Coach Harris would prefer me to eat during the season, we get back in the car. I narrow my eyes as Water Tower Place comes into view.

He's wearing a goofy grin when I turn to him.

"What are we doing here?"

"You'll see," he sings.

He parks the car in the underground parking garage, and once we're in the elevator, he hits the button for the second floor. He's shifting on his feet excitedly, which only causes my suspicions to rise.

"What are you playing at?"

"Nothing," he says coyly.

I narrow my eyes and pull on his hand until he's pressed up against me. Leaning in, I nuzzle my nose up the thick column of his neck, then nip his lobe with my teeth. His low moan goes straight to my cock, and I make a mental note to do that again when we're naked.

"Tell me," I whisper.

"No."

The doors open, and he smacks a quick kiss on my lips before leading me toward the LEGO store.

"Carter…" I warn.

The sheer amount of love shining in his eyes hits me square in the chest.

"Look, you have some time on your hands." He looks down at my cast and grimaces. "Okay, *hand*. You can't start physio yet, and you're still on screen downtime, so I thought you could use something else to keep your brain busy."

I'm trying to process his words when he leads me over to the Star Wars section, then crouches down. My jaw drops as he pulls a large box from the shelf.

Licking my dry lips, my voice goes an octave higher when I ask, "You're buying me the Millennium Falcon?"

"Damn right, I am. I thought maybe we could build it together. There's over seven thousand five hundred pieces in here, which should keep us busy for a while."

I blink at him, completely speechless.

"I read online that you can buy these LED light kits too," he rambles, shifting nervously on his feet when I still haven't said anything. "I called up the store before we left to make sure they had plenty of stock, but if there's a different set you want instead…"

I love you is on the tip of my tongue. We might have said those three little words easily before, but he'll know it has a whole other meaning now.

And while I'm sure Han Solo and Princess Leia would

appreciate it, I don't want the first time I tell him I love him to be over the Millennium Falcon.

"If we weren't in the middle of the LEGO store right now, I'd kiss you."

He drags his teeth over his bottom lip as his eyes drop to my mouth. "Yeah?"

"Hell yeah." I round the box so I'm at his side. I squeeze his bicep, loving the feel of his solid muscle beneath my hand, and lean in to whisper in his ear. "Thank you."

"For what?"

"Being amazing. Knowing what I need before I do. Being here for me and not running when I told you to." I swallow the lump in my throat. "Thank you for staying."

"Like I said, I'm not going anywhere, Reid." He winks. "But can we go and pay for this thing because you're gonna make me pop a boner soon, looking all adorable in your hat."

I flip him off, and we're both laughing all the way to the checkout.

Chapter Fourteen

Carter

Leaning against the doorframe, I simply stand there and watch Zach sleep. There's a slight crease between his brows, almost like he's thinking really hard about something. The covers have been kicked off, exposing one tattooed leg and his casted arm, while the other arm is tucked underneath his pillow. I've noticed he does that a lot. Like he needs to regulate his body temperature, but it's too cold to be completely uncovered.

The headache-free days were short-lived, and they've returned with a vengeance. We only managed to build the base of the Falcon before they struck him down again.

I feel so helpless. I wish there was something I could do to help him aside from supplying him water and massaging his head and neck. I've spent hours scrolling the internet, trying to find alternate means to help ease the pain. Ice caps, vitamins, massage techniques, soaking his feet in hot water. Each of them has only given him a small reprieve, and when I called the doctor yesterday, she said it was normal and it will ease up in time.

Well, it's easy for her to say when she's not the one watching someone you love be in constant pain day after day.

What if they don't go away? What if these migraines are the reason he has to retire early? He's twenty-nine years old. It's too early for him to hang up his skates.

Don't think like that, my conscience scolds me.

It's hard not to, though. I've seen firsthand how concussions have ended people's careers over the years. In football, head injuries weren't taken seriously for a long time, and even so, strict concussion protocols have only been in place recently. I know how much hockey means to Zach, and it will break my heart if this is it for him.

He's due back at the training facility tomorrow, and I know how much he's been looking forward to seeing everyone again. I just hope he's well enough to go.

I step into the hall, closing the door softly behind me so as not to disturb him, and head into the living room.

"I don't know what to do," I grumble to myself, falling back onto the couch and tipping my head against the cushion.

Whenever Zach was away on the road before, I would go to the gym or take a drive to find some random cute coffee shop somewhere. But I can't leave the apartment. I don't want to leave Zach alone in case he needs me.

Fetching my phone from the coffee table, I scroll through my contact list, and my thumb hovers over Raegan's name.

Since we broke up a few months back, we've remained friends. I don't harbor any ill feelings toward her for breaking up with me. In fact, come to think of it, some of the things she said make a lot of sense now. I hit Call before I can second-guess it. Maybe speaking with her will help clear up a few things in my head.

She answers on the third ring. "Carter, hey. I wasn't expecting to hear from you."

I smile at her familiar voice. "Hey, Raegan. I hope I haven't caught you at a bad time."

"No, no, not at all. I've actually been meaning to call you for a few days now and ask how Zach's doing. I saw it while I was scrolling on social media. Not going to lie, it made me feel a little sick."

"Yeah, me too. I've never felt fear like when I was watching him lying there unconscious."

"Shit, I'll bet. I would've been terrified."

"I was, but he's recovering. He's got some shit side effects from the concussion, but his wrist is healing up nicely. So, depending on how his head is, he'll be back on the ice in a month or so."

"Wow, that soon?"

"Yeah, I think he'd go out now if they cleared him."

She snorts. "Of course he would."

"I…" I let out a shaky breath. My palms are beginning to sweat, so I wipe them down the front of my sweatpants. "I was hoping I could talk to you, and I need you to be honest with me."

"Uh-oh, that sounds ominous."

I laugh. "No, nothing like that. It's just… When you broke up with me, you said we were on different paths. Did that have anything to do with Zach… and my very oblivious feelings for him?"

A heavy silence passes between us before a small sigh filters through the line. "Yes. I thought there was something there the first time I saw you in that bar in Oahu, because of the way he looked at you, and vice versa. Then there was the couple hitting on him and the jealousy pouring off you in waves, but I just put it down to the fact that you were on vacation, and you didn't want someone else taking his time and attention. But then when he left Denver…" I hear the sadness in her voice. "Carter, you were more devastated about him leaving than when I broke up with you."

Squeezing my eyes shut, I run a hand down my face. "Why didn't you tell me?"

The sadness that was in her tone is now replaced with amusement.

"And say what? 'Hey, Carter, I think you might be bi or pan and be in love with your best friend, who, by the way, is totally head over heels in love with you?'"

"Well, yeah," I reply, and we both laugh.

"I figured you were either in denial about your feelings for him, or you had no clue how you really felt, and I didn't want to stand in the way of that when you finally came to the realization that you're meant to be together. You two have such a special connection. I didn't want to be a roadblock and stop you from exploring those feelings."

Fuck, I was such a terrible boyfriend. And a terrible friend. The signs were there all along, and I was clueless. How could I get it so catastrophically wrong?

"I'm sorry."

"There's nothing to be sorry for. I kinda knew what I was getting myself into. Maybe I was a little in denial myself, but I don't blame you for anything. I want you to be happy, Carter, and I'm hoping the fact that you've called me today means you've come to acknowledge your feelings, perhaps?"

"Yeah, so… We're kind of a thing now?" I say, but it comes out as a question.

She laughs. "Are you telling me, or asking me?"

"No, we *are* a thing now. We're taking things slow. There's a lot at stake, you know? He's been my best friend for pretty much my whole life. I don't want to risk jeopardizing that, but at the same time, I can't see myself with anyone but him. We haven't done anything except kiss, but holy shit, Raegan, the kissing is so good." I grimace. "And now I'm nervous-rambling to my ex-girlfriend about how good it is to kiss the guy I'm dating."

She bursts into laughter, and the tension I was feeling eases. I rub my hand over my face, trying to scrub away the smile. I'm glad there's no hard feelings between us.

"Are you done?" she asks between fits of laughter.

"Yeah, I think so."

"Good, because I want you to know I'm so freaking happy for you. All along, I've been hoping one of you got his head out of his ass and realized you two are meant to be together. And Carter?"

"Yeah?"

"I might be your ex-girlfriend, but I'm still your friend, and it makes me so happy to hear the happiness in your voice, especially knowing Zach is the reason behind it."

Oh, fuck. My eyes burn at her words. Who decided to cut onions around me?

I pick at the loose thread on my sweatpants. I didn't realize how much I needed someone to talk to about this. Yeah, I've spoken to Zach about it, but it's almost like we're in our own bubble, blissfully blocking out the rest of the world while we navigate the grounds of our new relationship. But there's something that's been playing in my mind on repeat. Something that I don't want to place on Zach's shoulders since he's recovering.

"The night he ended up in the hospital, seeing him lying there in that bed and then being told he had swelling on his brain…" I let out a shuddering breath as my vision begins to blur. "Fuck, I had to stay strong for him, but inside I was terrified he was going to be taken away from me. I was ready to make a deal with whatever higher power there is to take his place. To plead for him to be all right because there was no way on earth I was living without him, and it was like everything started making sense. Me being jealous. Me always putting him before girls. How I always need to be close to him, touching him in some way…"

There's no malice in her voice when she asks, "Have you always found him attractive?"

"Always. He's the hottest person I've ever known." I wince. "Fuck, I'm sorry. That wasn't cool of me."

"It's okay, I'm not offended." She chuckles softly. "Sweetie, I think the series of events led you to have an epiphany. Sometimes it takes nearly losing someone, or the concept of losing someone, for you to acknowledge feelings that have been there all along. You don't need to justify it to anyone. You've got to do what's best for both of you, in your own time."

"Thank you. You're awesome, you know that?"

"Yeah, I know." I can sense her smile through her words.

I chuckle, shaking my head. "Thanks for being so great about this."

"I meant what I said earlier, Carter. I want you to be happy—both of you. And make sure I'm a bridesmaid at the wedding."

I snort. "Whoa, okay. On that note, I'm gonna go before we get way ahead of ourselves."

She cackles.

We say our goodbyes with the promise to speak soon, and when I hang up, I feel lighter. Like a load has been lifted from my shoulders.

Maybe I've been oblivious all this time, but I can't dwell on what I could have done differently. It's about how I move forward that's important. I can sense Zach's apprehension, and it might just take time and patience to show him that my feelings are genuine, and I'm all his, if he wants me.

"You know you're never gonna lose me, right?"

I jump two feet off the couch at the sound of Zach's voice behind me. Dressed in nothing but his black boxer briefs, I take in his sleep-tousled hair and kind eyes, and my heart skips a beat.

"You heard all that?"

He nods softly, and I sit back down as he moves to sit next to me. He rests his legs on top of mine, then takes my hand and holds it on his thigh.

"I'm sorry I put you through all that."

I open my mouth to argue that it wasn't his fault, but he silences me with a pointed look.

"I can't even begin to imagine how you felt, but I know I would have felt the same if the roles were reversed. But me and you? We're endgame. If there were such a thing as fated mates, I'd like to think we would be that. You've always been my person, Carter."

His face goes blurry as tears fill my eyes again. I quickly wipe them away with my palm.

"I don't know why I'm getting so emotional about it all because I know you're okay. Like, you're right in front of me, in flesh and blood. I just…" I shake my head. "That was Raegan. She said some things when we broke up that I wanted to clarify."

His smile is genuine as he asks, "How is she?"

"Good. She asked about you. I think hearing her say all she wants is for us to be happy kinda struck a chord and opened up the floodgates."

"That's understandable. You've had a lot to deal with. What with my grumpy ass, then the hit, and now looking after me." He shrugs and squeezes my hand. "It's normal to be emotional, but you're not going to lose me."

Closing the gap between us, I press a kiss to his lips. "How's your head?"

"Eased up, luckily." He murmurs against my mouth. "Great. In fact… I was wondering if you wanted to join me in bed for a bit."

I pull back so I can see his face. His blue eyes glisten with heat, and my dick instantly takes notice of the smirk lifting the corner of his lips. I've been thinking about this nonstop.

"That good, huh?"

He nods. "Only if you want?"

"Oh, I *want*, all right." I stand up so fast, my phone drops to the floor with a clatter. "Time to show me what you've got, Reid."

Chapter Fifteen

Zach

I follow Carter as he rushes down the hall to my room, chuckling under my breath at his eagerness. I'm also trying not to let the little voice in the back of my mind think too hard about where this has come from. We've always been affectionate. Ever since we were kids, it was like physical touch was our thing. But it's different now. Each touch means something more than just two best friends.

So much *more*.

When I walked into the living room, it wasn't with the intention to eavesdrop on his conversation. I didn't hear all of it, but I'm glad I caught the end. I could tell that there was something Carter was trying to deal with on his own, but I wanted—no, *needed*—to remind him he wasn't alone in this. That just because I was recovering didn't mean he couldn't lean on me when he needed it.

His laughter fills the room as Carter throws himself onto

my bed and tries to pull off his sweats as he bounces on the mattress, the springs groaning under his weight.

I try to hide my amusement behind my casted hand.

"What have *you* got in mind? Because I was thinking more of a cuddle session…" I deadpan.

Brown eyes sparkle back at me, a wicked smirk on his full lips. "I dunno. Blow jobs? Frothing?"

My eyes widen as I gape at him. "Frothing?"

"Yeah, you know." He mimics jerking off with his hand. "Jerking each other off at the same time, same hand."

I press my lips together, swallowing down the bark of laughter that threatens to escape as I pinch the bridge of my nose. "I think you mean frotting."

He snaps his fingers and points at me. "That's it!"

I snicker as he finally kicks his sweats onto the floor, then pulls off his hoodie, tossing it away, leaving him in only his light gray boxer briefs. My eyes linger on his almost naked body. The slight opening in my drapes casts the perfect spotlight on his smooth, light brown skin.

Shadows fall in the dips and grooves of his solid muscle, and I want to trace every decadent inch of his smooth skin with my tongue. Worship him until he's wrung out with pleasure before doing it all over again.

It's not the first time I've seen Carter in only his boxers. Hell, I've seen his bare ass more times than I can count. But this is the first time I've seen him like *this*. His half-hard cock straining against the cotton. The desire burning bright in his eyes because of *me*.

For me.

A shiver travels down my spine at the overwhelming emotion swirling in my chest. I've wanted this for so long.

Carter is the only person I've ever wanted, and now I finally get to have him, I'm not sure whether to scream in celebration or cry from gratitude.

"Zach? You getting over here or what?"

His voice snaps me out of the daze, and I close the distance. Climbing on the bed next to him, he grabs hold of my hips and motions for me to straddle his lap. My eyes shoot to his, looking for… something. Nerves? Hesitation? Any sign that he's freaking out about being with a man? Surely it can't be this easy.

Maybe you're overthinking this.

True, but I don't want Carter to run before he can walk. I don't want him to be scared off because he's going faster than he's ready for. Because he thinks he owes me this or some shit.

Or he's going at the exact speed that's right for him.

Fuck off, conscience. Stop being so logical.

When I don't see anything but pure want shining bright in his eyes, I throw my leg over his waist. My cock thickens in my briefs at being near his shaft. My arms remain at my sides as his warm palms run up the front of my legs, his thumbs grazing the sensitive skin on my inner thigh. By the time the tips of his fingers slip beneath the hem of my boxers, I'm impossibly hard, and if he's fazed by the tent my hard cock is creating, he doesn't let it show. In fact, his eyes dip lower, and I'm unable to miss the audible hitch in his breath before he licks his bottom lip and tugs it between his teeth in a seductive move.

"Fuck, I can't get over how hot you are," he says, his voice dripping in wonderment. "I've always thought you were hot, but I never let myself see you in the 'I really wanna fuck you' kinda hot way before."

I force myself to swallow, and my voice comes out raspy as I ask, "And you see me like that now?"

"Fuck yeah, I do." He nods in earnest. "I want to do it all, but I don't want to fuck it up by doing something wrong."

"You won't do it wrong, Carter."

He ignores my reassurance. "I mean, I've watched a lot of porn. Like this week, I've gone through an entire jumbo bottle of lube. I feel like I've been missing out all this time. I'm suffering from some major FOMO."

I bite down on my lower lip, trying not to laugh as he continues his ramble.

"I know you can't judge it on porn, but still, I don't want to hurt you because I'm all eager and excited and curious."

"Carter."

He blinks up at me. "Yeah?"

"Shut up and kiss me."

His relaxed grin warms me. He reaches up, both hands sliding into my hair as I lean down and kiss him. It starts off slow and sensual with lazy sweeps of our tongues, but it doesn't stay that way. Carter moans, and he drops his hands to cup my ass. He presses me down as he rolls his hips, grinding his erection against mine.

It's like something snaps. The kisses turn hungry, almost frantic. All nipping lips and clashing teeth.

I'm gasping for air when I ease myself up with my good hand and move further down the bed. I graze my teeth over his Adam's apple, eliciting a hot gasp from Carter as his hand goes instinctively into my hair. His day-old stubble scratches against my lips, the sensation causing my cock to throb.

"Mmm, that feels so good." He practically purrs as I kiss down his chest, stopping at his nipple.

I run the tip of my tongue around it before sucking it into my mouth and nipping it with my teeth. He trembles beneath me as his cock presses against my stomach, a hot iron bar branding me through his briefs. I repeat the action on his other nipple before trailing my tongue down the center of his abs, watching his muscles rippling as I descend. The soft, dark hair that runs from his navel to the band of his boxers tickles my chin.

Kneeling between his parted legs, I glance up. Carter's watching me with heavy-lidded eyes, his full lips parted. Without taking my eyes off him, I curl my fingers into the elastic waistband, waiting for the inevitable *Stop*, but it never comes.

"Here," he whispers when I struggle to pull down his underwear one-handed. He quickly lifts his hips and tugs them off, tossing them over my shoulder before lying back down.

My mouth practically waters at the sight. Carter shifts one leg, bending his knee out to provide the perfect access to his taint and balls that are sitting high and tight. His long, thick erection bobs against his abdomen, almost begging for attention as it leaves a trail of precome against his gorgeous skin.

I always knew he was packing. It kinda makes sense, being six foot five and two hundred and sixty-five pounds. It was only natural for his cock to be just as big as the rest of him.

Wetting my lips, I ask him with my eyes if I can touch him, and when he nods, I nuzzle my face into his groin, inhaling his scent and tonguing his heavy sac before licking a path up the underside of his shaft. His hips buck as I suck the swollen head into my mouth.

"Oh my fucking god, Zach," he groans.

I massage his glans with my tongue and bob my head, taking him further into my mouth. His salty taste on my tongue lights up every one of my nerve endings.

Fuck. I've dreamed about this for so long.

As I suck him down, I'm hit with a bout of insecurity. The need to impress him and to make him feel good is stronger than I've ever felt before. Will he be comparing me to the women he's been with in the past? Will he realize that being sucked off by a dude isn't as good and decide it was fun while it lasted?

But before I can dwell on that thought and allow it to take root, his fingers brush my hair away from my face, and he holds it in his fist.

"You're so fuckin' good at that." His voice is laced with arousal, as his chest rises and falls with his heavy breathing. "You're gonna make me come."

I whimper—fucking *whimper*—around his shaft, want pooling in my stomach. Relaxing my jaw, I flatten my tongue and take him in deeper. His moan is loud, and his thighs tense next to my shoulders. He's close, really close, but so am I. I've been grinding my hips against the bedsheet, and one more drop of his impeccable taste down my throat will have me coming in my boxers.

I release him with a pop and rise up on my knees to remove my boxers.

"Get on top of me," I say as I move to lie down next to him.

He follows willingly, nuzzling his face into my neck and peppering kisses along my traps.

When he lifts his head, his forehead creases in a frown. "I don't want to hurt you."

"You won't hurt me, Carter. Just fucking get on top of me."

There's a beat of hesitation before he shifts until he's lying on me, settling his weight between my legs. He rolls his hips against mine, and the new position means our hard cocks line up perfectly. I'm unable to stop a low grunt as he grinds his length against mine.

"Fuck! I never knew this could feel so good." His hands are in my hair again. I move my hand around to grab his ass, pulling him even closer.

"There's lube in the drawer," I tell him.

He quickly retrieves the bottle and pours a generous amount into his hand.

"Take us both in your hand."

Carter does what I say and wraps his hand around our cocks and squeezes. My spine arches, toes curling into the sheet. He thrusts his hips in quick, shallow movements, and the combination of his tight fist, his husky moans, and the underside of his cock rubbing against mine causes pleasure to shoot down my spine.

I'm unable to warn him as my brain short-circuits. I come in hot spurts across his hand, my stomach, and my chest.

"Holy fuck, Zach, I'm gonna come."

The sound of my name coming from his lips will replay

in my mind on a loop for the rest of my life. His release lands against my heated skin as he strokes through his climax before coming some more. My body trembles as I come down from the highest high I've ever experienced.

Holy shit. I don't think I've come this hard before. The lightheaded buzz in my head tells me my body needs a minute to recuperate.

"Holy shit." He lets out a breathy chuckle. "So, what's your recovery time like so we can do that again?"

"You're so eager," I tease.

He nips my chin as he flops beside me, wrapping an arm and heavy leg over me. "Is that a problem?"

"No, not at all." I lean down and press a kiss to his swollen lips. "Give me fifteen minutes, and I'll be good for round two."

His grin hits me square in the chest, and that small bout of insecurity fully disappears.

"Text me when you're ready and I'll come pick you up," Carter says as he pulls my car into the practice facility parking lot the next day.

I may not be skating today, but I'm really looking forward to being back with the team and getting back a slice of normality. The boys returned from a road trip late last night, and the group chat has been blowing up all morning in excitement over the fact I'm coming in.

Luckily, my appointment with the team's physician won't take too long. My wrist is still in a cast for at least another few weeks before we begin intense physiotherapy to get me back on the ice as soon as possible, but today's assessment will let me know if I can start training lower body.

Which means I'll have more time to spend with the guys.

"You don't need to wait around for me. I'm sure I can catch a ride with Blaine or Elliot," I offer, knowing Carter is planning on speaking with Hayden today and hitting the gym.

The twins both live in the same building as me, and we often carpool to the rink. Blaine bought an apartment not long after I got mine, then Elliot bought one a few floors down when he was traded from Vancouver.

Carter turns slightly in his seat to face me. "No, I want you to text me. I want to pick you up."

A small noise escapes my throat as I try not to laugh at his serious expression. "Okay, okay. I'll text you when I'm done." I lean over and squeeze his thigh. "Maybe we can hit up the bakery after?"

His features soften as a bright smile lights up his face. "Yeah, okay, let's do that."

Leaning over the center console, I give him a kiss good-bye. A quick peck because I don't want to risk getting caught lip-locked before I've had the chance to tell the guys.

I get out of the car and flash him a smile before closing the door and sauntering inside. The second I head down the hallway, a wave of familiarity washes over me. The smell, the sound of skates on ice and sticks hitting pucks bring me a sense of relief. It's only been just under two weeks, but it feels like forever. Having a bout of amnesia and consistent migraines really fucks with your sense of time.

The guys are on the ice already, running through some drills, so they don't see me as I slip behind the bench and lean against the boards. I feel like I haven't seen them in so long. Carter mentioned they all came to the hospital the night of the incident, but in my delirious state, I don't remember. I also missed out on the times they came to the apartment for a visit because I was asleep.

But just being here again, feeling the chill from the ice against my skin, reminds me that it's not always going to be this rough.

"Hey! I didn't know you were here already."

I turn to see Chris stepping up beside me on the bench. He's been with the Thunder as the team's head physician for coming up to seventeen seasons now. He's treated me through a number of injuries, and this is just another one to add to the list. He also doesn't like us calling him Doc, as apparently it makes him feel old.

"I'm a little early. Just wanted to…" I trail off, motioning to the ice with my hand.

"Glad to be out of the apartment, huh?" He chuckles.

"Yeah. As much as I love Carter's company, it's nice to be back here."

"And how have you been feeling?" He motions to my wrist with his chin as he rests against the boards. "They're changing the cast in a few days, right? It's looking a little loose now."

"Yeah, they are, and honestly? I've had no issues with my wrist. It's my head that I've been struggling with."

His dark brows furrow in concern. "Post-concussion syndrome?"

"Yeah. I had constant dizziness for the first few days, and I'll occasionally have a dizzy spell, but I've been getting a lot of headaches. Some have completely wiped me out and given me some sensory issues."

I hate the look of worry that crosses his face. It's what I've been dreading the most.

As a defenseman, *statistically* I'm less likely to get my bell rung than a forward, but this is my second concussion in my professional career, and regardless of my position on the ice, I know that the more concussions I have, the higher the risk of developing post-concussion syndrome or other neurodegenerative diseases.

I love hockey. It's been my first love for as long as I can remember. I learned to skate before I could walk. But I need to think about my future after I hang up my skates. I have Carter now in the way I've always wanted him, and I don't want to risk potentially missing out on our time together once I'm done with the game.

I'm only twenty-nine, after all. I don't want to be thinking about what happens after hockey.

But of course, Chris will be thinking about it too. While it's his job to declare whether I'm fit to return to the ice—which won't happen while I'm experiencing these symptoms—he will want to ensure I have a decent quality of life after I retire.

"Come, let's have a look."

I follow him into the training room, where he goes through the usual checks, one of them being my weight. I've lost a few pounds, but that's understandable, and I make a joke that Carter will enjoy feeding me. He goes through a few concussion-related assessments, and types away on his laptop in between checks.

"Headache dependent, you're good to begin training

lower body and low-impact cardio as we don't want any pressure being put on your wrist." When he levels me with a pointed stare, my spine stiffens. "I would suggest speaking with your neurologist about your PCS. The symptoms can last for weeks, or even months, but it's important they are aware too. And please don't downplay your symptoms, Zach. Head trauma needs to be taken seriously."

"I know." My voice is quiet. "And I will. Speak to her, I mean."

I move to sit on the edge of the table when the door swings open and bounces off the wall with a loud bang. Elliot storms in like the hurricane he is. He's dressed in his Thunder-branded athletic shorts and T-shirt with calf-high socks and his most recent obsession: a pair of bright red Crocs.

I'm completely unprepared for his tight embrace as he wraps his arms around me, knocking the breath from my lungs.

"I'm so glad to see you. I was so fucking scared," he murmurs into my shoulder, and if it were possible, he tightens his hold on me even more. "You were just lying there. You weren't moving. I didn't know what to do."

Carefully wrapping my arms around him, I close my eyes and take a deep breath. Carter told me how Elliot was the first one to get to me when I didn't get up from the ice after the hit and how his terrified voice could be heard from where Carter was sitting in the stands. He also came to the hospital and spent all night at my bedside with him.

To the world, Elliot always appears to be the life and energy of every room he enters, but what a lot of people don't realize is that Elliot's a very sensitive soul. He feels things on a deeper level than most, especially when it comes to those he cares about, so I can't even begin to imagine how he must have been feeling.

Plus, this is the first time he's been able to see me awake and alert since the incident.

"I'm okay," I whisper reassuringly. "I'm gonna be all right."

Elliot lifts his head, and his mossy green eyes shimmer with so much emotion. His breath trembles as he exhales, collecting himself. A moment later, he places his hands on his hips and scowls at me. "Don't ever do that again. You scared the fuck out of me. I thought you were dead."

"Hey." I smile softly, squeezing his shoulder with my good hand. "I'm okay. Once my migraines fuck off and this heals up—" I raise my casted wrist "—I'll be right as rain, and we'll be back on that ice together."

"Damn right." He grins, and just like that, the darkness that was clouding him disappears. "I need my big D-man protecting me. So, how's it healing up? Have they given you a time frame of when you'll be back on the ice? Can I draw on it?"

"Sure, you can draw on it, but I'm getting a new one tomorrow. And I may be back in a couple of weeks. The cast comes off in three weeks, so they'll probably do another scan then before we start physio."

"Ew, physio sucks. I remember when I strained my groin, and it was not fun." Elliot grimaces, then turns to face Chris. "Hey, Doc, you got a Sharpie? I wanna draw on his cast."

The rest of the guys filter into the room, and I tell them everything while Elliot draws on my cast. I tell them about what the doctor said at the hospital—at least what Carter told me she said as I wasn't fully with it—to how my recovery has been and what we've got planned for my return.

I tell them everything except for how things have progressed with Carter.

I don't know why I'm being so... reserved about sharing this news with anyone. I'm hanging back in the defensive zone, not wanting to break the cycle I've been in since I was a teenager. I'm not worried about the guys' reaction. I mean, shit, I think they're half expecting it. And it's not because I'm concerned Carter is going to change his mind, especially after yesterday.

I guess I'm not ready to share him yet, because I've had to share him for twenty-three years, and now he's finally *mine*.

"Maybe we can have a boys' night soon? Do it at your place?" Peyton suggests.

"Or mine," Blaine offers. "Alex has a night out with Nate planned soon, so it'll just be me and the dog."

Peyton mock-gasps, his hand flailing to the side of his face. "You're letting Alex out without you? Alone? Are you unwell?"

Blaine scowls and flips him off. "Fuck off, I'm not that bad."

We all burst into laughter. If there's one guy here who's whipped, it's Blaine.

"I'm not!" He lifts his hands in protest. "But seriously,

I'm happy to host. It might be nice to get out of your apartment for a few hours. And you can bring Carter."

"Yeah." I smile. "We'd really like that."

Maybe we can share the news with them then, together.

Chapter Sixteen

Carter

After I drop Zach off at the Thunder practice facility, I make my way over to Lincoln Park. There's a gym that I started going to last year, which is the one where Nate works. I met him through Blaine's fiancé, Alex, as they usually attend the games together and Zach's comp seats are next to Blaine's. We struck up a conversation when I mentioned needing a gym in Chicago that was more advanced than the one in Zach's building, and Nate, being a personal trainer himself, hooked me up with a membership. But I haven't been here since before we left for Hawaii last year, and I also haven't worked out once during the off-season.

Oops.

But I've had a valid reason. Zach needed me, and I wasn't going to break my word and leave him, even if it was only to go to the gym. This is the first day I've been apart from him since I got here, and I'm itching out of my skin to get back to him.

"A workout will be good for you," I say to myself as I park Zach's SUV in the gym's parking lot.

The off-season is supposed to be for relaxing and going a little easier on yourself after pushing hard during the season, but I know if I let myself relax too much, it will be ten times harder when I need to start upping my training regime to get ready for the next one.

"He's going to be busy, and you need to do a workout. Blow jobs and frotting do not abs make." I roll my eyes at myself and snort.

They really should, though. That would be epic.

I'm about to switch the ignition off when a name flashes on the screen with an incoming call. Picking up my phone from the center console, I swipe to answer and bring it to my ear as I turn the engine off.

"Hey, Hayden. You good?" I greet my agent.

"All good here, bud. How are you? How's the big guy?"

We've not spoken since I landed in Chicago, only exchanging texts touching briefly on Zach's recovery.

"He's doing good at the minute. His wrist is healing up nicely, but he's still struggling with the headaches."

Hayden sighs. "Oh, fuck, really? I was hoping they would have eased up by now."

"Yeah, me too. I think if anything's going to keep him on IR, it'll be these damn migraines."

Zach was placed on the team's Long-Term Injured Reserve List as he was going to miss at least ten games and twenty-four calendar days of the season with his broken wrist. While I know the Thunder are hoping to get him back in a few weeks, if these headaches don't subside, he could potentially be out for the rest of the season.

I'm worried about him. And if there was ever a time I wished to be proven wrong, it's now.

"Damn, that sucks. But how about you? Are you holding up all right?"

A smile tugs at my lips. If I ignore the fact Zach's hurting and my last season was the worst I've ever had, I'm the happiest I've ever been.

Ghosting my fingers over my bottom lip, I'm pretty sure he can sense the smile in my voice when I say, "I'm really good."

"Oh, boy," Hayden chortles. "Come on, tell me everything. That sounded like a 'getting laid often' kinda good. Who is she?"

"*He*," I quickly correct, then grimace. We haven't exactly discussed what we're going to tell people, or if we're telling people at all right now.

There's a beat of silence before Hayden's laughter filters through the line. "Fuckin' hell, Lockwood. Finally, fucking *finally*! I have been waiting for this day to come for years."

A swarm of embarrassment floods my veins. "Don't tell me you knew, too."

"It wasn't so much as knowing; more like I had this feeling there was something going on between you two. Let's face it, you spend more time together than a married couple does. I mean, shit, you were together more than I was with my ex-wife. I always assumed you were either having a secret relationship, or it was some unrequited love and the other was in denial."

Sighing, I rest my head against the headrest and close

my eyes. I know Hayden means well and his words are not meant to hurt me, but knowing that other people seemed to know about Zach's feelings for me while I had no clue makes me feel like the biggest asshole.

"It seems everyone knew except me," I say, echoing my thoughts.

"Hey, sometimes it's all about divine timing, right? At least you know now, but…" He trails off. "Do I need to start approaching your contract from a different angle? You know the trade window opens soon…"

And that's the million-dollar question: do I want to go back to Denver?

The thought of being away from Zach for six months makes me antsy. Hell, I'm restless already, and it's been less than an hour. It would be different if I were here and he was on the road, but being states apart and seeing each other maybe twice during that time? I was able to deal with it before, but now that we've crossed the line into relationship territory, I don't know if I could do it, even for the final year of my contract.

I know it's not as simple as just upping and moving to a different team. Hayden can try to work on different deals, but ultimately, the team could trade me anywhere if they do decide to trade me. I don't have a no-trade clause in my contract or optional teams, after all.

If I end up getting traded somewhere else, would I give it up? I love my job, and I've been fortunate enough to get incredible contracts and sponsorship deals, meaning money isn't a concern for me, but still. Football has been all I've known, and I wasn't planning on hanging up my cleats just yet.

This is something I really need to talk about with Zach. Figure out how we're going to navigate this new version of us. We've been blissfully ignorant in our bubble, where nothing else matters except us.

But as much as we can ignore it right now, reality is going to come calling at some point, and I don't want us to go through another six months of pain like we just did.

"I… I don't know. I know that I don't want to resign with Denver if the offer comes up, but I also don't want to go anywhere else except—"

"Chicago," he supplies.

"Yeah."

"I get it. Let me see if I can work my magic, but for now, just enjoy your time together."

"I will, thanks," I say, relieved.

"Anytime. This wasn't why I was calling, but it's still good to know where your head is at. The reason for my call is that I'll be in Chicago at some point in the next few weeks and wanted to ask if you and the big guy wanted to get dinner."

"Oh, yeah, for sure. Let me know when, and we'll figure something out."

After we say goodbye and hang up, I make my way into the gym, feeling a little lighter than I did before.

"Can I get you anything?" I whisper, carding my fingers through Zach's hair a couple of hours later.

He's curled up against my side where we're lying on the couch, one muscular leg hooked over mine. His head rests against my chest, and his casted wrist lies on my stomach.

It seems that going into the training facility has completely wiped him out. He complained about a headache forming on one side of his head the moment he got back in the car, which meant we didn't end up making it to the bakery for donuts, much to his dismay.

"No, I'm okay," he murmurs. "I'll be good in twenty minutes, just need to shut my eyes."

I laugh under my breath as he snuggles even closer. It was a good thing I showered at the gym because we weren't in the apartment for a minute before he tackled me onto the couch and has been hanging on to me like a koala since.

Not that I'm complaining. I will happily stay like this for as long as he wants.

"I heard from Hayden today."

He angles his head up toward me but keeps his eyes closed. "Yeah?"

"He's coming to visit in a couple of weeks and wants to grab dinner."

"I won't say no to food."

I scoff, reaching down to pinch his ass. "I know. I… I told him about us."

Zach opens one eye and looks up at me. "You did?"

"Mhm. Is that okay?" I move my hand back into his hair. "He seemed happy for us, but also made me feel kinda shit because it's like everyone knew but me."

"Of course it's okay." Zach sighs heavily and shifts to lean up on his elbow. His eyes are weary when he opens them, but I know it's because of his headache rather than me. "But you've gotta stop beating yourself up for it,

Carter. You didn't know because I didn't want you to know."

"I know, I'm sorry."

"No, don't be sorry." He takes my chin awkwardly in his hand. "This isn't going to work if you keep holding on to it. We're here now, and we're in this together, yeah?"

I know he's right. We've had this conversation so many times, but I can't seem to ignore the guilt nestled in my chest over my obliviousness. I know I need to get over this because it will end up driving us apart, and that's the last thing I want.

"Yeah, we are."

"So, let's not focus on what we can't change and focus on the now and the future." He leans down and kisses me before settling back down on my chest. "Did Hayden say anything about your contract? Does he think Denver will keep you?"

I'm about to reply when there's a knock at the door. Furrowing my brows, I ask, "Are you expecting anyone?"

"No."

The buzzer didn't go off, so it's either someone in the building, like the twins, or someone on Zach's pre-approved list. He groans when I try to peel myself out from underneath him, then grabs hold of my thigh with such force I'm unable to move.

"Ignore it, they'll go away," he grumbles.

I laugh. "Zach, if you let me go, I'll get rid of them, and we can have naked cuddles in bed."

He drops his hand so fast, you would think my leg burned him.

"That's what I thought," I snicker.

Making my way over to the door, I peer through the peephole to see a familiar figure. I swing the door open and greet Jacob with an easy smile.

"Hey, Jacob! Come in."

"Hi." He gives me a quick, tight smile as I take a step back to let him inside.

I've only met Jacob a few times. He's dating Zach's captain, Ethan Parkes, and he's Alex's brother. We first met last summer, and I could tell he was unsure about me. His posture was rigid, and I noticed he kept watching me cautiously. Zach explained later it was because he didn't know me, and he had acted the same when he first met the guys because he was nervous. But I haven't seen him since to let him know he doesn't need to be nervous around me.

Jacob bypasses me and heads straight to Zach, who is now propped up in the corner of the sectional, and sits down beside him, holding a plastic container in his lap.

"Can I get you something to drink?" I ask, trying to offer an olive branch.

"No, thank you. I can't stay long but wanted to check in and see how this one is doing." He motions with his hand toward Zach before turning to him. "I've missed you. It's been a while since you've been in the bakery. How are you doing?"

"I'm fine," Zach murmurs, a ghost of a smile on his lips.

I know he's trying to put on a brave face. The last thing an athlete wants is to look weak, but there's nothing weak about him. Every day since he's come out of the hospital, he's been fighting whether it's migraines or other symptoms that are a result of his injury.

Silently, Jacob assesses him with narrowed eyes. There's

a small crease in his brows, like he's debating whether to call him out or not. But he must decide against it because he holds up the plastic container. "I brought you two of your favorite donuts."

"For me?" Zach instantly perks up and takes hold of the box with his good hand. Placing it on his thigh, he flips open the lid, and a wide smile spreads across his lips as he picks up one of the donuts. "Oh, thanks, Jacob. You're the best."

Jacob smiles shyly at his compliment and looks over his shoulder at me. "One is for you. If he doesn't eat it first, that is."

I want to fist-bump the air. Maybe he is warming up to me after all. "Thank you. I don't normally get a look in unless I go into the bakery myself."

He chuckles and turns back to Zach. "Ethan mentioned you've been getting migraines?"

Zach grunts, stuffing more of the donut into his mouth to avoid answering.

"Almost daily." I answer for him, walking over and taking a seat on the edge of the couch by Zach's outstretched legs. "But the doctor doesn't seem concerned right now, so it's just a case of resting and hoping they will eventually go away."

Those icy blue eyes lock on mine, and there's a shimmer of heat sparking in them. A look that says, *Do orgasms count as resting?*

I arch a brow, lifting my lips in a smirk. *We take a nap after, don't we?*

Jacob clears his throat, and we both turn our attention to him.

"Something you want to tell me?" he asks, a teasing tone to his voice.

"Nope." Zach shakes his head slightly.

Jacob narrows his eyes, then quickly takes the box away from him and snatches the half-eaten donut out of his hand. Zach's mouth drops open as a choked noise leaves him, and I have to smother my laughter with my hand.

Jacob may be small, but shit, he is feisty. I met him before he started dating Ethan, and there was a time when I thought Jacob and Zach would be well-suited. I also remember there was a moment in Blaine and Alex's apartment where Zach gave Jacob a hug, and the surge of jealousy that whipped through me was alarming. They are both quiet and gentle, and seemed to share this mutual connection that no one else was privy to.

But now, I can't picture Jacob with anyone except Ethan. And well, Zach's mine.

Zach groans, reaching out for the donut. "Jacob. Give me the donut back," he whines.

"No. I will not give you these back until you tell me what you're hiding."

"I'm not hiding anything."

He gives him a pointed look, then quickly looks at me. He flashes me a wink and a small smile.

"Don't make me tell Ethan you're hiding something from me." He pouts.

Zach sighs and reaches out to me with his good hand. I take it, lacing our fingers together and giving his hand a small squeeze. "Carter and I are together."

Jacob's face morphs into the widest smile I've ever seen on him. "Really? Like *together* together?"

"Yeah, really." I nod, unable to stop my own smile. "I got my head out of my ass and finally realized what's been in front of me all this time."

Jacob drops the donut into the box and claps his hands excitedly before wrapping his arms around both our necks, bringing us in for a hug. "I'm so happy for you. Oh, gosh, this is like a book I've read. Best friends forever, finally falling in love. Aw! It's so amazing."

Zach rolls his eyes, but his expression is soft and adoring. "I haven't told the guys yet, so if you tell Ethan, make sure to tell him to keep it quiet."

I try to hide my hurt by looking down at our linked hands. I know we haven't spoken about what we were going to tell people, but knowing he didn't tell the guys he's closest to stings.

Is he still unsure about this?

Jacob's face falls. "Why haven't you told them?"

"I was planning on telling them at boys' night so they can interrogate Carter, and it can be my entertainment for the evening." Zach grins.

"Thanks. Setting me up for the wolves. Nice," I deadpan, but inside, I'm relieved.

I'm so fucking nervous about messing this up. Zach means everything to me, and I'm so desperate to make him happy that I keep forgetting he's had nearly two decades of suppressing his feelings for me. Hiding them from those around him.

I'll take every doubt going forward as long as it means I get to call Zach mine and continue to show him I'm in this for real, no matter how long it takes for him to believe me.

Chapter Seventeen

Zach

I'm not sure if Carter is purposely trying to torture me or if he simply doesn't realize the impact his touch has on me.

With his head propped up on one fist, he drifts his fingers lazily down my bare chest, tracing over the curves of my pecs before grazing featherlight strokes over the hair on my chest. He circles my nipple with a fingertip, and I shiver.

"You like that?" His face lights up with a grin.

"Yeah, I do."

It's been a week since I introduced him to the magical world of frotting, and to say he's been curious would be an understatement. Carter is eager. Very eager. To the point I've had to slow him down at times because I haven't wanted to rush this.

Showering together has become a regular occurrence since the time Carter kissed me. He claims it's to save the environment by sharing water and to keep an eye on me in case I have a dizzy spell, but I think he likes having an excuse to take care of me.

So, with nothing else better to do, we decided to spend the afternoon watching a movie in bed. Though it seems Carter isn't interested in watching the movie anymore and has made it his mission to make me lose my mind.

His cock rests semi-erect against my hip, and my mouth waters at the sight of his incredible body on display for me. My hands itch to touch him, but I keep them at my sides as his hand travels further down my body. I want to give him this time to become familiar with me.

His fingers coast over my navel and the trail of hair leading down to my cock. I can tell he wants to touch me, but he's holding himself back. Like he's afraid he'll do something wrong.

"You can touch me," I manage to croak out.

"Will you tell me how you like it?" His voice is barely audible over the blood pounding in my ears.

I give him a shaky nod and guide his hand over my closely cropped pubic hair, down to my aching shaft. He wraps his fingers around it, and I motion for him to pump his fist in slow strokes.

His tongue darts out to lick a wet path across his lips as he watches his hand work me over. His dark eyes are molten, filled with desire.

"Use your thumb over the head," I say all breathy, and when he sweeps his thumb over the sensitive head, I hiss. "Yesss! That's it."

The look he gives me is full of pride. Like he can't quite believe he's turning me on so much. His thumb collects a bead of precome on the next upstroke before he twists his palm around the swollen head. His movements become more confident, alternating between massaging my balls and pumping my cock.

My spine arches up as he squeezes my shaft.

"Harder," I demand between gritted teeth.

His breath comes out in rapid bursts as he jerks me harder and faster. I groan, fisting the bedsheet as my thighs and abs tense. My climax is imminent. Pooling at the base of my spine as my balls draw up tight.

Carter must sense I'm close. I'm leaking more precome, giving him the perfect glide.

"Carter," I moan, only it's muffled when he slams his mouth against mine and I'm unable to hold back much longer. The kiss is desperate. Hard and hungry. It's almost like he's starving, and sucking on my tongue is his only salvation.

"I want to fuck you," he murmurs against my lips, and it's those five words that set my world alight.

Stars blind my eyes as I let go. He strokes me through my orgasm, gliding his tongue lazily into my mouth as my release paints his fist and my stomach. The sheer force with which my orgasm hits me causes my brain to go offline for a few seconds.

"Holy shit." He grins widely. "That was so hot." His thumb teases the sensitive glans on my cockhead, and my body jolts from the ripples of aftershocks it sends through me.

"Carter," I hiss, trying to slap his hand away with shaky movements as my legs melt into the bed.

He releases me with a quiet snicker and brings his hand to his mouth, licking the evidence of my release off his skin.

If I hadn't just come as hard as I did, I would come again at the sight. My softening cock gives an appreciative throb.

He's so fucking beautiful.

His dark hair is damp from the shower and beginning to curl. A light sheen of sweat glistens against his smooth skin, emphasizing his sculpted muscles, and his full lips are swollen and his mouth is slightly red with beard burn.

But it's the magnitude of pleasure shining in his eyes that has my breath hitching.

Fuck, I can't believe this is really happening.

With Carter. My best friend. The man I've been in love with since I was ten years old.

Smiling proudly, he leans down and captures my mouth in a slow kiss. I can taste myself on his tongue.

Carter has *me* on his tongue.

"Can I fuck you?" he whispers against my lips.

I nod several times, unable to find my words as I gasp for breath.

Without a word, he rises up on his knees and retrieves the bottle of lube from my bedside table and a condom. A small frown lines his brows as he eyes the square packet in his hand, but it disappears just as quickly.

"What is it?" I ask.

Soulful, brown eyes latch on to mine, a bashful smile lifting his lips at being caught. "I know it sounds stupid, but I don't like the idea of you being with anyone else."

I pinch his nipple. "Right back 'atcha."

"Fuck." He slaps my hand away and rubs over his pec. "I know I have no right to be jealous, but I am. Is that bad?"

"Is it weird I kinda like your jealousy?" I card my fingers through his curls. I love that his hair is getting longer. "As long as it's not coming from a place of distrust, I kinda dig it."

He shakes his head vehemently. "No, I do trust you, implicitly. I just…" He pauses, and his eyes bore into mine, almost like he's hoping to find the right words. "I've always felt very possessive of you, but you remember that couple in Hawaii? I wanted to rip their hands off when they touched you, and I know I shouldn't have felt that way at the time, but you're *mine,* and even back then I knew I didn't want anyone touching what's mine."

Sliding my hand around his head to cup his cheek, I bring his face to mine, nipping his bottom lip between my teeth before kissing him again.

"I am yours. I've always been yours, and I'm not going anywhere."

He answers by pushing his tongue into my mouth, and I groan.

"And I'm yours. All yours," he mumbles between kisses.

"Good. Now get me ready, Lockwood. I'm going to need a lot of prep to take your big cock."

His grin is wicked as he sits back on his haunches and slowly jerks himself.

"Damn right," he says with a cocky wink.

Bending one knee to my chest, Carter kneels between my thighs and lifts my other leg, pressing it toward my chest. He rubs lubed fingers in slow circles around my rim, flicking his eyes between my hole and my face. A shuddering breath whooshes out of me as he presses one finger inside.

"You okay?" he asks, halting his movements.

"Yeah," I rasp. "Keep going."

He eases his finger in further and a low groan rumbles in

my chest as pleasure ripples through me. He thrusts his finger in and out in slow, controlled movements until he breaches the rings of muscle, and his knuckles are pressed up against my skin.

"Holy shit. You're so tight," he gasps, curling his finger inside me.

My eyes roll to the back of my head as he brushes my prostate. I came less than ten minutes ago, but the ache in my balls grows stronger as he works me over. One finger becomes two, and before I know it, he's three fingers deep, and my cock is a steel bar against my thigh again.

I'm rocking against him, seeking him out with every thrust of his fingers.

"Carter," I beg, my nails digging into my skin as I try to keep hold of my knee. "I need you."

He removes his fingers, and I whimper at the loss. His hand trembles slightly with nerves as he rolls the condom on his cock and covers himself with lube before adding more to my hole. He tosses the bottle to the floor and moves up the bed, resting my ankle on his shoulder and lining up his cock.

But he doesn't push in right away.

His breath hitches as he takes me in. Starting at my face, his gaze makes its way down my torso to where my cock rests heavy against my heated skin. It throbs under his watchful eye, before moving further down to where the head of his cock is pressing against my stretched hole. His tongue peeks out to lick his lips, and when his eyes land back on mine, there's a slight flush to his cheeks.

"You're so fucking beautiful, you know that?"

I want to argue with him that he's the beautiful one here. That I thought he was beautiful the first moment I saw him, and I thought it every day since, but I can't speak. I can barely breathe from the thick emotion threatening to burst from inside me.

I've wanted this for so long. Craved it, even. I've imagined this moment so many times that it was the only fuel I needed to make myself come.

And now that it's actually happening, I could cry.

But it's not the time to get emotional, not when my body is humming with the familiar burn as Carter slowly starts to sink his cock inside me. Despite the fact that Carter had three fingers inside me, I wasn't kidding when I said he's *big*.

Planting his hands on either side of my head, he watches intently as he slowly slides his cock in and out. There's a slight furrow in his dark brows as he concentrates, sweat beading at his hairline, and his parted lips allow quiet whimpers to escape as he moves his hips in shallow thrusts.

"Carter," I pant. "You feel so fucking good, but I need you to move. You don't need to go easy on me."

His eyes lock onto mine, seeking my approval to know he isn't going to mess this up. I give a small nod, and it's all it takes for him to move. It's like the tightly strung band he was holding on to snaps. His hips piston into me, switching it up between short, erratic thrusts and slow, long drags that have my toes curling. His cock pegs my prostate every time, and I've never felt so fucking full in my life.

"Zach," he cries into my mouth.

We're not kissing, but our open mouths are pressed together. Exchanging heavy breaths and pleasured grunts as the sound of skin slapping against skin fills my ears.

His thrusts become jagged as he climbs closer to his release. I let go of my leg and grasp his face in my hand, pulling him down until our sweaty foreheads are pressed together.

Staring up into those gorgeous eyes, I demand, "Come for me, Carter."

He doesn't break my stare as his body jerks, and I feel the heat of his release as it fills the condom. My name is a mantra he repeats over and over as he continues to pump his cock inside me, riding out his orgasm. The friction of his abdomen against the underside of my shaft is the only stimulation I need to come again, spilling my release between our bodies.

"Carter," I moan against his lips.

I don't know how long we lie there for, exchanging lazy kisses and gentle caresses of heated skin. I let out a soft cry as Carter slips his soft cock from my ass. I'm vaguely aware of him disposing of the condom, but my brain is too blissed out. Floating on a sex cloud, not ready to come down from the high.

"We're going to need another shower," he says quietly between kisses. "You've made a mess."

"Yeah, in a minute."

My release is drying against our skin where we're pressed together, but neither of us makes a move. We end up falling asleep, Carter still lying on top of me, and it's the best afternoon I've ever had.

Chapter Eighteen

Carter

"Are you sure you're up for this?" I ask Zach as he steps out of the bathroom.

We're heading over to Blaine's apartment for their regular "boys' night," but Zach's been asleep for most of the afternoon. He said he's feeling a lot better now, but I know him, and I know when he's hiding his pain.

The perk of having known him for pretty much my entire life.

"Yeah, I'm fine. I'll just tell them not to get rowdy and that we won't be staying too long." He moves to stand in between my legs where I'm sitting on the bed, and my hands instantly go to his hips. He runs his fingers through my hair, and I can't help but close my eyes and let out a satisfied hum.

"Okay, tell me if you can feel one coming on."

"I will."

His hands remain on my head as I stand up, slipping my arms around his back as my lips find his neck.

Since we had sex the other day, we haven't been able to keep our hands off each other. I wondered if maybe the amount of orgasms Zach's having on the regular is playing a part in his headaches due to the increased heart rate and blood pressure that comes with them, but he insists it's worth it, so who am I to judge? I love making him come.

His hand slides around to grab my ass, hauling me closer until we're pressed up against one another. I graze my teeth over his pulse point and kiss up to his jaw.

"You're going to make me face your friends with a boner."

He snickers. "Nothing they haven't seen before. It's like part of the team bonding ritual, seeing each other's accidental hard-ons."

"Are you kidding me?" I snort.

"Your teammates don't do that?"

"No." I shake my head. "We don't."

"Shame, you're missing out." He winks and takes a step back. I follow him out of the bedroom, my eyes glued to his delicious ass as we head out of the door and down the hall to Blaine's apartment.

When we're inside, it seems we're the last to arrive. Ethan Parkes is sitting on the couch with Jonathan Peyton and Jackson Wilde. Adam Kendrick is stacking beers in the fridge, and the Olsen twins are sitting on the rug with Blaine's dog, Ernie. There are a few notable absences, such as the young gun Mitch Henry, but Zach mentioned he's got a new girlfriend, so they weren't expecting him to turn up.

"You got a new cast!" Elliot gasps when he notices

Zach's new addition. He pushes himself off the floor and rushes over to take hold of Zach's arm, turning it over in his hand before turning back toward his brother. "Blaine, you got a Sharpie?"

When Zach got it changed, I was so relieved when the doctor said the break is healing up perfectly. He's only got less than two weeks before they will take it off and he can begin his hardcore physiotherapy sessions.

Which means one step closer to him getting back on the ice.

I don't really know how I feel about it yet. I've loved being with him these last couple of weeks, taking care of him, *loving* him. He goes in for a few hours every morning to train lower body, and when he's given the green light to play again, he'll be back training every day and going on the road, and the needy part inside me is anxious about being away from him. About what might happen when we're separated.

I thank Kendrick as he hands over a beer, and Zach moves to stand in the middle of the living room, jerking his head at me when he realizes I haven't followed him.

"I've got something I want to tell you guys," he announces as I step up beside him, and the room goes quiet.

"You're not retiring, are you?" Peyton asks with a frown.

Zach shakes his head. "No, as soon as I've been cleared by the doc, I'll be back out on the ice."

Elliot lets out a sigh of relief. "Oh, thank fuck for that."

"I… uh…" Zach stammers. He throws me a quick smile and grabs my hand. "So, me and Carter are dating."

There's a moment of complete silence, and my heart rate begins to kick up in panic. Are they going to disapprove and tell him this is a terrible idea? Try to talk him out of it? These guys are like his family. He often tells me how they are more like his brothers than Brody is. I know their opinion is important to him.

Fuck. What if they hate me for what I've put Zach through over the years?

But before I can spiral, the silence is broken by a flurry of excitement. I sag in relief, feeling the weight of their approval like a physical thing.

"I knew it!" Blaine beams, wrapping his arms around us both in a hug. "Wait until I tell Alex, he's going to be so stoked."

"Does this mean you're boyfriends now?" Elliot asks, bouncing on his toes.

"El!" Blaine scolds.

"What? It's a valid question!"

I'm about to open my mouth to confirm, but I'm cut off.

"I thought you were already dating?" Kendrick asks, a puzzled expression on his face. "I thought you had an open relationship or something."

Zach huffs out a laugh. "No. I was just an idiot in love for a long time."

I squeeze his hand. "We're both idiots in love now."

"Aw! You're so cute, it hurts." Elliot hoots, placing both hands on Zach's face and squishing his cheeks together. The goalie takes a step in front of me, and gone is his playful expression. His eyes narrow as he crosses his arms over his chest. "What's your intentions with my favorite D-man?"

"Hey!" Kendrick protests. "What about me?"

"This isn't about you, Kenny," Elliot says over his shoulder before glaring back at me. "So?"

Pressing my lips together, I cast Zach a quick look before focusing on Elliot again. "My intentions are good, you don't need to worry about that."

Unconvinced, Elliot cocks his head to the side, brows arched.

"Since I was six years old, he's always been my favorite person in the world, but I've come to realize that he's more than that."

I'm aware that his teammates have stopped talking and are all listening intently, but I ignore them. My eyes find Zach again. He's chewing on the inside of his cheek as he listens.

"He's my entire world. My soulmate, in every way. It's like for my entire life, I've been building this LEGO set, and I've always been missing one piece, but it's always been there, right in front of me. I just wasn't ready to see it."

Zach visibly swallows, and I continue.

"So, Elliot, the answer to your question is… I'd really like to love your favorite D-man for the rest of my life, if he'll let me."

Elliot grins widely, knowing he achieved exactly what he intended to and have me say the words out loud.

Zach closes the distance between us and cups my face with his hand, pressing his lips hard against mine. Resting his forehead against mine, he murmurs, "You mean it?"

"Yeah, I mean it. I'm in this, Reid, if you'll have me."

His answering kiss tells me everything I need to know. We're doing this. Together. It might have taken me years to catch up, but I'm here now, and he's got all of me.

Peyton attempts to lift Zach up off his feet when we pull

apart, swinging him in a circle like a toddler before righting him again.

"Fuck, I'm the only single one left," Peyton cries when he puts him down.

"Uh, no, you're not," Blaine replies, then points to Elliot and Jackson. "What about those two?"

"Jackson's a dad, he doesn't count, and Elliot's in love with the fireman."

"Am *not*," Elliot retorts.

"Yeah, you kinda are," Blaine quips.

"Fine, maybe I am. Only a little bit, though." Elliot sighs with a roll of his eyes. "But it still means I'm single. So, quit being all mopey, Pey, and order some pizza. I am *hungry*."

Peyton blinks at him. "It's not my apartment!"

"Ugh. Can't you be the responsible adult for once?"

"I'll order it," Ethan grumbles from the back of the group and makes his way over to us. He puts his hand on my shoulder and squeezes. "I'm pleased for you both, truly."

"Thanks, Ethan." Zach smiles.

When the guys disperse and follow Ethan to give him their pizza order, Zach turns to me and lets out a relieved sigh. "I was really nervous about telling them."

"Why?"

"I don't know. I knew they would be nothing but supportive and happy for us, but I was still nervous about their reaction."

"No, I get it. They're important to you." I take his hand, lacing our fingers together. "I'm glad you've had this, though. This support network around you. I never really understood until now just kinda… how alone you were without me, I guess. I'm glad you've got these guys."

Zach presses his lips to mine in a gentle kiss, and when we move to sit on the couch, Elliot's standing in front of us, blocking our path.

"Okay, so I'm like super happy for you both. If I had pom-poms, I'd be doing some kind of cheer right now and making a song out of your names, but how about we do a little less kissing and more gaming?" He holds out the game controller, but his face falls when Zach holds up his casted wrist.

"No can do, bud. I'll be on your team though for moral support."

Elliot seems content with that, and Zach gives me a quick kiss before taking a seat next to Elliot and Blaine as they power up the game console.

Heading into the kitchen, I place my beer down and lean against the counter next to Ethan.

"How's he doing?" Ethan asks quietly. "He mentioned the other day his cast is coming off soon, but he didn't say anything about the headaches."

"He's doing okay, but the migraines are still knocking him around. The doctor doesn't seem too concerned, though. She said it's pretty normal, given the severity of the concussion." I chew on my bottom lip. Ethan's been the Thunder's captain for over a decade, and as the oldest guy on the team, he's naturally taken on the "papa bear" role.

"I had a word with Chris and told him that Zach might not always tell us about it. He will try and play through it, so we need to watch for signs. I've been reading up on it so I can keep my eye on him. Any slight sign of a migraine, and I'll be getting him checked."

My breath whooshes out of me. Ethan's hit the nail on

the head regarding the concern that's been swirling in my chest. Zach can be stubborn as fuck. I know that, and I'm so fucking relieved that his captain knows that too.

"Thank you, it means a lot knowing he has you looking out for him," I say, genuinely grateful. "I'm not going to lie to you, it's been stressing me out. I've felt helpless these last few weeks, you know? I wish there was more I could do to help him, take some of that pain away, because I know that the second the doctor says his wrist is good, it'll all come down to his headaches, and I know he'll downplay his pain just so he can get back out there."

"Just being here for him is helping him. He's an intelligent guy, but it's a case of making sure he knows hockey isn't everything, and now that you're here and you're together, I'm hoping he'll make the right decision and put his health first."

Swallowing roughly, I ask the question that's been playing on my mind since Jacob came over. "Did… did you know?"

"That he's been in love with you all this time?" He lifts a brow and smirks.

"Yeah…"

He nods. "Yeah, I did. I've always had an inkling because of your level of codependency. You've been so close for a long time, and I often wondered if there was more to it, but I knew for sure when he came over as soon as he got back from Denver and told us."

"Us?"

"Jacob and me," Ethan confirms.

"Oh." I nod, letting out a shaky breath. Well, that

explains Jacob's excitement when he found out the other day.

Glancing over at the couch where everyone's sitting, I watch as Zach tilts his head back and laughs at something Peyton's said, and something warms my chest at seeing him happy.

"It broke me when he left. Don't get me wrong, I don't blame him for leaving, especially now that I know the reason why, but it was the first time I experienced heartbreak in a sense." I rub the back of my neck. "When I spoke with my ex-girlfriend the other week, she pointed out that I was more upset over him leaving than when she broke up with me."

Ethan laughs softly under his breath, and it's almost strange to see. Ethan's always been this impenetrable force. Always so serious and guarded, but since he met Jacob, it's like those sharp edges have softened, and the walls he kept so high have slowly lowered and allowed people in.

"I think the time apart was good for you. Hell, look at where you are now. It might hurt to think about those pockets of your past, but it also got you here. You're together. Sometimes it takes seeing someone you love walk away from you to realize what's important."

"I think it was when the doctor told me I was listed as his emergency contact. It was like something clicked in my brain. He's always been my person. The one I feel most connected to, who I feel at home with, and I realized what I've been looking for has been right in front of me all this time. It scared me that it could have been taken away from me before I had the chance to do something about it. And now I'm so scared about fucking this up because I'm desperate to show him that my feelings are real. That this isn't some flippant choice I've made because I found out his secret."

Ethan sighs and gives a reassuring smile. "If you're genuine, I don't believe he'll see it like that. I mean, I get why you'd think he would question your motives, but I also think you need to be mindful that these feelings aren't new to him. They're decades old, and he's been so worried about losing you that he's bound to be a little hesitant. He's just as scared as you are, but you've just got to be patient and continue to show him he doesn't need to be. Like that speech you made earlier." He points with his beer bottle to the middle of the living room. "That was genuine. I could tell it was from the heart, and that's what's important. I nearly lost Jacob because I didn't speak from my heart when it counted, so don't make the same mistake I did."

"Thank you. I really appreciate—" The sound of the buzzer makes me jump, and Ethan chuckles under his breath.

"Pizza's here!" Elliot shouts as he leaps off the couch to get the door, causing Ernie to scramble behind him.

"Anytime." He nudges me with his elbow, grabbing my attention as everyone begins to filter into the kitchen. "You know where to find me if you need anything, and Jacob's around when I'm on the road. He adores Zach, so I know he'll jump at the chance to help where he can."

Zach sidles up next to me before I have the chance to reply. He wraps an arm around my waist as he presses a kiss to my neck.

"Thank you," I mouth over his shoulder, and Ethan winks before turning to take his pizza.

"You good?" Zach asks, grabbing a bottle of water from the fridge and handing me a beer.

"Yeah, just been catching up with your captain."

His blue eyes sparkle as he smiles brightly. The happiness he's feeling being here with his teammates, with me, is visceral. It wraps around my heart, flooding my body with warmth.

There might still be some anxiety about the what-ifs when he eventually returns to the ice, but after speaking with Ethan and seeing the look of adoration shining in Zach's eyes, I know we're going to be okay.

Chapter Nineteen

Zach

It's official, I'm back. I've finally been given the OK to return to the ice by both my doctor and the team's physician, and tonight's game in Pittsburgh will mark my return.

I've been itching to get back. It felt a lot longer than seven weeks, but the second I was given the thumbs-up to return to practice, I've been doing every practice session and spending some time with the defensive coach doing some one-on-one drills. I put one hundred and ten percent into my physiotherapy sessions once my cast was removed, and made sure to do everything that was advised to ensure there weren't any holdups.

Of course, it wasn't my wrist that held me up—it was my damn head.

My migraines haven't gone away. They're still frequent, and I'm not sure they will ever go away at this point, but I've been managing to push through most of the time. Carter has been supportive too, spending his free time researching alternative methods to try and help ease the throbbing ache that seems to be a regular occurrence now.

But if I thought I could get away with hiding it, I would be wrong. I've caught Ethan watching me like a hawk, calling me out over the slightest wince during practice.

I'd like to say I'm pissed off about it, but I'm not. How can I be when I've got someone looking out for me? I only wish he wouldn't look so closely because if I admitted to every headache, I'd never get back out here.

Luckily, Ethan's on the other side of the ice while I'm going through my groin and glute stretches when Jackson drops down beside me and begins to stretch out his hamstrings.

"Have you heard anything from your brother?"

I found out that my brother, Brody, had been traded from New Jersey to Toronto as soon as we landed in Pittsburgh. He's been unhappy in New Jersey for quite some time, and I knew he had been pushing for a trade, but we're not as close as people expect us to be.

Growing up, I was constantly compared to Brody. Even our dad would pit us against each other—who could score the most goals, who had more time on ice per game, who had the highest shooting percentage. Brody reveled in the fact he was drafted and I wasn't because I decided against entering the draft as I wanted to graduate college with Carter. My dad said I was a disappointment to the Reid family name for not following tradition and didn't speak to me for weeks because of it. Still, I held my head high and worked my ass off in the AHL to make sure I was valuable enough for the Thunder when they called me up that they wouldn't send me back down.

The hard work paid off, too, because they ended up offering me a full contract, and I've been here since.

Turning to Jackson, I shake my head. "No, but we're playing Toronto when we're home, so I'll probably catch him then."

Jackson's brows furrow in confusion behind his visor.

I've come to accept that while we aren't that close, Brody loves me in his own weird way. He only checked in on me twice while I was recovering, but I didn't let it get to me. I just put it down to the fact it's Brody, and he's got bigger things to worry about. It's always bothered Carter more than me. But now isn't the time to be thinking about my big brother.

The first period goes scoreless and is pretty uneventful. Pittsburgh is on a four-game losing streak, so they're hungry for a win, but they're not being very aggressive about it. Elliot slapped every shot on goal away like a bored cat playing with a mouse.

"This game needs to spice up a bit. I'm almost taking a nap out there, boys," he complains during the intermission while flossing in the middle of the locker room. As in the dance move, not his teeth. "Can you guys get a penalty or something? Make it exciting, like five on three or something, because I'm *bored*—"

"No," Ethan quickly interrupts, throwing a glare at everyone around the room. "No penalties."

When we go back out for the second period, Blaine

manages to slip one in the top left corner with me getting a point for the assist and putting us up by one. I skate back to the bench, a wide grin on my face as I sit down and squirt some water in my mouth.

"Doing good, Reid?" Peyton asks, knocking my helmet with his.

"Yeah, I'm good." I nod truthfully.

I'm not sure if I'm just having a good day or if it's the adrenaline of being back on the ice keeping the headache at bay and I'll have a migraine when we get back. Either way, I'm taking it as a win.

The game ends with a win of 1-0. Since Elliot had a shutout, he's been granted control of the post-W playlist. As Kylie Minogue's "The Loco-Motion" blasts through the speakers in the locker room, a few of the guys dance in their hockey pants and skates, having tossed their jerseys in the laundry hamper. Elliot's in the middle of the pack, goalie pads still on as he mimics a train with Peyton.

"How did I end up here?" Ethan grumbles under his breath, pinching the bridge of his nose.

I grin. "You love it."

The dance-off continues as I hit the showers then change into my suit. There's no rush to catch a flight as we're only leaving for New York in the morning, from where we'll fly back to Chicago after the game. We all pile on the waiting bus that takes us to our hotel before deciding to eat our weight in food and have a beer while running through tonight's game.

"I think I'm gonna head up," I say, pushing my chair back and standing up.

"Already?" Elliot frowns. "But we haven't played darts yet."

I tap my head with my finger. "I'm tired, and I don't wanna overdo it by not resting."

I'm also dying to talk to Carter, but I don't want to admit that and open myself up to the ribbing we give Blaine over Alex.

"Oh, yeah, for sure." Elliot nods a few times. "Breakfast at eight, yeah? I hear they have pancakes."

"You got it, bud." I hold my fist out and he bumps it, then I say goodnight to the rest of the guys.

I slide my phone out of my pocket as I weave through the tables toward the lobby, quickly typing out a text to Carter.

ZACH

I'm about to head up to my room. Are you still awake?

CARTER

Yeah I am. I've been rocking a boner ever since I saw your gorgeous face on the TV.

I might send those camera people a bottle of nice scotch for the close-up. When you were squirting that water in your mouth, I imagined it was me shooting come down your throat.

ZACH

eye roll emoji You're such a horndog.

CARTER

Get back to your room, Reid. It's time to get naked. *devil emoji* *eggplant emoji*

. . .

Grinning, I make my way toward the elevator bank, only to end up stopping short when I see Jackson sitting in one of the plush armchairs tapping away on his phone. There's a deep crease between his brows, and his mouth is tipped downward.

"Hey, you good?" I ask quietly as I approach.

He lifts his head and plasters on a tired smile. "Hey. Yeah, I just checked in with my mom. I missed bedtime, and Isabela wasn't happy about it." He sighs, scrubbing a hand over his face. "Sometimes she's fine when I go on the road, but then she can also give my mom such a hard time. I feel like such a shit dad at times."

I take the seat next to him. The hotel lobby is quiet, despite the noise filtering in from the guys at the bar. "You're not a shit dad. It's hard to explain it to them when they're young."

Isabela is almost four years old, whereas Ryan is seven and understands Jackson's job better. Staying with his parents while he's on the road means they have more stability, but this life is tough. It's not always glamorous. It's spending a lot of time separated from the people you love most, and when they're kids, it can be confusing for them. I know from experience, growing up with my dad in the NHL.

"Exactly." Jackson drops his phone into his lap and runs a hand through his hair. "Enough about me. How's your head? How's Carter doing? Is he missing you yet?" He gives me a teasing smirk, and I can't stop the wide smile from appearing on my face.

Jackson chuckles. "I take that as a good thing."

"Yeah, he's good. I just…" I huff a laugh, almost in disbelief. "Sometimes it doesn't feel real, you know? It was a pipe dream for so long. I'd accepted that I was never going to be able to act on my feelings, and I was becoming okay with that, but now… Now he feels the same way, and sometimes I have to pinch myself to make sure it's not a dream. It's real."

"I'm really happy it worked out for you both." He smiles fondly. "Have you discussed what's going to happen when he goes back to Denver? He's got a year left on his contract, right?"

"Yeah, that's right." I let out a long sigh. "But we haven't spoken about it, no. I know it's only six months, seven at most if they make it through to the playoffs, and it'll help that we'll both be busy either training or on the road, but it's still six months…"

He's silent for a moment, his fingers mindlessly brushing the scruff on his chin. I can sense the wheels turning in his head, but instead of pushing, I wait for him to speak.

"Long distance relationships can be hard, especially when you both play professional sports. Communication is the most important thing, along with trust. You have to make sure you share when you're uncertain about something, be vulnerable with each other, and be prepared to get creative when it comes to satisfying your needs, if you know what I mean." He winks.

I chuckle. "You sound like you're speaking from experience."

He shocks me when he says, "I am."

"I thought you and your ex-wife lived together before the divorce?"

"I'm not talking about Laura. This happened over ten years ago. It was in my early days playing in Boston. We met in my rookie year. You know how it goes, puppy love. We thought we could make it work, but when I got traded to Los Angeles, it crumbled. We were on opposite ends of the country, and the distance broke us. We didn't do any of the things I just advised you to do, and we ended up resenting each other. We fought all the time, and in the end, we called it quits."

"Shit, I'm sorry. I had no idea."

He waves it off. "It was a long time ago. Ancient history now. We both moved on—marriage, kids." He wiggles his phone, and the screen lights up with a photo of Ryan and Isabela on his lock screen. "What I'm trying to say, probably not in the best way, is that you both need to know for certain how it's going to be when he goes back to Denver and you're in Chicago. Set your expectations. Nothing will break this down faster than shit communication."

My phone buzzes in my hand, Carter's name flashing on the screen with an incoming call.

"You better get that." Jackson winks and gets up. "I'm gonna have a drink, then head to bed. Go speak to your guy, and I'll see you in the morning."

"Night," I say, waiting until he's walked away to bring the phone to my ear. "Hey, sorry. I got chatting with Jackson. Give me a minute and I'll head up to my room."

Carter doesn't answer, but I can hear his labored breathing through the line.

Dropping my voice low, I ask, "You didn't wait for me?"

"I don't think you understand how horny seeing you on TV made me," he rasps, and I hear the familiar sound of the lube cap being popped open.

"Fuck," I groan under my breath, hitting the elevator call button a little harder than necessary. "I'm on my way to my room. Don't touch yourself until I'm naked. It's time we discovered just how good video sex can be."

Chapter Twenty

Zach

The second I'm inside my hotel room and the door clicks closed behind me, I pull the phone from my ear and switch to FaceTime. Within moments, the image of Carter fills my phone screen, and the sight of him naked in my bed causes my breath to catch in my throat.

How did I get so fucking lucky?

"Hey there, handsome." He grins. The phone is positioned against his thigh, giving me the perfect view of his smooth, expansive chest. His abs ripple as he moves his hand that's just out of shot, and a low growl rumbles in my throat.

"Didn't I tell you not to touch yourself?"

"Maybe." His eyes sparkle with mischief and arousal. "But I told you, I've been horny all evening, then you left me hanging to talk to your teammate. I didn't know I was so into edging until now. Maybe we can try it some more when you come home to me."

Home.

I don't know why hearing him call my apartment *home* does something to me. My heart swells in my chest, pride blooming through my veins at how casually he said it.

Doesn't he realize that *he* is my home?

It's not some geographical location. I could be anywhere in the world, but as long as I had him at my side, I'd be home.

I tip my head back with a groan. "You're cruel."

"That makes two of us," he teases. "Anyway, we've been on video call for nearly a minute now. One of us is wearing too many clothes, and it's definitely not me. Prop the phone up and strip for me."

Not wanting to keep him waiting any longer than I already have, I flick the desk lamp on and place my phone upright on the dresser, angling it so he can see down to my knees. I kick off my shoes and then undo my cufflinks. He hums the intro to "The Stripper" by David Rose & His Orchestra as I slowly unbutton my shirt and pull it from where it's tucked into my pants.

"Stop that." I laugh with a shake of my head.

He lets out a low whistle when I part my shirt to show off my chest. "Damn, you look so hot. Now turn around and take it off."

I arch a brow. "You don't want to look at me?"

I run my hand down my chest and flick my thumb over my nipple.

"Oh, I want to look at you, all right. I want to look at that sexy back and peachy ass, too. Have you seen yourself in those pants?" He sticks his tongue out and pretends to pant. "I'm surprised they haven't ripped from all that luscious cake being contained."

"They're custom-made pants."

I can't find pants that fit my ass and thighs. Hockey player problems.

"Of course they are." He snickers, then twirls his finger in the air. "Turn around. Show me the goods."

Laughing, I turn around and slowly slip my shirt from my shoulders, making sure to flex the muscles in my back as the cotton slides down. Carter's strangled moan goes straight to my cock that's now pulsing in my boxers. I toss my shirt onto the chair and pull my belt free, throwing that aside before glancing over my shoulder.

Carter's watching with rapt attention. His phone has moved slightly, allowing me a better view of him stroking his hard cock.

"Stop teasing me, Zach," Carter pleads.

I give him a wink before turning my back to him again. I unbutton my dress pants, and push them down, sliding them over my ass slowly, almost like my ass has been confined just as he said, and it's finally being let loose. When they sit beneath my buttocks, emphasizing my cheeks, he lets out a whimper.

"Off. Now. No more teasing," he demands. "I can't wait anymore. I need to see you. All of you."

Without a word, I do as I'm told, discarding my pants over the chair and quickly removing my boxers. I don't bother taking off my socks, too impatient to pick up my phone again and get onto the bed.

I position one of the pillows between my parted legs and

use it to hold my phone, allowing me to have both my hands free to jerk my cock and tug on my heavy balls.

Carter's breath comes out in a whoosh. "Fuck, I want to suck you off so bad."

I don't know why his confession catches me by surprise. Just like with everything else, he's been eager, and it's been me who has stopped him before he could even begin, distracting him with my mouth, my hand or my ass.

But he hasn't stopped mentioning it, dropping a mix of subtle hints and outright comments.

He wants this. He wants me, and who am I to keep denying him that?

"You'd look so good with your lips wrapped around my cock."

His dark eyes heat at my words, chest rising and falling as his breathing comes heavier. His tongue darts out, licking his lips as his gaze fixates on where my thumb brushes over the slit, collecting the bead of precome.

"I want you to feed it to me. I want to suck you deep. Suck your balls into my mouth." His hand moves so fast, it becomes a blur on the screen, and it doesn't take long until his breathing is coming out in short, quick bursts. "I want it all, Zach. I want all of you. Will you give me that?"

My hips jerk, the impact of his words making my cock throb and balls ache. They're pulled up so tight, I'm not going to last much longer.

"Holy shit, you're gonna make me come if you keep talking to me like that."

"Good," he rasps. "I want you to come knowing the next time you do, it'll be down my throat."

"Fuck!" I grunt, pumping myself faster. "Carter."

"I'm gonna come," he warns. His body jolts as his release spills over his hand, landing on his stomach. He strokes himself through his orgasm, moaning my name as his head tips back into the pillow.

My cock swells in my fist, and when my eyes catch sight of his come dripping down the inside of his thigh, my orgasm rushes down my spine in a hot rush.

I'm gasping for air as I paint myself with my release that seems never-ending. I'm strung so tight, my muscles begin to cramp up.

"Ah, fuck!" I hiss, letting go of my cock to massage my calf.

Carter chuckles softly, rubbing his hand over his face as he melts back into the bed. His soft cock rests against his thigh, and he's unfazed about the come drying on his skin. When he drops his hand, his smile is tired and sleepy. "I miss you."

I duck my head, trying to hide how happy I am to hear those three little words fall from his lips. "You saw me this morning."

"I know, but still. Tomorrow night feels so far away. I don't want to think about what it's going to be like when football starts again."

Sighing, I lean back into the pillow and use my forearm to push my hair from my face. "We probably need to talk about that at some point."

"Yeah," he whispers before yawning.

"You get some sleep. I'll speak to you in the morning."

"Okay, sounds good."

He smiles, and I'm about to say goodnight when his lips tremble, like he's trying to suppress a laugh.

"What?" I ask.

He waves his hand near the side of his face. "You've got come in your hair."

I pull the phone closer so I can look in the camera, and sure enough, there's a pearly rope of come drying in my hair. "Guess it's a good thing I need to have my second post-game shower then."

He snickers. "Okay, I'll let you go. Night, Zach. Miss you."

Warmth spreads through my body. My heart feels so fucking full, emotion burns the back of my eyes. Placing my palm over my chest, feeling my heart beating wildly in my chest, I'm unable to disguise my smile when I say, "Miss you, too. Night, Carter."

It's 2 a.m. when I finally walk through the door to my apartment the next day.

The game against New York… sucked. There is no other way to describe it. We played like shit. You wouldn't have thought we were at the top of the league standings given the way we played tonight.

But there's always next time.

The mood was somber on the flight back home. Everyone was quiet, reflecting on how we fell apart. Me, on the other hand? I'm disappointed we lost, but I'm more disappointed in myself. A headache bloomed behind my eyes during the third period, and I didn't want to risk being taken out of the game, especially when we were down by two goals, so I kept quiet. I caught Ethan watching me a few times, but I made sure not to let my discomfort show. I took some pain killers and pushed through the throbbing ache in my head and ignored the burn in my eyes from the glare off the ice, choosing to focus on how close I was to slipping into bed and cuddling up to Carter.

This has been the first time we've been apart since my injury, and I knew Carter was feeling a little anxious about it, even if he didn't say it outright. Luckily it was for less than forty-eight hours, but I don't think I truly realized the impact my actions had on him. Shutting him out for the sake of protecting myself. But despite him saying he trusts me explicitly, I know I need to rebuild his trust in a way. I need to show him that I'm not going to shut him out like I did before when we can't be physically together.

Quietly closing the door, I carry my luggage inside to prevent the wheels from making a noise against the hardwood floor and waking Carter up. I toe off my shoes and leave them by the door with my luggage before heading straight to my room.

Unlike me, Carter likes to sleep with the drapes open. He says he likes the natural light to wake him up in the morning, but he doesn't complain when I close them, needing the darkness the blackout material gives.

The cover is half thrown off him, exposing one side of his incredible body. The lights of downtown Chicago dance over his naked skin, illuminating the smooth lines and sculpted curves of his muscles. He looks so peaceful, lips slightly parted as he breathes softly, his face pressed into my pillow, like he needed to smell me to fall asleep. One thick, muscular leg is bent outward, and I want to go over there and use his big thigh as a pillow.

Silently, I get undressed, not caring that my suit will become creased on the floor and slip under the covers next to him. He stirs, murmuring something unintelligible as I ghost my hand over the warm skin of his stomach.

"Mhm, yeah, nice," he mumbles in his sleep, then rolls into me.

He slowly blinks awake at the sound of my quiet chuckle, and his face lights up with a sleepy smile when he sees me. "Hey, baby."

My heart rate kicks up from that one little word.

Baby.

We've never said it to each other before. It's almost too gentle for guys our size. We're both over six foot five, and our combined weight is over five hundred pounds, but somehow, hearing that word coming from Carter, it's… significant.

In one little word, I feel loved and cherished. It's powerful, in a weird way.

"Hey, baby," I echo, leaning in to kiss him.

He wraps his arms around me, tucking me close against his warm body. I melt into him as we exchange lazy kisses and our hands stroke each other's skin. The feel of his soft cock brushing against mine has me groaning into his mouth, and next thing I know, his hand slides down between us and he's coaxing me to full hardness.

Without a word, Carter pulls away from my mouth and shifts further down the bed until he's lying between my legs. He wraps a hand around the base of my shaft, then slaps it against the side of his face, grinning up at me. "It's almost as big as my head."

I let out a bark of laughter. Only Carter could make me

laugh when he's about to suck my cock for the first time. But my laughter soon dies off as he lowers his head, keeping his eyes locked on mine as he takes me into his mouth and sucks on the swollen head.

I moan, fisting the sheet as he flicks his tongue over the tip before taking me deeper. There's nothing tentative about his touch. No sign of nerves or hesitation.

He wants this.

"Fuck, Carter," I gasp, my eyes rolling to the back of my head. "Just like that, mmm, yeah, feels so good."

The praise seems to spark something in him. He releases my cock with a wet pop and ducks his head, licking and sucking my balls before using the flat of his tongue to lick over my taint. The muscles in my thighs tremble as I try to keep my hips from thrusting, wanting Carter to have complete control.

"I want you to fuck my mouth," he declares, pumping his fist over my shaft before taking me again, deeper with each bob of his head.

Releasing the sheet from my grasp, I place one hand on each side of his head and hold him still as I thrust my cock in and out of his mouth. I let out a cursed cry as he relaxes to let me all the way in, and my balls draw up tighter when I hit the back of his throat. He gags and pulls off me. His eyes water as he coughs, lips swollen and wet with saliva.

"Again," he demands, his eyes fixed on mine as he swallows me back down, cheeks hollowing as he sucks hard.

"Ngh," I groan, fisting his hair. "I'm gonna come."

My orgasm burns at the base of my spine as I wait for Carter to react, and it doesn't surprise me when he doesn't lift his head. Instead, he looks up at me, heat burning in those dark brown eyes as he continues to suck on the head of my cock. The tip of his tongue teases the sensitive glans, and I come with a low growl.

He swallows every drop of my release. His moan around my cock sends aftershocks straight to my balls, causing another spurt of come to land on his tongue. I collapse into the bed, limbs weightless; the only thing I can hear are my labored breaths and pounding heartbeat.

Carter crawls up over me, nestling against my side and throwing a leg between mine. He nuzzles his face into my neck, peppering gentle kisses against my hot skin.

We lie there for several minutes. Carter wrapped around me, the feel of his lips against my neck and his hard cock digging into my hip bringing me back down to earth.

"Wow," is all I manage to say.

He chuckles into my neck, then lifts his head. His lips are puffy, and his hair is a mess from my hands, but he's never looked more beautiful.

"So, we're definitely doing that again." He beams. "A lot. Oh, and we're going to be sixty-nining, like, every day."

"Is that so?" I huff a laugh and curl my hand around the back of his neck, pulling him down to kiss him. Just like that first time I tasted myself on his lips, I'm overcome with emotion. Maybe it's the post-orgasm high, or maybe it's just because it's Carter.

The man I've loved for nearly twenty years.

"Welcome home, baby," he murmurs against my lips.

And I'm right where I need to be.

In Carter's arms. *Home.*

Chapter Twenty-One

Carter

"I can't believe it has taken us this long," Zach says with a light chuckle. "I thought we would have finished it by now."

There's still over a dozen bags of pieces left for the LEGO Millennium Falcon, all currently scattered across the coffee table in the living room. Between his migraine attacks, which are now a regular occurrence, him returning back to the ice, and us having copious amounts of sex, the build was pushed to the back of our minds.

Not that I'm complaining about the sex part because, shit, I didn't know sex could be like that. Mind-altering, out-of-this-world sex. There's still so much we haven't done though, one of them being me bottoming. I didn't know it was even a phrase until I started researching one afternoon when Zach was taking a headache-induced nap. He's told me so many times not to worry, that we'll take things slow, but I don't want to take things slow. I want *all* of it, so I've been making sure I know what I need to do for when that day finally comes.

But it won't be today, because as soon as he got back from practice this morning, we had sex in the shower, and then he decided this would be a good day to finish the set as he doesn't have a game tonight.

The Falcon is looking awesome, though, and when we finally get to add the LED light pack I ordered online, it's going to look epic.

"Where are you going to display it?" I ask, sorting through the pieces and placing them in small piles so it's easy for him to pick up.

"Probably the game room. I've seen some people display it on coffee tables, but…" He waves his hand, motioning to the coffee table we're currently sitting at.

I got it custom-made as a birthday gift a few years ago when I found a guy in California who made Star Wars-themed wood and resin tables. It looks fucking amazing, like the spacecrafts are flying through the galaxy.

Getting it from California to Chicago was a bit of a feat, but it was totally worth it to see the look of amazement on Zach's face.

"Maybe we could get a display cabinet for it in the game room," I suggest. "Like a cube, so you can see it from all angles."

There's a soft smile on his face when he looks up.

"What?"

Tugging the corner of his lip between his teeth, he shakes his head slightly as his smile turns bashful. "I just love how you say 'we,' like this is our home."

"What do you mean?" I furrow my brows. "It is our home."

"I mean, you say it like this is the home where we live together. That your home in Denver is just temporary."

"Because it is." I scoot forward on the couch. He's wearing half of his hair up in a bun today, but a few tendrils have fallen out around his face, so I tuck them behind his ear. "My home has always been wherever you are, Zach. My house in Denver has never felt like home to me, not like this place does."

He doesn't say anything to that, just leans forward and presses his lips to mine. I sink into the kiss, loving the feel of his stubble against my clean-shaven face and the lingering taste of the glazed donut he ate not long ago on his tongue. When he pulls away, he has this dreamy look in his eyes.

"What was that for?"

"Because I can." He winks. "Now, let's get this finished before you distract me even more. If we're late for dinner with Blaine, he won't let me hear the end of it."

We're meeting Blaine and Alex tonight for dinner. Zach mentioned how eager Blaine's been for us to double-date since that night in his apartment, and this is the first night that has worked out for everyone.

Chuckling, we return our focus to the building instructions, listening to Sports Network in the background as we work.

I'm not sure how much time has passed when I hear, "What do you think? There's one year left on his contract, but should Denver trade Carter Lockwood?"

Both of us snap our heads to the TV when the talk show host mentions my name.

"Hell no. I agree, last season was a disappointment, but Carter Lockwood is the strength and power of their defensive line. Without him, they will flop harder than they did last season. I think they would be foolish to trade him over one fluke season," one of the presenters replies.

"But it's a business. He's one of the highest-paid non-quarterback players in the NFL. He definitely did not earn his eight million dollar salary this year," another argues. "Why should they keep him?"

My cheeks burn as shame lodges thick in my throat. I've managed to avoid most media opinions, only going on social media to look at my private Instagram, where I don't follow any of the sports pages. I didn't want to see other people agreeing to what I've been thinking or confirming that I don't deserve my spot on the team—or my salary. But I didn't think they would talk about it on the TV segments, given it's the off-season and all.

"What the fuck?" Zach growls, picking up the TV remote and changing the channel.

My voice is quiet when I say, "Well, they're not wrong."

His face is pinched in frustration when he turns to face me. "The fuck, Carter? Of course they're wrong. They don't know shit."

I grunt, flopping back into the cushions and covering my face with my arms.

"Carter." He tugs at my hand, trying to get me to uncover my face.

I move my arm slightly so I can look at him with one eye.

"I suppose it's time we talk about what's going to happen when you need to go back for training camp."

"Yeah, I guess so." I sigh. "I told Hayden that I won't be resigning with Denver or going anywhere except Chicago."

Zach's eyes widen. "Are you serious?"

"Yup." I nod and sit back up. "I don't want to think about it happening again."

He opens his mouth, but I hold my hand up, silencing him.

"Not the shit with us. I mean, if something happens to you and I'm not here to take care of you. You ending up in the hospital was a real wake-up call for me in a lot of ways. It made me realize how much we're both risking when we step out onto the ice or the field. Sure, I've had teammates who have been injured, but fuck, Zach, I'm just as likely to get a concussion as you are."

Understanding seems to dawn on him.

"It would drive me crazy not being able to be with you if that happened," he says quietly.

"Exactly. So, while football is here—" I hold my hand out, indicating a level, then put my other one a lot higher. "—you're here on my list of priorities, and if that means Denver lets me go and I don't get signed by Chicago for the next season, I'm okay with that. I love playing football, and I've had some great years, but my heart is here with you. I've accepted that if I need to retire earlier than I'd originally planned to be with you, then I'll do that."

He chews on the inside of his cheek, eyeing me. A beat goes by, then another. When he finally speaks again, his voice is more determined. "And you're sure about this?"

I nod vehemently. "Yeah, I've never been surer of anything in my life."

He lets out a shaky breath and nods, almost like he's agreeing to something in his brain.

"During those six months you're in Denver, we need to make sure we talk every day. Video call at every opportunity," Zach insists.

"And phone sex." I grin, wiggling my brows. "*All* the phone sex."

He laughs. "Yeah, there will be a lot of phone sex."

Pressing a knee on the couch, I lean forward and tackle him until he's lying beneath me. His hands slip under my sweater, caressing my back. I capture his lips in a kiss, trying to tell him without words that we're going to be okay. That this new path I'm going to take will be worth it, and the only regret I have is not realizing what we could be sooner.

✕

"Running late, I see." Blaine smirks, one eyebrow arched as we walk up to the table.

It's a good thing we planned to meet Blaine and Alex at a steak restaurant that's just around the corner from our apartment building because we are running *very* late.

One look at Zach in his tight black dress pants and open charcoal shirt, and I immediately dropped to my knees. One thing led to another, and next thing we knew, we were having to tuck our shirts into our pants in the elevator, and I'm pretty sure my mouth is still a little red with stubble burn.

"Leave them alone." Alex playfully hits Blaine's chest with the back of his hand. "It's not like you can talk. If I didn't threaten to withhold sex from you if we were late, we would still be in the apartment."

"I would flip you off if we weren't in a classy establishment," Zach retorts as we both sit down opposite the other couple. "We're not that late."

He looks at his watch before looking back at Zach with a pointed expression. "You're twenty-five minutes late."

"Blaine." Alex laughs. "Don't act like you're a saint when *we* only got here five minutes ago."

His fiancé's mouth drops open in a mock gasp. "Baby, will you please stop being so perfect and let me tease my friend?"

I snicker as I pour some water into my and Zach's glasses. "You can blame me for being late. I seem to have some trouble keeping my hands to myself around Zach."

A wicked grin appears on Blaine's face, but the waiter comes to take our orders before he can say anything. Once we've ordered, we settle into an easy conversation about the Thunder's season. They clinched their spot in the playoffs two nights ago, becoming the first team to secure a place in the postseason. Then Alex tells us about their wedding planning. They've decided on a date in July, and they've found a place in California right on the beach.

"Maybe we can plan to head there from Hawaii? Spend some time in California before we need to be in Denver?" I suggest to Zach.

He turns his head to me. The low, ambient lighting of the restaurant does nothing to diminish the love shining in Zach's blue eyes. He's tied his hair up completely tonight, showing off his handsome-as-fuck face. I want to trace his cheekbones and the sharp lines of his lips with my fingers.

How can the simple sight of someone make your heart leap in your chest?

"Yeah, that sounds great." He smiles softly.

"So, how's Brody finding it in Toronto, Zach? You looking forward to facing him next week?" Blaine asks, breaking the moment.

My teeth grind on instinct at the sound of his brother's name. Don't get me wrong, I don't hate the guy, but growing up, he was a real asshole to Zach. I hated how upset he got, not knowing why his brother had become his biggest rival. However, in recent years, he seems to have accepted that he and Brody aren't going to be as close as siblings should typically be.

But also, I'm an only child, so I don't understand why Brody is the way he is.

Zach shrugs. "Okay, I think? I've not really heard from him."

And that's another thing that pisses me off. Brody only messaged Zach twice since his injury in January. It's been nearly three months. Doesn't he give a shit?

"How about you, Carter?" Alex smiles at me. "Will you be seeing any of your teammates in the off-season?"

I blink at him, a little confused. I mean, his question is totally normal. Anyone would think that I'd make plans to see a few of the guys, even if it's to grab dinner or a round of golf. But I'm not like everyone else, and realization hits me full force, knocking my breath from my lungs.

Here I am getting pissed off about Brody, but none of my teammates have checked in on how Zach was doing. Not once have they dropped a text or a DM checking in on me. We spend so much time together during the season, so they know how important Zach is to me. Hell, I've come to realize that we've almost been in a relationship without knowing we were in a relationship. Surely that should mean something?

But then again, I've never looked at the people in Denver and thought of them as family. Not like the Thunder guys, who have welcomed me into the fold as an extension to Zach.

But fuck, other than Zach, I have no one.

He's got them—Elliot, Blaine, Jackson, Peyton, Ethan, and all the others. He's got people who care for him, almost as much as I do. They were there for him when he was injured. They were there for *me* when he was injured, but my own teammates were nowhere to be seen.

But then again, maybe my teammates are simply not like these guys. The Thunder guys have a unique bond, and a lot of teams don't have that.

"Carter, you okay?" Zach asks quietly, his hand squeezing my thigh.

Letting out a steady breath, I place my hand on top of his and nod. "Yeah, I'm okay."

If I hadn't already made my mind up about leaving Denver, this would have settled it for me. My home is here in Chicago. It's with Zach and this extended Thunder family.

I've just got to make it through to January.

Chapter Twenty-Two

Carter

"Are you sure about this?" Zach asks, turning to me once he's put his car into park. We've just arrived at the private terminal where the Thunder travel from, ready to board the plane heading to Denver. "Not that I don't want you to come, because I do, but are you sure you want to do this?"

The whole thing with my teammates has been playing on my mind since we went for dinner with Blaine and Alex the other night, and when I noticed Zach had an away game in Denver tomorrow, I asked if I could come along. I knew I needed to speak to them, and it wasn't the kind of conversation I wanted to have over the phone, but I also didn't want to leave Zach. Luckily, he managed to pull some strings with the team, and once I got the OK to travel with him, I sent a text to some of the guys asking if we could meet tonight for a catch-up.

I'm aware it's most likely a whole big misunderstanding

on my part, but if I'm going to be returning to Denver for training camp in the summer—which seems more and more likely considering I haven't heard anything—I need to know where I stand. Once I have something in my head, it's like I can't rest until it's resolved. I can be a little impatient like that.

Wetting my lips, I give a clipped nod. "Yeah, I'm sure. It'll give me the chance to see if they've heard anything as well."

Zach smiles, nodding once before getting out of his car and collecting our bags from the trunk. They tend to travel to Denver the day before the game to give them some time to adjust to the altitude. It took me a while to get used to it when I first moved to Denver too, along with being apart from Zach for the first time in my life.

"Well, lookee who we have here!" Elliot chirps as we approach the steps of the plane. With a lopsided grin, he wiggles his finger between us. "Don't think about joining the Mile High Club while we're on our way to the Mile High City, broskis. You two won't fit in the toilet together. It'll make for some wild turbulence, and I don't wanna bring up the delicious turkey and Swiss flatbread I had earlier."

I snort as Zach flips him off and nudges him up the steps. "Get on the plane, Olsen."

"What? It was a really good sandwich!" Elliot replies before tipping his head back with a laugh when Zach rolls his eyes.

I follow Zach as he makes his way toward the back of the plane, saying hello to everyone as I pass and making sure to thank Coach Harris for letting me tag along. Stowing my bag in the overhead bin, I drop into the aisle seat as Zach settles into the window seat with his Nintendo Switch and noise-canceling headphones. I've traveled with him so much, I know his in-flight routine as well as my own, and I don't want my presence here to interfere with that.

I'm about to tell him to just go about his normal routine as if I'm not here when he asks quietly, "Have you thought about what you're going to say to them?"

I shake my head. "No, not yet, but I've got some time to think about it."

He laughs quietly under his breath and loads up his Switch. "I think you're worrying about nothing, but it's good you're speaking to them. It would've been unhealthy to stew on it until July."

"I know." I squeeze his thigh, then lean over to smack a kiss to the corner of his mouth. "You do your thing. Pretend I'm not here."

"Like I'll ever be able to do that." He winks then puts on his headphones as I sit back into the seat and think about how I'm going to bring it up to the boys.

A few hours later, I'm walking through the doors to the steakhouse where I've arranged to meet Palmer and Walker. They were the reason why I bought a house in this area. We play on the same line together, as they are both defensive tackles and I'm a defensive end, and we naturally gravitated toward each other being around the same age too. But they're both married with kids, and I'm… well… I've been hypothetically married to Zach all this time.

"Look what the cat dragged in," Palmer drawls as I approach the table.

Grinning, I hold my hands out to the side and give a

careless shrug. "What can I say? I've missed both of you and couldn't stay away any longer."

"Fuck off." Walker scoffs. "You couldn't get out of here fast enough. It was like your ass was on fire."

"I'm pretty sure I saw a trail of smoke following you out the door," Palmer jokes.

I give them both a one-armed bro-hug before sitting down at the table. "You know how it is. I needed to lick my wounds in Chicago, and there's only one thing that can help me."

And he goes by the name Zach Reid.

The three of us catch up over amazing food and drinks, and I'm glad they don't mention anything when I stick to water. I have plans for tonight when I get back to the hotel, and I don't want to fog my head with alcohol.

"You haven't heard anything? At all?" Palmer asks, brows raised in surprise.

I shake my head, sipping on my water. "No, nothing. I know I played like shit last season, but—"

"Hey, whoa, no. We all played like shit last season, but that was *last* season. Coach Jefferson knows how much hard work you put into your training and into your game," Walker protests. "It wasn't your fault you were unlucky, getting hit with injury after injury."

I missed a couple of games here and there thanks to things such as torn muscles, bruised ribs, and a fractured finger. I had blocked it out of my mind, because to me, they were minor injuries. It wasn't anything like what Zach had sustained.

I didn't see it at the time, but these guys were there for me when Zach couldn't be. We might not be as close as the

Thunder boys, but they were there through the tough times, even if I did shut myself away.

"It's hard to be on top of your game when you recover from one thing, only to be taken down two weeks later by something else." Palmer sighs, his thumb idly peeling the label from his bottle of beer. "If it helps, I haven't heard anything either. I'm kinda taking it as no news is good news."

"Both your contracts are up after next season, right? Maybe they're working on offering an extension?" Walker suggests, his tone hopeful.

"Maybe." I rub my hand over my face and lean back in my chair.

"Anyway, enough about stuff that's out of our hands. Tell us how your man is doing," Palmer says, resting his forearms on the table in front of him. "I mean, I can't say we're surprised to hear that you and Zach are boyfriends." He shares an amused look with Walker. "We all thought you were secretly dating, and the girlfriends were just to warm your bed during the season because they didn't seem to stick around for very long."

"Would you believe me if I said I had no idea people thought that?" I chuckle, shaking my head softly. "But he's doing good, thanks. I'll be honest... I... I didn't think you cared. I didn't hear from you when he was in the hospital, and it was only the other day that I realized that I never heard from you at all and it kinda stung."

Hurt flashes through Walker's eyes. "Of course we fucking care, dude. I know Melissa sent flowers to your apartment with a note telling you we were here for you if you needed us. Didn't you get them?"

"Uhh… No?"

"Fuck, let me find out where she sent them." He types away on his phone, and moments later, he holds it up with an address.

"That's his old apartment. He hasn't lived there for a few years."

"Fuck. Well, whoever lives there now received a nice bouquet of flowers and a box of those fancy chocolates you like."

"I sent some too, and I didn't want to text you because I knew you would be busy. I knew you'd reach out when you had a chance," Palmer adds.

I rub my hand over my chest, trying to ease the ache as guilt claws at me. Fuck, these guys. I can't believe I let myself believe they didn't care.

"I'm really sorry for doubting you guys."

"We've always cared about you, Lockwood. We only stopped inviting you to things because you never leave the house. We knew the answer would be no because you always want to speak with Zach and we don't hold it against you. We never have. It's not that we don't care about you, you idiot. We knew Zach was more important to you and we accepted that." Palmer's face is full of sympathy. "I'm sorry it felt that way to you, though."

"Thanks for this. I…" I let out a shuddering breath and chew on the inside of my cheek. I feel like a huge idiot. Not only was I clueless about Zach, but I also completely missed the signs of my teammates trying to include me too. "I really appreciate it, and I'm sorry for doubting you guys."

"Nothing to be sorry for, brother. We'll come back better and stronger. It's gonna be our year," Walker says, his mouth morphing into a bright grin. "So, how the hell did you not know you were in love with Zach? And also… When's the wedding?"

A few hours later, I'm swiping the key card to our hotel room, feeling so relieved with how dinner went with the guys. Zach was right—there was no way I would have been able to wait until July to get it off my chest. And knowing Palmer also hasn't heard anything makes me feel better too. Maybe I am overthinking the whole trade thing.

When I step inside the room, Zach's already in bed with his Nintendo Switch in his hand. He's watching me with questioning eyes, trying to gauge my mood.

"How did it go?" he asks after a beat.

"Really good," I reply, kicking off my shoes. "Turns out, I wasn't just oblivious about you. I was oblivious about how I behaved with them, too. You might as well call me Carter 'Oblivious' Lockwood."

He puts his Switch down on the bedside table and gives me his full attention. "What do you mean?"

As I strip out of my clothes, I tell him everything. By the time I'm down to my boxers, Zach's eyebrows are raised in surprise.

"Wow. I can kinda understand Ethan's point about us being codependent."

"I know, me too."

"Do you feel better about it now?"

Pressing a knee on the bed by his thigh, I throw my leg over him and straddle his lap. His hands immediately go to my hips, his thumbs tracing the lines of my V as I curve my hands around the back of his neck and thread my fingers into his hair.

"Yeah, I do, and I think if Denver does want to keep me, it'll help make the upcoming season a little more special because I know it'll be my last with these guys, and I want to do good for them. I want to be the best for them."

"That makes sense."

Leaning forward, I capture his lips in a gentle kiss. He tastes like toothpaste and the lingering taste of his mouth-wash. "How was your evening?"

"Good," he murmurs. "Had dinner with the guys, then came to bed and played Pokémon for a bit. Elliot's beating me, so I had to catch up."

I grin against his mouth then nip his bottom lip between my teeth before pushing my tongue into his mouth. I'll never get over how good kissing Zach is. The feel of his tongue against mine gets me hard in an instant. I roll my hips, rubbing our hard cocks together through our under-wear and he moans. His hands snake around and squeeze the swell of my ass.

"I want you to fuck me," I announce in a whisper.

Zach freezes his movements and opens his eyes. His tongue is still in my mouth, hands mid-squeeze of my ass cheeks.

A second passes, then another, before I pull back an inch. My favorite pair of icy blue eyes are filled with so much emotion as he blinks up at me.

"Really?" he asks, barely above a whisper.

"Yeah, Zach, really." I nod. "I want you to own me in

every way. I want you to take me to a place that no one has ever taken me before."

He swallows roughly as I lift my hand to his face, tracing the shape of his lips with my thumb.

"Will you do that for me?"

"Y-yeah." His answering nod is shaky, and I grin down at him before slamming my mouth to his. It's a duel of eager tongues and hungry kisses as I grind my hips against his. When I sit up, he lets out a groan and chases my mouth.

"I need to…" I wave my hand. "Freshen up."

"Who told you that?"

"The internet."

Zach presses his lips together like he's trying not to laugh, but the sparkle in his eyes gives him away. "You've been looking it up on the internet?"

"Well, yeah. I didn't want to go into it blind. I wanted to know what I needed to do to make it easier for you and good for me."

An adoring smile tips his lips as he shakes his head softly, curving his hand around the back of my head and bringing me in for another kiss. It's not as frantic as before, but it's still filled with need.

"Okay, you go. I'll be waiting out here," he says, giving my ass a soft slap.

I climb off him and head into the bathroom, taking a quick shower, making sure to clean thoroughly like I'd read, and when I step back out, the lights are off except the ambient lighting behind the headboard. Zach is lying in the center of the bed with the covers kicked off, languidly stroking his hard erection, and the sight instantly makes my cock throb.

Zach's heated stare trails over my body as I walk over to the bed and climb onto his lap.

"Damn, you're so fucking hot," he says, his voice turning a little husky.

My hands go straight into his hair as our mouths meet. His hands move to grab my ass cheeks, kneading and massaging the solid muscle of my glutes as I thrust my cock along the underside of his.

Dipping my head, I graze my teeth up the side of his neck and suck on the delicate skin just below his jaw.

"Get up on your hands and knees," Zach growls.

I don't miss a beat. I'm on all fours in an instant, arching my back in a way that has Zach letting out a low moan.

"You are so fucking perfect, Carter." He begins by smoothing a hand over my spine to the top of my crease as he shifts on his knees until he's behind me. "Your body is a work of art. I could spend hours exploring every inch of you. Tasting you." He presses his lips against the back of my thigh, and a shiver travels up my spine as he runs his tongue up to the curve of my ass cheek. "I want to know what makes your body *sing*, so I can take you to heaven and make you see stars."

"I want all of that," I beg, curling my hands into the bedsheet beneath me.

He hums, and I'm so turned on it's like I can feel the vibrations from deep in his throat rippling across my skin. A small whimper escapes me as his hot breath fans across my exposed hole before he licks a hot, wet stripe over the furled skin.

"Holy fuck," I hiss.

I feel so exposed like this, like I'm on display for him to

take what he wants. Knowing Zach has probably thought about this moment so many times over the years makes heat coil at the base of my spine.

I moan into the bedsheet as he eats me out, teasing me with flicks of his tongue and deep, satisfied rumbles. I'm a whimpering mess when he moves to lick over my taint and suck on my heavy balls. His hand moves between my legs to take hold of my cock that's dripping with precome, angling it back so he can take me into his mouth.

"Ngh, fuck, Zach. *More*."

It's like my body is coiled tight, ready to let go at any second.

He sucks me down as deep as he can in this angle before moving back up to my ass.

The sound of the lube cap being clicked open breaks through the thumping in my ears from the blood rushing through my head. Moments later, the feel of cool liquid being spread around my hole causes my toes to curl.

Zach circles his finger around my hole a few times before pushing inside.

I'm unaware I'm holding my breath until he whispers, "Breathe, Carter," and the breath I was holding whooshes out of me, allowing him to ease all the way inside. He whispers reassuring words and presses kisses to my skin as he works me open, and by the time he's got a third finger inside me, I'm rocking back on his hand, seeking more.

"Now," I demand, peering over my shoulder. "I want you inside me, now."

He moves up on his knees behind me, and there's a feral glint in his eyes when our gazes lock. His chest rises and falls with each heavy breath he takes.

"I need you to relax," he whispers, gripping my hip with one hand as the other guides his cock to my hole.

I do, and he slowly slips inside. It's nothing like the times I've been pegged. Zach is big, girthy, and long. It's incredible. It's the kind of pleasure I've never experienced, and I know I'll never get enough of it. Of him.

The hair on his legs tickles the back of my thighs and the arousal coursing through me like a rapid wave only heightening my senses. He doesn't move for a moment. I can hear his fast, heavy breathing, like it's taking every ounce of willpower not to lose the steady grip on his control.

But I want him to lose it. I want him to let go. I want him to give me everything he's ever wanted, so I can give it to him right back.

"I think this is the stage where you move," I tease, squeezing my muscles around his cock, causing him to groan.

"I want to be gentle for your first time," he admits with gritted teeth.

Both hands grip my hips, fingers digging into my flesh, no doubt leaving bruises.

"What if I don't want you to be gentle, Zach? What if I want you to fuck me like you're desperate for me? Starved for me, and the only way to make it right is to fuck me so good."

He growls, and the sound that leaves his throat makes my cock throb.

After what feels like a lifetime, he moves. His hips snap, and my toes curl as my body lights up with arousal. The bed creaks under our weight, the sound of our skin slapping and his balls hitting my taint fills the room along with our joined moans.

I drop to the bed, my arms unable to hold me up any longer. Snaking a hand beneath my chest, I wrap my fist around my cock and thrust into my hand in time with the thrust of his hips.

"Carter," he breathes. "I'm gonna come."

"Come for me, Zach. Fill me up."

He blankets my back with his chest, holding his weight up with his elbows. I angle my head, feeling his hot breath against my cheek as the steady rhythm of his hips begins to falter just before he shudders. His cock pulses inside me as the heat of his release filling me triggers my own orgasm, and hot spurts of come land on the sheet.

We don't move. I can feel his pounding heart against my back as we both work to try and catch our breath. I don't know how much time has passed when he slowly slips his softening cock out and flops down on the bed beside me. I collapse onto the bed, not giving a shit about the pool of come I'm now lying in, and I turn my head to face him.

The look in his eyes is something I'll never forget.

Pure, devoted love shines in his light blue eyes, and it's directed at me.

"I love you," I confess, sliding my hand across the bed to his and linking our pinkies together.

His eyes turn glassy, and my heart skyrockets when he says, "I love you too."

I've loved Zach Reid since we were six years old, and it might have taken me twenty-three years to catch up, but I'm so glad I get to love him now.

Chapter Twenty-Three

Zach

We're less than two weeks away until the start of the postseason, and tonight we're facing off against Toronto. I haven't heard from Brody since his trade, and I haven't seen him since we played in New Jersey before the holidays. I would usually be a little cheerier about seeing my brother again, but this headache I've had since we played in Denver has put a damper on my mood. First I put it down to the altitude and the powerful tidal wave of endorphins that came from having sex with Carter, but it hasn't eased up.

If anything, it's progressively getting worse.

So, this morning I decided to skip out on the optional skate to play two-on-two soccer with some of the guys instead, then after I had lunch, I went home for my pregame nap and slept for longer than usual in hopes it would help.

It didn't make a single bit of difference.

But am I going to tell anyone about it? Hell no. We're about to head into the playoffs, and I'm not going to let it get the better of me. I've played through injuries multiple times over the years, and this headache will be another one to add to the list.

I will *not* let my team down now.

The mood in the locker room is calm and collected as we get dressed ahead of warm-up. I have my headphones, listening to my pregame playlist as I lace up my skates. Occasionally, I close my eyes, willing the dull throb behind the back of my eyes to go away.

Ten minutes later, we're heading down the tunnel and stepping out onto the ice. I immediately wince as the glare off the ice burns my retinas and the sound of the loud music hits my ears. A wave of nausea comes over me, but I push through a few laps of our end of the ice.

Movement catches my eye in one of the corners on one of my laps. I look up and come to a stop when I see Jackson's kids, Isabela and Ryan, standing up against the boards with wide, excited smiles on their faces. They're both wearing Thunder jerseys with "Daddy" on the back and Jackson's number, Isabela jumps up and down, slapping her little hands against the plexi as she tries to get our attention.

"Well, if it isn't the coolest Wildes!" Elliot grins, knocking his blocker against the glass.

"I would take offense to that if it wasn't true." Jackson chuckles, appearing next to me to greet his kids.

Picking up two pucks from the ice, I take off my glove and pass them to the kids through the small opening photographers use before heading back to the bench and having a drink. As I squirt some water into my mouth, I look up toward where Carter normally sits a few rows behind home bench with Alex. He's watching me with a slight frown on his gorgeous face.

Sometimes I hate that he knows me so well, because he can read me like the back of his hand, and he knows something's up.

But before I can react, Elliot knocks his shoulder against mine and asks, "You okay, big guy?"

"Yeah, I'm good." The lie tastes bitter on my tongue, but I'm not going to confess my pain.

The doctor said that it could be months until it eases up —if ever—but it's not good enough, and the more headaches I have, the more I wonder if the decision on when my career comes to an end is going to be taken away from me.

"Have you spoken to the big bro yet?" he asks.

I glance over to where Toronto are warming up on the other side of the ice, and a lump thickens in my throat when I spot Brody waiting at the blue line, watching me with a scrutinizing glare. That's nothing new. Brody always seemed to have an issue with everything I did, even about the way I tied my laces or the way I taped my stick. I would always do something wrong in his eyes, and clearly, there's something he's unhappy about now.

"No, but I better go as it looks like I'm being summoned."

Elliot snorts, tapping my ass with his stick before skating off toward the net.

With a sigh, I skate over to the blue line where he's

shifting from skate to skate. His brows pinch as I get closer, and I'm about to make a snide remark when he asks, "Are you okay?"

I let out a choked noise in surprise. Holy shit. This is new, and I'm not quite sure how to take it.

"I'm fine," I say, trying to hide my shock at his genuine concern.

His frown deepens, but I'm glad when he doesn't push me on it.

"Shall we get this over with?" I ask, motioning to the waiting reporter.

We smile for the mandatory brotherly love photo we always have to take for the media whenever we play against each other, then he motions for me to follow him to center ice.

"So, how are you liking Toronto?" I ask. Hopefully I can distract him from the fact that he knows something's up, and he'll leave me alone.

"It's good. I like it. Nice city, nice people."

"It's Canada, what do you expect? Everyone's nice in Canada." I chuckle, and that earns me a small laugh.

Holy *shiiiit*. What is going on right now?

"True, but… I dunno, I feel better now that I'm out of New Jersey. I didn't realize how much I needed to get out until I got out, if that makes sense."

I nod. "Yeah, it makes sense."

He eyes me for a beat, his gaze bouncing over my face like he's trying to figure me out. My shoulders stiffen on instinct beneath my pads, preparing myself for whatever verbal jab he'll throw my way, but it doesn't come.

"How's your head? Mom mentioned you've been getting migraines."

"It's fine," I quickly dismiss. "I'm fine."

The muscle in Brody's jaw ticks as he seems to bite back his response.

"I better go warm up." I motion behind me with my stick. "It was good to see you."

I don't turn around to see if he's gone back to his own warm-up as I skate off, dropping down onto the ice and going through my stretches before I join the rest of the guys taking shots on net. As I skate around, my vision begins to swim. My teammates become blurry, and the dull, throbbing pain begins to grow behind my eyes.

Fuck, not now.

Taking off my glove, I rub at my eyes under my visor, trying to do it as subtly as possible so I don't get the attention of eagle-eyed Ethan, but it's no use. The brightness of the ice causes my head to pulsate, the pressure increasing until it feels like it's about to split in two. Yep, it's definitely turning into a migraine.

I startle slightly when Jackson skates up to me and places a hand on my shoulder.

"Hey, man, are you okay?" he asks, but his voice sounds so far away.

There's only two minutes left of warm-up. Maybe if I head back to the locker room now, I can sit down and drink some water, and it'll pass. Maybe Joe will be able to give me some pain meds to take the edge off so I can get through the game, then I can rest tonight and all of tomorrow. The painted lines on the ice blur as I make my way toward the bench, stumbling slightly when I step over the ledge and head down the tunnel.

"Zach?" someone calls out, but I ignore them and move toward the locker room.

I feel so fucking woozy, like I could throw up from the pain in my head. If I could sit down and close my eyes for five minutes, I'd be okay.

I'm aware of someone gripping my bicep and guiding me into the training room. I slump onto the nearest chair, dropping my stick and gloves to the floor before taking off my helmet. Pressing the heels of my palms into my temples, I close my eyes and rest my elbows on my knees.

Fuck, it's like my head is trapped in a vise and the only bit of relief is the pressure I'm applying to my temples, which sounds crazy as fuck considering the pain I'm experiencing is the pressure building in my head.

I take slow, measured breaths through my nose, hoping the nausea will soon subside. An ice pack is pressed to my forehead, and I stiffen. When I open my eyes, Joe is crouched in front of me, concern etched into every inch of his face.

"How long have you had a headache for?" he asks.

"When do I not have a headache?" I grumble, "Sometimes it's fine, it's more tolerable. But this one has been here for days. It started when we were in Denver. I didn't say anything because if I told anyone I have them that often, I'd never get out on the ice."

He frowns. "Zach, you need to tell us when you're struggling. Migraines are common after a concussion, but we can't help you if you don't work with us."

Rubbing a hand over my face, I let out a heavy sigh. "I

know. It's just… It's exhausting, you know? Every day I wake up and I don't know how I'm going to feel. I'm constantly on edge, wondering if one is going to strike and knock me on my ass."

"I understand that, but if we don't know, we can't try and prevent it from progressing into a full-blown migraine. Chris is a magician, if you didn't know," he says teasingly.

I huff out a laugh. "I'm sorry."

"Don't be sorry." He taps my knee pad. "Just talk to us. We can help you, but you've got to stop hiding how you're feeling."

"I'm going to be scratched tonight, aren't I?"

He nods solemnly. "Yeah, most likely. I'll go and speak with Coach Harris, but I think it's best."

I close my eyes again as he leaves the room to find Coach, and I rest my head back against the wall. The ice pack gives some relief, and I'm thankful the training room is pretty quiet and dark.

I'm so fucking pissed at myself, at my head, at Mueller for knocking me into the boards in the first place.

I'm not sure how much time has passed until the door creaks open, and I hear Carter's voice. "Zach? What happened?"

Opening my eyes, I tilt my head to look at him and give him a small smile. "Tried to be strong. Thought I could fight through it."

He sighs, sitting down on the seat next to me and curving his hand over my thigh. "You don't have to be strong all the time. Maybe instead of putting you on IR, they can assess it game by game?"

"Mhm, yeah, maybe."

Carter wraps his arm around my shoulders, hauling me closer. It's awkward with my padding, but I rest my head on his shoulder as his hand finds my hair, massaging my scalp in that relaxing way he always does.

As expected, Coach agrees with Joe that I'm going to be scratched from tonight's line-up, and I need to see Chris tomorrow for an assessment. I stay in the training room with Carter until the nausea eases off, and then during the first period, I head into the locker room and take a shower with the lights off. Carter sticks close by in case I need him.

"I saw you speaking to Brody. Did he have much to say?"

I shrug. "No, but it was really weird… He seemed genuinely concerned about me. He didn't make any back-handed comments or anything."

His eyes widen in surprise. "Wow. Maybe this move has been good for him?"

"Yeah, maybe."

I hope so. I know we haven't always gotten along, but I do want the best for my brother. So, I hope this move to Toronto works out well for him.

We wait until the first intermission before leaving so I can say goodbye to the guys and reassure them that I'm okay, and as we head down the corridor and pass the visitors' locker room, I stop in my tracks when I see Brody step out.

"Hey, lil' bro," he says, a sheepish smile on his face.

We couldn't be any more different. His hair is cut short on the sides with only a few inches of length on top. His eyes are brown, matching our dad's. He's a few inches shorter and a hell of a lot lighter than me too.

"Hey."

Nothing could have prepared me for Brody wrapping his arms around me in a hug. This is the first time I think he hugged me since he was drafted at eighteen, and that was only because it was being aired on national TV and he had to keep up appearances.

I eye Carter over Brody's shoulder as I return the hug, and his expression tells me he's just as shocked as I am.

When Brody takes a step back, he runs a hand through his damp hair and lets out a shaky exhale. "I know I haven't always been a good brother to you, and I'm really sorry for everything. I just… Fuck." His voice cracks as he looks up at the ceiling, as if the concrete beams will give him answers. "If I hadn't been such an asshole to you over the years, maybe I could have been there for you through all of this. I didn't realize how severe your concussion was. I didn't know that it was still impacting you like this, and I wish there was something I could do to help."

My mouth drops open as I blink at my older brother. If it weren't for Carter standing beside me, I would think I'm imagining it.

My brother just… apologized.

To *me*.

I didn't think he was capable of showing remorse toward me.

"I appreciate that, Brody. I'm doing okay in the grand scheme of things. Yeah, I struggle with migraines, but I'm okay." I squeeze his bicep and clear my throat. "Thanks for this. It means a lot."

He nods a few times, rolling his lips between his teeth.

The door to the locker room opens, and he thumbs over his shoulder. "I better get back in there."

"Yeah… It was good to see you."

He nods again, then looks at Carter. "It's about time you realized he's the best thing to ever happen to you."

Carter's eyes light up in a smile as they meet mine. "I know. I'm one lucky guy."

"You are. Make sure you look after him."

"Always have, always will," Carter replies.

Brody smiles, then disappears back into the locker room.

"Whoa," Carter says in disbelief as we make our way to the parking lot. "Who would've thought the day would come when he acknowledged he has been an asshole to you?"

I shrug, taking his hand in mine. "I didn't, but I'm glad he did. Like you said, maybe the trade has been the best thing that could happen to him."

We're quiet as Carter drives us back to my apartment. I close my eyes, resting my head against the headrest, and twenty minutes later, we're in my bedroom. Carter closes the blackout curtains as I strip out of my clothes, leaving them in a pile on the floor before climbing under the duvet as he quickly gets undressed and slips under the covers with me.

On instinct, I curl into him. Reveling in his body heat and the feel of his warm skin against mine and the prickly hair on his legs as he thrusts his thigh between mine. He wraps his arms around me and presses a kiss to my forehead, and my eyes burn at the tender move.

"I'm sick of feeling like this, Carter." My voice breaks as I allow my emotions from the night to come to the surface.

"I'm sick of these headaches. I'm sick of them impacting my game."

"I know, baby. I wish there was something I could do to make it better for you."

"But what if they don't go away? I don't know if I'm ready to give up hockey just yet."

I always thought I would retire on my terms. Right now, I'm not so sure, and I don't know how to feel about that.

Chapter Twenty-Four

Carter

As I expected, Coach Harris put Zach as a game-time decision. With only a handful of games left in the regular season, he prefers Zach gets some rest to be ready for the playoffs. So, while he missed the game against Toronto, and the one after that, he returned to the ice last night. There are only three games left before the postseason begins, where they will face St. Louis in round one, and Chris and Joe have started trying a few different targeted relief methods such as acupuncture and acupressure. Zach says they seem to be helping, so I'm keeping my hopes up that this is the beginning of the end for these headaches.

Plus, we do our own kind of *relief* method when he's home.

"Fuck, do that again," Zach moans, his back arching off the couch.

I do as I'm told. I look up at him from where I'm lying

between his parted legs as I swirl my tongue around the swollen head of his cock and pump him with my fist. He has one foot planted on the floor, the other on the cushion, his knee bent for stability.

I wrap my lips around him and suck him into my mouth, holding the base of his erection as I continue my torment. It's safe to say that, since his trip to New York and our phone sex session, we've dipped our toes into edging. Something I've enjoyed immensely.

Zach, though? I've been sucking on his cock for nearly thirty minutes now, bringing him to the brink of release before pulling off. And the death grip he has on my hair right now tells me I'm not going to get away with it for much longer unless I want to go bald.

His hold halts my movements as he begins to buck his hips, tunneling his cock in and out of my mouth. His body trembles, letting me know he's close before he can say the words.

"Carter. Ngh, fuck, I'm gonna come. I wanna fill your mouth with my come. Don't you fucking dare stop me."

Smiling around his thick shaft, I relax my jaw, allowing him to hit the back of my throat with each thrust. I swallow around him, and he lets out a roar as he comes so hard, some of his release seeps from the corner of my mouth. I use my thumb to catch it and suck it into my mouth.

"Shit, why is that so hot?" he says as he pants, gasping for breath.

"Who knew you had such a hot, dirty mouth?" I smirk before mimicking his moan, rolling my eyes to the back of my head. "I wanna fill your mouth with my come."

"Fuck off. You make me lose my brain." He snickers and shoves my shoulder. "Anyway, you love it."

"Yeah." I nip the soft skin at the juncture of his thigh. "I do."

Zach's boneless body melts into the couch with a satisfied sigh, and I push myself up, adjusting my erection that's currently trying to punch a hole through my sweatpants.

Patience, padawan, I tell my eager dick.

I head into the kitchen to grab two bottles of water from the fridge and hand one over to Zach as I sit back down.

"What time is Hayden getting in again?" he asks, taking a quick swig before pulling his sweatpants back up and sprawling back onto the couch.

I look down at my watch. "His flight lands any minute now."

Placing my water down on the coffee table, I move to settle between his parted legs, and he lets out a satisfied noise. I curl my arms under his arms, my fingers threading through the long strands of his hair. I nuzzle my face into the crook of his neck and pepper kisses along the thick column of his throat.

"Mmm, I suppose I better get changed," he murmurs.

"Or we'll wait until he's downstairs and do this a little longer." I roll my hips, eliciting a delicious moan from his throat.

"We don't have time for that."

Lifting my head, I glance down at him under hooded eyes and suck his bottom lip into my mouth. "But we have time for me to grind myself on you and make out."

Thankfully, he doesn't argue with me on that. His tongue pushes into my mouth, tangling and exploring as I lose myself in the feel of his lips. I lose track of time and place as I grind my hips against his and his hands massage my ass cheeks beneath the waistband of my sweatpants. I'm so close when the sound of the door buzzer makes me jump.

Startled, I look down at Zach in confusion. "That can't be him already?"

Zach huffs out a breath, shifting beneath me and adjusting his erection in his sweatpants. "I doubt it, but I wouldn't put it past Hayden. I swear that guy has some magical skills. I wouldn't be surprised if he could teleport."

Chuckling, I make my way to the intercom as it buzzes again.

"Hello?"

"Hello, Mr. Lockwood, I have Mr. and Miss Wilde here to see Mr. Reid," Steve, the doorman, says.

"Okay, uh, send them up. Oh, and Steve? When Hayden Cassidy arrives, send him straight up. He should be here soon."

"No problem, Mr. Lockwood."

I hang up and turn to Zach, who hasn't moved an inch. "Jackson's here with Isabela."

His brows furrow before he widens his eyes in realization. He looks down at his lap then jumps off the couch so fast, he's a blur as he runs into the bedroom.

I tip my head back and laugh before I walk over to the freezer and open the door, allowing the cold air and mundane thoughts to deflate my cock.

Zach returns wearing jeans and a sheepish expression as there's a knock on the door.

"That was close." He lets out a relieved sigh and sits down on the couch.

I head toward the door, opening it to greet Jackson and his daughter Isabela on the other side. She's bouncing on her toes, wearing a bright smile on her face as she clutches a piece of paper in her hands.

"Hey, I'm sorry for dropping by unannounced. Iz drew a picture for Zach at school and wanted to hand-deliver it herself," Jackson says, stroking his hand over her head. "She didn't want to wait until tomorrow."

"Hey, no worries at all. Come in." I open the door wider to let them in, and Isabela dashes inside, dumping her backpack on the floor before launching herself on the couch next to Zach in a fit of giggles.

"Isabela, this isn't your home. You need to be more mindful of—" Jackson's words cut off with a sigh as Isabela's sneakers land haphazardly on the floor as she kicks them off. He leans down to pick up her backpack and her sneakers before sending an apologetic look our way. "I'm sorry. It seems I've created a monster."

Laughing, I wave it off. "It's no problem. Can I get you a drink?"

"Coffee, please," he pleads.

"No Ryan today?" I ask.

He shakes his head. "No, he's gone over to his friend's for dinner, so we're having a daddy and daughter dinner, which I'm pretty sure will consist of hot dogs and fries."

I snort. "Sounds like a great time."

"This is for you." Isabela grins up at Zach as she hands over the artwork.

My heart practically bursts from my chest at his gentle excitement toward her.

"Wow, Isabela, this is amazing! You really did this?"

She nods enthusiastically, a beaming smile on her face.

"Wow! You did such a good job. What's this?" Zach asks her, pointing to something on the drawing.

"Daddy said you had a head boo-boo." She stands up on the couch cushion and places her small hands on his head. "So, I made you into Mr. Bump."

I hand Jackson his coffee and look over Zach's shoulder at the drawing as I sit down next to him. It's Zach dressed in his hockey gear, but instead of a helmet, he's got bandages around his head and a speech bubble that reads "Ouch."

"This is so awesome." I chuckle. "We'll have to hang it up."

Isabela lets out an excited whoop, then climbs off the couch and runs to the floor-to-ceiling windows that overlook the lake.

"So, how's your head today?" Jackson asks.

"It's good. Saw Joe this morning for another round of acupuncture. I don't know why I didn't try it before, but it seems to be helping," Zach replies, resting his hand on my thigh. "We're meeting Hayden shortly to talk about what's happening next season."

I notice a quick flash of something I can't decipher in Jackson's eyes, but it disappears before I can get a read on it.

"Oh yeah? How do you feel about it?" Jackson asks me. "Think you'll be heading back to Denver?"

"Yeah, I think so. I've got a year left on my contract, so I'm going to play this season, then see if I can get signed by Chicago."

"And what happens if you don't?"

"Then I'll be taking an early retirement."

I'm assuming Hayden's coming to tell me that the

rumors aren't true and I'm staying in Denver, but I'm not worried about it like I was before. I have complete trust and faith in our relationship, and I know we will be perfectly fine seeing through the five months we'll be apart. We've talked about our expectations if we do need to do long distance, and once we get his schedule in the summer, hopefully we won't have any away games when we're in each other's city, but if we do, we have a plan.

We have a new pact now. One that we made while eating donuts after having the most mind-blowing sex.

I think that's why the last one didn't work out in the end. We didn't seal the deal with orgasms and fried dough.

Jackson fills us in on how Ryan's under-8's hockey program is going when there's a knock on the door. Now this is more likely to be Hayden.

I open the door, and he's standing there, full of swagger with his pressed dress pants, a turtleneck sweater, and wool overcoat. He knows he's a good-looking guy.

Glancing at my watch, I arch a brow. "What time do you call this?"

"What is it with O'Hare and delays?" He grunts with a roll of his eyes. "I could probably walk here by the time it takes to get through that airport."

He steps inside, and I give him a fist bump before leading him into the living area.

"Where is the——" His words cut off as he almost stumbles over his feet. His eyes widen at the sight of Jackson, who is looking equally caught off guard. I cast a confused glance to Zach, who looks as puzzled as I am.

I know Hayden and Jackson used to be teammates back in Boston. The media even called Hayden a formidable power forward before an ACL injury led to his early retirement. But I didn't hear anything about there being any bad blood between the two of them when Jackson was traded to Los Angeles. Then again, it was a fair few years ago.

"Hayden, you know Jackson Wilde, right?" I ask, motioning to the guy sitting next to my man. "And this is his daughter, Isabela."

The little blonde chaos gremlin in question comes running over to her dad, throwing her arms around his neck as she suddenly goes shy.

"Y-yeah, I know Jackson." Hayden clears his throat a few times and gives a stilted nod. "You're looking really well, Wilde."

"You're looking good too, Cassidy," Jackson says, then stands up with Isabela on his arm. "I'll leave you guys to it, I've gotta get this one fed." He picks up her backpack and shoes, then turns to Zach. "I'll see you in the morning."

"See you tomorrow, and thanks for my artwork, Isabela." Zach waves, and she waves back over Jackson's shoulder.

"Good to see you, Cassidy." Jackson gives Hayden a clipped nod before heading out of the door.

The three of us stand there in awkward silence as the door clicks closed. I'm not quite sure what to do or say. It's like the awkwardness when I'm doing an interview with the press, and I don't know what to do with my hands. But luckily, Hayden breaks the silence by clapping his hands and heading back toward the door.

"You boys feeding me or what?" He sounds like he's trying to be cheery, but it's clear his confidence has wavered slightly.

We both follow, and as we're slipping on our shoes, I look over to Zach and mouth, "What the hell happened there?"

Twenty minutes later, we're sitting opposite Hayden in our favorite Italian restaurant. He seems to have shaken off whatever came over him and is back to being his charming self.

"How's the vibe heading into the postseason?" he asks Zach, tearing off a piece of bread to dip into the small dish of oil.

"Good. We're focused and working hard every day. I just hope my migraines don't make another appearance."

"Yeah, that's tough. I've played through migraines before, not to the same extent but it's not something I would recommend. The Thunder are supporting you with treatment, right?"

"Yeah, we have daily sessions now, and I have follow-ups with my neurologist."

Hayden nods approvingly, taking a bite of his bread before turning his attention to me. "And what about you, Lockwood? How do you feel about next season?"

"You tell me, Cassidy." I shrug and give him a lazy smile. "I was hoping you were here to bring me some news."

His eyes twinkle behind his dark-framed glasses as he chuckles. "I had a feeling you'd say that."

"Come on then, spit it out."

"Okay, okay. So, Denver is keeping you through to the end of your contract," Hayden announces.

I hold my breath as his words confirm what I have been expecting. Since there was no news for Palmer or me, I'm not surprised that the whole trade rumor mill was just that. A rumor.

I glance over to Zach and catch him looking at me with a small smile.

We've got this, his eyes tell me. And I believe him.

It might be the hardest, longest five months of our lives, but we can do this. We've come a long way in the last few months, and once we get past this time apart, we will have the rest of our lives together.

"Okay." I nod slowly, drawing on the table with my finger. "And?"

"They're also offering a two-year extension."

I immediately shake my head. "I don't want it."

If Hayden's surprised by my quick rejection, he doesn't show it. "Okay… So, do you have a plan of what you'll do once your contract expires?"

"Well, kinda. Like I said before, if Chicago sends me an offer, I'll take it, but if I don't hear from them, then I'll be retiring."

"Retiring?" He gapes at me, and I can't help but laugh.

"With what happened with the concussion and the development in our relationship, I don't believe I'll be able to play at my highest standard if I'm away from Zach. I know it'll come as a shock to some people, especially since I'm going to be turning thirty next week and there's still a few years left in me, but my heart is here in Chicago, and I can't ignore that."

"Are you sure about this?" Zach asks, but I know it isn't

from insecurity. I know he will support me in whatever decision I make.

"I haven't been surer of anything in my life," I echo the words I said to him after our first kiss.

Hayden whistles under his breath and raises his glass. "You guys, I can't tell you how long I've been championing you two getting together, and I can't deny, I fucking love it."

We both lift our glasses and clink them against Hayden's.

"I'll let Denver know your decision, then once the season's ended, I'll work on Chicago."

Under the table, Zach places his hand on my thigh and squeezes, and when I turn to face him, his eyes are filled with pride. I know Zach had his doubts at the beginning, and they were completely valid. If I were in his shoes, I would most likely feel the same, but I would give up everything for Zach Reid. That includes a decade's worth of hard work to get me to where I am today in the NFL.

He's fucking worth it.

Chapter Twenty-Five

Zach

"Are you sure you don't mind hosting?" I ask Peyton as I carry a trash bag full of helium-filled balloons into the living room.

His living room currently looks like a party store has thrown up all over it. It's filled wall to ceiling with colorful balloons and streamers, and I know this isn't the last of it. He's taken the role of party planner very seriously, and I'm starting to wonder if he's gone slightly overboard.

"Of course I don't mind, dude. I have this huge house for just me and the dog. It'll be nice to have some liveliness going on between these walls that doesn't include me having a nap in my armchair while watching Family Feud with a packet of Oreos." He grins.

I laugh. "You're really leaning into that lonely old man vibe, huh?"

Peyton separated from his wife before the holidays and

has since been adjusting to the single life. I think he's lonely in this big house by himself, and that's why he's always offering to host whatever get-together we plan.

"You know it! But a little less of the *old*, Reid, I'm only thirty-one," he teases, and playfully slaps my shoulder before motioning to the front door with his head. "I think there's two more sacks of balloons left to bring in, then we've got to put the banners up. Oh, and I think Ethan and Jacob are due any minute with the cakes."

I nod and get to work with the rest of the decorations.

When I mentioned to the boys the other day that I wanted to do something for Carter's thirtieth birthday, Peyton immediately offered his house for the party. It just so happens that Alex's birthday is the day after Carter's, so we decided to do a joint birthday celebration. And with the postseason now well underway, we're having a very civilized party starting at 3 p.m. so us Thunder boys can be in bed by nine.

It might not be an all-out wild party for the history books, but it will still be a good time because we have eight different pasta dishes available.

Amazing, I know.

Peyton rips open the last bag of balloons, and they float up toward the ceiling, joining the other two dozen.

"So, do you have a plan to get them down?" I point up to the high ceilings. Even if I stand on a table, I can't reach them, and I'm the tallest one out of us all.

He gives a careless shrug. "I dunno. I guess I'll just wait for them to deflate and start to sag down to the floor."

I arch a brow, pressing my lips together to avoid making an inappropriate joke.

Ethan and Jacob arrive with the cakes as we're pinning the last banner up. Knowing Jacob promised to bring some donuts, I follow them into the kitchen.

Ethan carefully places several boxes down on the kitchen counter before turning to us. "Is there anything you need me to do?"

My stomach grumbles at the sight of the familiar boxes, and it gets worse as the sweet smell of baked goods fills my nose. I'm pretty sure they are the to-go boxes that Jacob uses to transport cupcakes at the bakery or when someone orders a dozen donuts—something I know firsthand because I've ordered them on a few occasions.

Rounding the corner, I carefully lift the lid of the top box, wanting to take a sneak peek to see what delights we have today, but Ethan slaps my hand away before I can get a look.

"Hey, get your paws out of there. You can't eat them yet, not until the birthday boys get here at least."

"Ugh, fine." I sigh defeatedly, dropping my hands onto the counter. "And no, I think we're good. The caterer came earlier, so it's a case of warming up the food when everyone's here. Decorations are done, and the fridge is stocked with drinks. Last thing is putting the snacks out." I wave my hand in the direction of the pile of chips, pretzels, crackers, and other quick snacks.

"It looks amazing. You've done a great job." Jacob beams. "They're going to love it."

My chest warms at his compliment. "I hope so."

It took a lot of convincing to get Carter to stay home while I helped Peyton get his house ready, but once I made him see stars with a blow job, he caved. He even promised he would stay there until three before driving up to Peyton's house in Lakeview with Elliot.

The house slowly fills as the others turn up. Jackson, Ryan and Isabela are the first to arrive, soon followed by Kendrick and his wife Maria, who's about to give birth any day now.

We've joked that he could have timed it better, considering we're in the middle of playoffs, and he may even miss the birth of their first child, but he just shrugged and said he couldn't control his swimmers. Luckily, Maria has both his and her parents to help her out.

Two of Alex and Jacob's co-workers, Daniel and Aria, are next to turn up, along with Alex's best friend Nate, before a few more of the Thunder guys make an appearance.

The living room is bustling with activity by the time Blaine and Alex arrive, and the second Alex steps through the door, we release confetti poppers, showering him in colorful paper.

"Oh my god!" Alex squawks, raising his hands in surprise as it rains down over him.

"Happy birthday!" we all shout in unison.

Alex laughs, shaking the confetti out of his hair before Blaine hauls him into a tight embrace and slams his mouth over his.

"Okay, okay. Enough of that, there's children present, Olsen." Kendrick walks over to the couple and pushes them apart. "It isn't that kind of party."

When they step apart, Alex's cheeks turn a deep shade of red, and we all burst into laughter. It's not long until the door opens again, and I turn, hoping it's my man. And despite the ribbing I'm bound to get from the guys, I'm not ashamed of the wide grin that spreads across my face at the sight of Carter. His dark eyes bounce around the hallway before lighting up when they land on me, and his equally bright smile hits me square in the chest.

Fuck, he's so fucking handsome it hurts. It doesn't matter that I've known him almost my entire life, every time I see him takes my breath away.

I close the distance and wrap my arms around his waist, greeting him with a kiss. It's not as ravenous as Blaine's claim on Alex, though. It's a gentle peck to his lips, just as another wave of confetti is let loose, covering both of us.

"Wow, look at this place," Carter praises, looking around the decorated room in amazement. "Whoa, Peyton, did you get a special deal on the balloons or something? Hell, did you leave any in the store for other people to buy?"

Peyton flips him the bird, then his eyes widen slightly as Isabela runs up beside him and tries to copy him.

"No, don't do that! Oh fuck. I mean shit. Ahh, someone help me!" He grimaces.

Jackson chuckles, swooping his daughter up into his arms and gently pushing her middle finger back into her tiny fist. "Stop corrupting my kids, Peyton."

Laughing, I turn to face Carter, sliding my hand to rest on the base of his spine.

"Surprise," I say, my voice just above a whisper.

"Mhm, this is an awesome surprise." A soft smile is on his lips as he wraps his arms around my waist.

"Wait, didn't you come with Elliot?" I ask, but before he can reply, the sound of plastic wheels rolling against the hardwood echoes down the hall.

Carter snickers guiltily, like he knows he's been caught.

"What did you do?" I give him a pointed look.

But he doesn't get the chance to answer because Elliot appears. He's managed to fit his tall, lean frame onto a ride-on unicorn—all six foot one of him sitting on a children's horse.

There's a ripple of surprised laughter as Peyton scolds our goalie, "You better not be scratching my floor with that thing, Olsen!"

"Hey, it can't be a party without a pony," Elliot calls out and rides the damn thing into the kitchen with Isabela hot on his heels, squealing in excitement.

"What… How… Do I want to know how you ended up with a unicorn?" I ask.

"We had some time on our hands, and somehow we ended up in the toy store, and I dared him to ride it there." He shrugs. "I didn't think he would buy it."

I roll my eyes and sigh. "Carter, please don't dare Elliot to do anything because he will do it and then take it a step further."

"So I've learned." He chuckles and leans in to nip my bottom lip. "Thank you for organizing this for me. I really appreciate it."

"Always. You only turn thirty once, and I know the next few weeks are going to be hectic with the playoffs, so I wanted to do something nice for you."

His eyes shine with fondness as he tries to hide his bashful smile by tugging his bottom lip between his teeth. "I love you."

No matter how many times he says those three little words, it always makes my heart skip a beat. We've exchanged them so many times since we became friends over twenty years ago, but now it's different. It's... more.

It's that big love that not everyone gets to experience in their life—an all-consuming love. It's knowing someone so thoroughly, you're almost one. Where you can read each other's thoughts and feelings without speaking a single word. It's trusting that person—*your* person—with your life, knowing they will hold your heart in their hands like it's the most precious thing in the world. It's getting lost in someone, knowing that you're already home. Because they are your home.

It's everything, and every day that I get to share those three little words with Carter, I thank my lucky stars that I've been given the chance to love him the way I've always wanted to love him.

"I love you too."

He captures my lips in a sweet kiss, then entwines his fingers in mine as we make our way into the kitchen. Jacob, Ethan, and Jackson have heated up all the food, laying the trays of various pasta dishes on the island, along with so many snacks, you can't see an inch of the countertop.

"It's not that I'm not grateful for all of this, because this is honestly one of the greatest birthdays I've ever had, but if I have to eat another bowl of pasta, I think I might cry." Alex chuckles.

"Welcome to the hockey life, Alex!" Maria sings, raising her glass of soda.

We all load up our plates and hang out in the living room, exchanging stories from the road and embarrassing tales, and once we've filled ourselves up with the amazing food, Ethan helps Jacob carry out the two cakes he made, one for each of the birthday boys. There are a couple of candles stuck in the top, and we gather round to sing happy birthday. Carter wraps an arm around my shoulder, swaying slightly to the song.

"Make a wish!" someone calls out when it comes to an end.

Alex and Carter blow out the candles, and the room erupts into hoots and applause. Carter takes the cake from Jacob and drags his finger through the frosting of his cake, bringing the digit to my mouth. His dark eyes shimmer with heat as I suck the sweet chocolate frosting off his finger before he leans in and kisses me.

"Mmm," I hum against his lips. "So, what did you wish for?"

"You." He kisses me again, and when he pulls away, his lips tilt up in a devilish smirk. "And that we can flip fuck later."

X

When we get home a few hours later, Carter's birthday wish comes true.

"Oh, fuck yes, this was a good wish," he moans, his hands gripping my hips tight as I bounce on his cock. "You feel so fucking good, Zach. Happy birthday to *me.*"

"It's not your birthday until tomorrow," I grunt out.

"Don't care." He thrusts his hips up, his cock pegs my prostate at the perfect angle, and my head falls back on a throaty moan. "Are we really getting literal right now while my cock is in your ass?"

I answer by rolling my hips, taking his cock as deep as I

can take him, and my name is a delicious cry on his lips. Placing my hands on his wide, solid chest to steady myself, I work us both thoroughly. My hard cock rubs against his stomach as I move on top of him, leaving a wet trail of precome. He wraps his arms around my back and tugs me forward. He plants both feet on the bed and bucks his hips up into me in hard and fast strokes, his balls slapping my ass with each thrust. I land on my forearms, unable to hold myself up with the pleasure coursing through me as our moans become garbled noises.

The rhythm of his thrusts becomes jerky, then his body stiffens beneath me and his cock throbs as he lets go of his release. I ride through his orgasm, smoothing my hands over his chest in a gentle caress, grazing my thumbs over his nipples as his body twitches with the post-orgasmic high. The moment his breathing stabilizes slightly, I sit upright.

"Time to switch it up. I'm close and I wanna come inside you," I demand, rising to my knees and letting his spent cock slip from my ass.

"How do you want me?" he asks.

"On your side," I instruct, and I lie down behind him, pulling his back to my chest.

Placing my hand under his knee, I bend it toward his chest to open him up. As we prepped each other when we got home from the party, he's ready for me, allowing me to slide my cock into his slicked hole.

"Fuck me." His head falls back onto my shoulder.

"That's the plan, baby." I nip his lobe as I ease into him in slow, languid strokes, trying to prolong my inevitable release.

He twists his head so I can see his face, and I press my

lips to his in a heated kiss. He lifts his hand, reaching back to hold the back of my head while our tongues meet in a desperate tangle, exchanging gasping breaths and low moans.

Letting go of his leg, I move my hand down, propping his heavy thigh up with my forearm as I take his half-hard cock in my hand. I alternate between deep and fast thrusts and long and slow strokes, and by the time my balls are drawn tight to my body, he's mumbling incoherently.

I'm not gonna last long. I never do when I'm inside Carter.

"Not that I'm not loving this, because I am, but you've got six minutes until you need to go to sleep, so I really need you to come now, baby," he says between heavy breaths. "Let me turn thirty with the ache from your big cock inside me."

I snort. It's no secret that I have a set time to go to sleep during the playoffs, so the fact that he's trying to help me stick to my routines, even while we're having sex, is why I'm so fucking in love with this guy.

He laughs, causing his muscles to squeeze around my cock.

"Fuuckk," I growl, my eyes rolling to the back of my head, and my hips falter.

Heat rushes down my spine, tingles spread up my legs from my toes, and I release inside him with a groan. Ribbons of come shoot from his cock, coating my hand and his stomach.

I hug him closer to me, pressing my sweat-coated chest up against his back, and kiss the back of his neck. All I can hear is our heavy breathing and the blood rushing in my ears from my rapid heartbeat. Minutes tick by while we just lie there, my cock softening inside Carter's ass and my limbs feeling like wet noodles.

"We need to move," he murmurs, his breath fanning across my arm.

"Yeah, and we need to change the sheets." I kiss his skin again, but neither of us takes the first step.

I can hear the smile in his voice when he says, "You're going to miss your bedtime."

Groaning, I slowly ease out of him and swing my legs over the edge of the bed.

We make quick work of cleaning up and changing the sheets, and when we slip under the covers, I curl into him, resting my head on his chest as our legs intertwine. His hand goes into my hair, his fingers lazily massaging my scalp.

"You better get some sleep, baby. You've got a cup to win," he murmurs sleepily and kisses my forehead.

Winning the cup might be at the forefront of our minds, but as far as I'm concerned, I've already won.

Because I have him, and he's the greatest prize of all.

Chapter Twenty-Six

December - eight months later

Carter

Having a game on New Year's Eve threw a wrench into my plans, but I wasn't going to let it get to me. I knew exactly how I wanted it to go, but I also knew I was going to be cutting it close, so I've pulled out all the stops and got creative. Along with the help of some others.

Within an hour of my game ending in Denver, I skipped out on the post-win celebrations with my teammates and jumped into a private car that took me to the airport, where I hopped on a charter flight to take me to Chicago. Now, I'm in another car heading toward downtown Chicago, and just my luck, it's bumper to bumper on the I-90, and the rain is coming down heavily.

Zach also has a game today, and it's currently into the

second intermission, so I'm only going to get a small window of time to get everything perfect.

It's going to be fine. I'm not going to let this slight inconvenience ruin my mood tonight.

The Thunder are having another stellar season. They are in strong contention for the postseason, as they are currently top of their conference and sitting second in the overall league. They were also crowned Stanley Cup Champions last season, and I'm hopeful they will retain the title for another year, especially if they can continue dominating the way they are.

Watching Zach lift the cup was one of the greatest moments of my life. It wasn't his first Stanley Cup win, but it was the most special because I knew how much he went through to be there. The struggles, the pain, the knowledge that his condition could stop him from getting on that ice.

Seeing his face light up as he held the Stanley Cup made it all worth it.

There was a point during round two where Zach missed two games due to his migraines, much to his frustration. Like every athlete, especially when they are in postseason mode, he tried to downplay his symptoms, but when he threw up on the bench during morning skate one day, Coach Harris stepped in and took him out from the line-up.

Zach mentioned there was a sense of uncertainty in the locker room regarding whether he could return, which made the win all the sweeter.

I went to every one of his games—even the away games in Boston—but there were times I felt scared watching him play, not that I would ever tell him that. A player thinking about concussions often invites one to happen, but the thought that one hit could set him back in his recovery or even change his entire life meant I spent every second he was on shift as a complete mess.

Even now, he still struggles with migraines, but thankfully they aren't as persistent as they were earlier on in the year. He has regular follow-ups with his neurologist to monitor for any signs of change, and the team continues to support him in every way.

I'm pleased that his neurologist is happy with his progress, but he's had to come to terms with the fact that these migraines are most likely here to stay, and he's going to need to learn how to live with it.

After the Thunder celebrated their win, we headed back to Hawaii. We rented the same villa as last year, only this time we spent more time naked and wrapped up in each other than exploring, but neither of us complained.

Who knew pool sex could be so much fun?

Given how hectic the first six months of the year had been, it did us both good to unwind and fully relax. Instead of going to Denver at the end of our trip, we went back to Chicago to celebrate Ethan's retirement from the NHL.

It came as a shock to the boys. I think they saw their captain as untouchable, having dedicated two decades of his life to the league, but Ethan said it was time.

Me, on the other hand? I'm keeping an open mind.

Hayden's heard some rumblings that Chicago might be interested in adding me to their defensive line-up, but I've told him if it doesn't happen, then I'm happy as I am. I've joked with Zach on a number of occasions that I'll be a stay-at-home husband, and maybe Ethan and I can start a retired athletes club. In fact, Ethan's recently started up a foundation that offers hockey programs to underprivileged kids, but depending on whether I get an offer from Chicago, I might ask him if he would be interested in expanding it to include football.

But I'm not thinking too hard about it for now.

There's only a few more weeks left of my season in Denver, then I'll be moving to Chicago permanently. I've got a realtor dealing with the sale of my house and I've started packing up my belongings. I don't have that much to pack anyway.

It turns out I lived quite a minimalist existence. I guess somehow, my subconscious knew I would end up here. I don't feel sad about it, though; if anything, I'm excited, especially since I've been having an incredible season, which I think helps because I'll potentially end my career on a high.

Zach was with me during my preseason, and I got to do something I've watched my teammates do for years. I got to run over to him on the sidelines before the game and kiss him in front of everyone.

I've never considered myself an overly superstitious guy —not like Zach who is strict when it comes to his pre and post-game routines—but clearly I am, because this season I'm on fire, and I have a feeling it's all because of him.

Zach's apartment building comes into view, and I can't stop the smile that appears on my face. To think in a few weeks, this will be *our* apartment building. Our home.

I thank the driver as he pulls up outside and make my way inside to see the doorman, Steve, waiting with a light pink box in his hands.

"Good evening, Mr. Lockwood." Steve bows his head in

greeting, a small smile playing on his lips as he holds out the box. "I have a special delivery for you."

"Amazing, thank you." I grin, accepting the box from him and following him to the elevator bank.

"Is he still unaware of your arrival?" he asks.

"He has no idea," I reply, and we both chuckle.

That's right, Zach has no idea that I'll be waiting for him when he gets home from his game. I said that I needed to stay in Denver as Coach Jefferson wanted us to run through some game tape ahead of our final games next week, but I've really been coordinating all of this behind his back, with the help of the likes of Steve, Jacob, and Zach's teammates.

I want this to be a night he will never forget, and I'm sure he'll forgive me for my little white lie.

"He's going to be pleased to see you. Happy New Year," Steve says as the elevator doors open.

"Happy New Year, Steve." I smile before stepping inside and pressing the button for Zach's floor.

Once I'm inside the apartment, I switch on the TV and find the Thunder game. They're currently winning 3-1 against Dallas, and it's halfway into the third period, which gives me a little bit of time to get everything in order.

I know Zach will be eager to get home after the game, thinking he's going to FaceTime me so we can watch *Return of the Jedi* together, but little does he know he's in for a surprise.

I get started preparing his chicken and broccoli Alfredo so it's ready for me to cook as soon as he gets home, then fetch blankets and pillows from the guest bedrooms and put them on the couch. It won't be exactly like that night when we were ten years old, because why would we put our bodies through sitting on the floor when he has a perfectly good couch?

It might have been the night he fell in love with me, but I plan on making tonight the night he knows I'm so fucking in love with him, he's the reason my heart beats.

Anxiety pools in the pit of my stomach as the game ends with a win for the Thunder, and the clock begins to count down. Blaine texts me to let me know as soon as Zach leaves the arena, and I have just under thirty minutes. When twenty have gone by, I start to cook the chicken and boil the water for the pasta.

My hands are literally shaking as I hear the electronic lock of his door engaging.

I watch as he walks in and stops just inside the hall, his brows furrowing when he sees the TV on. He still hasn't spotted me when he says, "Uhh…"

I round the counter and hold my hands out. "Hey, baby!"

Zach's mouth drops open, his eyes widening as he drops his bag on the floor with a heavy clunk. He closes the distance between us and engulfs me in his arms, squeezing the breath out of me and hiding his face in my neck.

"Hey, baby," I say again with a chuckle under my breath, wrapping my arms around his back.

I kiss the side of his head, and when he lifts it to look at me, his eyes are glassy. His hands cup the sides of my face, thumbs sweeping over my cheeks.

"I can't believe you're here," he whispers.

"I wanted to surprise you," I whisper back.

His wide smile lights up his face before he presses his lips to mine. The kiss is gentle, but it's filled with emotion. It says, *I miss you* and *I love you* and everything in between.

"Why don't you have your shower while I cook your dinner? Then we can watch a movie."

"*Return of the Jedi?*"

"You got it, baby." I give his ass a slap. "Go shower. If we're going to time it just right, you got five minutes until we need to hit Play."

With a final kiss, he collects his bag from the floor and rushes into his room. I finish cooking his pasta, and when he returns in only a pair of low-slung sweatpants, I let out a low whistle.

"Damn, you're so *fine!*"

He laughs and falls onto the couch next to me. He eyes the mountain of blankets, then notices the bowl of pasta waiting for him on the coffee table along with his favorite donut and a bottle of water.

"You got me a donut too?" He gasps.

"Yeah, I did." I nod, leaning in to steal a kiss from his lips because I can't help myself. "I had it on special delivery and everything."

"I fucking love you."

I grin. "I fucking love you too. Now eat up while I start the movie, or it's going to be all out of sync."

We settle back into the couch, cuddled under the blankets as he eats his dinner, then the donut. I subtly check my pocket under the blanket, and my heart rate begins to skyrocket as the scene comes closer and closer. From our spot on the couch, we have a perfect view of Navy Pier, where they will set off fireworks, making it even more perfect.

Slipping my hand under the blanket again, I grab hold of the box, and the second the Death Star explodes on the screen, fireworks paint the night sky over Lake Michigan in a multitude of colors.

It's my cue.

I slide off the couch and get onto one knee with the velvet ring box in hand, flicking the lid open to reveal the black platinum wedding band I had custom made.

Zach's eyes widen. "Carter…"

With a shaky smile, I begin the speech I've been rehearsing for the past week.

"Zach, I was six years old when I bulldozed my way into your life and decided we were going to be best friends. I didn't really give you a chance to argue, but it took less than a day together for me to realize you were my favorite person, and you've remained my favorite person ever since. Over the years, you have always been the first person I thought about when I woke up and the very last person on my mind before I went to sleep. It took me a long time to realize that everything I had been looking for in life had been right there all along. My home has never been a place, but a person. *You.* You are my home. You're my life, my soul, and I don't think I can ever show you how much I love you. You are the Han to my Leia—"

He snorts a laugh.

"Stop it, I'm serious. I couldn't use Han and Chewbacca because neither of us are hairy and they weren't in a relationship, and Anakin and Padmé seemed like a curse."

We both burst out laughing, then I take a deep, shaky inhale, dragging my teeth over my lower lip as nerves bubble in my chest.

"I want to grow old with you, eat donuts with you, and watch *Return of the Jedi* every New Year's Eve with you. I want to travel the world with you, and ultimately, I want to love you every day. And I would *really* love to do it all with you as my husband."

His breath hitches, and those icy blue eyes turn glassy as his eyes fill with tears.

"Carter…" His voice trembles.

With another deep breath, I ask, "Zach Reid, will you marry me?"

He nods several times, swallowing roughly as a bubble of laughter escapes him.

"Yes," he rasps. "Yes, I'll marry you, Carter Lockwood. I want all those things with you."

I'm unable to contain my grin as he drops to his knees in front of me. He grabs my face with both hands and kisses me. With the ring box in one hand, I wrap my arms around his neck, my own eyes burning with tears that soon fall down my cheeks.

When he pulls away, he rests his forehead against mine, and I stare back into my favorite pair of blue eyes.

"I love you so much," I whisper.

"I love you too." He slants his mouth over mine, guiding his tongue into my mouth. We exchange deep, slow kisses to the sound of fireworks over the lake and the movie behind us.

As we ease apart, I take the band out of the box and hold my hand out for his. Zach places his left hand in my palm, trembling slightly as I slide the ring onto his finger before bringing his hand to my mouth and kissing the ring and his palm.

"You said it was on this day twenty years ago that you first realized you were in love with me, but today marks the day you became my best friend, my lover, and my forever."

Zach's teeth dig into his bottom lip as a tear falls down his cheek. I hold the side of his face with my hand and wipe the tear away with my thumb.

"I was six years old when you came into my life and became my favorite person. I think even at that young age, I knew you were someone special. You brightened my day just by being in it, and you brought peace to my life by being by my side. But it was when we were ten that I knew you were my soulmate." His voice cracks, and he clears his throat. "I didn't know what it meant at the time, but my heart had always beaten a little faster around you. Your laugh was always my favorite sound, and your smile is my sun. I didn't know it was possible to love you more."

Tears pool in my eyes. My heart feels so fucking full that I don't know how to express everything I'm feeling, so instead I give him a wobbly grin. "That's because I'm awesome, baby."

He laughs, taking my face in both hands. "That's because you're mine, baby."

I kiss him, then we move to sit back on the couch. Our heads rest on the cushions, our legs locked together as we simply stare at each other, a soft, unbelieving smile on our faces. I trace the ring with the tip of my finger, marveling at how good it looks on him. And how fucking good it feels to know he's going to be *mine* in an official sense, too.

"I can't wait to see how this looks when you have your hand wrapped around my cock." I smirk.

Zach tips his head back and laughs. "What are you

waiting for, fiancé?" He gets off the couch and holds out his left hand with an arch of his brow. "Shall we start a new tradition of seeing the new year in with a bang?"

I jump to my feet and take his hand in mine while the other slides around to grab his ass. "I think we need a new pact. One where we always *come* first."

"Of course you do." Zach laughs and rolls his gorgeous eyes. "It's a good thing I love you."

"I'm all yours, baby." I grin. "I'm all yours."

Epilogue

July - two and a half years later

Zach

"Mmm, fuck. Yes, Carter, just like that." I throw my head back and bite down on my lip to muffle my moan as Carter takes me in quick but deep thrusts.

We don't normally need to worry about being quiet when we have sex anywhere in the house, but we have guests staying with us for the first time since we bought this house in Hawaii, and we learned the first day that the shower wasn't as soundproof as we thought. When we walked out the next morning, we found Elliot grinning at us around a mouthful of cereal with an amused expression.

It was the look of someone who had heard *everything* and was looking forward to giving us hell about it all day.

Since then, we've perfected having quiet sex, much to

Carter's disappointment because he's quite the vocal lover. Not that I'm complaining.

He presses his chest against my back and digs his fingers into my hips. His hot breath fans against the side of my neck, causing a shiver to race across my skin down to my toes.

"I fuckin' love being inside you, baby," he murmurs and nips my ear with his teeth. "So tight. So good."

Taking one hand off the tiled wall, I widen my stance slightly for balance and begin to stroke my cock to the rhythm of Carter's hips slapping against my ass.

"I need you to hurry up because the others are going to be here any minute," I say, my voice a mix of breathy and demanding.

Carter licks up the column of my neck. "Can you imagine if the first thing they heard as they walked through the door was the sound of you moaning my name while covering the wall with your come?"

"Not. Funny," I grind out between clenched teeth. My balls are so heavy and so full that I'm a second away from doing as Carter said and painting the wall with my release.

Carter snickers and presses his lips to my shoulder in a tender kiss, then lifts one hand to cover my mouth. His breath tickles my ear as he takes me hard and fast, just the way I like it. His hand muffles my moan as I come, and he instantly follows me over the edge.

We make quick work of cleaning ourselves up before stepping out of the shower.

"Happy anniversary, husband." Carter grins, then grabs my chin and takes my mouth in a heated kiss. His tongue slides into my mouth, tangling with mine, and my spent cock gives an appreciative throb as his delicious bergamot and clove scent fills my nose.

"Happy anniversary, husband," I echo.

It's been twelve months since we got married, and I still get goose bumps every time the word *husband* leaves Carter's lips.

We got married in Lake Como, Italy, at a villa where they filmed part of *Star Wars: Attack of the Clones*. I was a little surprised when he suggested getting married at the same venue as Anakin and Padmé, considering what he said about them being cursed in his proposal speech, but it couldn't have been more perfect. Not just because I'm a huge fan of the franchise, but because the venue was breathtaking. The photos online didn't do it justice. There were picturesque views of the lake behind us as we promised to love and cherish one another for the rest of our lives, and we were joined by a small group of our closest friends and family. We even got to take pictures reenacting iconic scenes from the movie. Carter had them framed the moment we returned to Chicago, and I often find him simply staring at them while he drinks his morning coffee.

Once we're both dry and dressed, we head out to the kitchen, and a rush of happiness sweeps through my chest to see the others are here and have made themselves at home.

As it's only a four-bedroom house, we don't have the room to host everyone, so the Kendricks and the Wildes rented a villa around the corner, allowing the kids to stay together, and they travel around on one of the resort's golf caddies.

"Is this how you imagined it?" Carter asks quietly as he steps up behind me where I'm standing in front of the coffee machine looking out at the pool. He wraps his arms around my waist and rests his chin on my shoulder.

I lean back into my husband, covering his hands with mine and smile. "Yeah, it's perfect."

When we first saw this house a year ago, I knew it was something special, but it was the moment I saw the floor-to-ceiling windows that fold out to create one huge open space, all I could think about was having *this*.

Being here with Carter and having my friends here with their partners and their kids, relaxing, laughing, having fun. We invited Brody too, but he politely declined. He came to our wedding and had dinner with me and Carter when he was last in Chicago. The move to Toronto was definitely the best thing for him, and while our relationship isn't fixed, it's improved.

We weren't looking to buy a house here so soon. We both thought we would wait until we both retired, and we hadn't even decided on an island, let alone started looking for houses. But Carter found himself scrolling through listings one night while we were on vacation, and as he was showing me the photos for this very house, we turned to look at each other, and we were both wearing the same expression. Something felt so right in our guts about it, and it was too good to pass up.

Not wanting to waste time, we booked a tour for the next day and made an offer within an hour. It's not on the beach, but it has the most picturesque views of the ocean. We have the best view of every sunrise and sunset, and we have the privacy we like as it's in a gated resort. It's so quiet and tranquil; I've never felt so relaxed. There's also an infinity pool overlooking the ocean and a jacuzzi, and it's located on a golf course, something Carter loves, as it's a new hobby he's picked up since he retired.

It's perfect for us.

Carter ended up retiring after his contract was up in Denver. He had various offers from almost every city except Chicago. Some of them were incredible, an eye-watering amount of money, but despite me asking him on more than one occasion to rethink his decision about hanging up his cleats so soon, he stood his ground and kept his word. He now works with Ethan at his foundation, helping underprivileged kids get into sports. He spent hours creating a full proposal presentation on how he would invest in the foundation to expand it to include football—not that Ethan needed or wanted that, but Carter wanted to prove he was committed to the cause. Now he's thriving.

We haven't decided if children are in our future or whether we're happy being the fun chosen uncles, but I know that Carter feels such an incredible sense of pride every time he gets to help a kid who wouldn't necessarily have had the support or the means to play football before.

I haven't quite figured out what my future holds yet. I announced my retirement at the end of our playoff run in early June. I took another big hit during the first round, and it made me nervous about getting another concussion. Every time I stepped out onto the ice and I was crushed into the boards or had a player collide with me, I was on edge, and I knew I couldn't continue to play with that mindset.

The Thunder organization understood my reasoning, and the boys didn't try to fight me on it, which was something I was glad about. But I haven't figured out what's next. I would still like to be involved in hockey in some form, but I need to make sure I don't become a liability with my headaches, so I've decided to take it easy for now and see what opportunities arise.

"Here they are!" Jackson's son, Ryan, shouts and rushes over to us, giving us both a high five. "Happy anniversary!"

We make quick work of grabbing our coffees, then head out toward the pool, taking a seat at the sectional we keep outside. Ethan's in the pool with his and Jacob's daughter Olivia. She's sitting on an inflatable pool ring, giggling and splashing around excitedly. Jacob sits on the edge with his feet in the water, watching them both with love and adoration. They've taken to parenthood so well, and it's been such an honor to be included in their chosen family to be able to see Olivia grow up.

"It's about time you joined us!" Elliot calls out from where he's lying on his own inflatable pool float that's shaped like a pizza slice. "I was starting to wonder if we would see you today or whether it would be a private anniversary celebration." He wiggles his brows.

"We had a nice, chill morning," Carter replies and takes a sip of his coffee, not taking his bait.

Elliot raises a brow and smirks. "Oh, I'll bet."

"Don't act like you're all innocent, Olsen." I wag my finger.

"Oh, I never claimed to be. Why else do you think I put your washer on to clean my sheets?" He winks before turning his float around to face his partner, who simply shakes his head with a soft smile on his face.

I'm glad Elliot finally has someone who loves him unconditionally. He deserves it all.

We chat with the Kendricks as they get their two kids

ready for a day in the pool, and the Wildes as they get the kids covered in sunscreen. Blaine and Alex are in the cabana kitchen chopping some mangoes that I assume they picked from one of our trees. One of the other reasons why this house was so perfect. Fresh mangoes.

The only person who's missing is Peyton. His life shifted slightly when he became captain once Ethan retired, and this summer he had to stay back in Chicago. We've spoken to him on FaceTime a few times because we've been missing him, but there's always next year for him to visit.

The day is filled with laughter, dips in the pool, and amazing food, thanks to Elliot's partner and Ethan, and by the time the sun sets, the kids are fast asleep inside, and the adults are enjoying a drink under the clear night sky.

These last few years have been the happiest ever for me. Yeah, I got injured, and it changed my life because I'm never going to be free of migraines; it also changed my life in a completely different way. It gave me and Carter the opportunity to explore a new version of us. A version where I can love Carter the way I always dreamed I would. Fiercely, with no limitations. A version where he loves me back, so purely and entirely. There isn't a day that goes by where I'm not grateful for him and for the family we have around us.

I might not know what the future holds for me, but I know that as long as I have him by my side, I'll be the happiest man I can be.

"Come with me a sec," he whispers.

He stands up, and without a word, I follow him inside to our bedroom, where the moon basks the room in a soft glow.

"So, you know how our tradition has always involved Star Wars?" he begins.

"Yeah?"

"I wanted to do something special for our anniversary, and I was going through a few different ideas, then it came to me."

I'm half expecting him to reveal another LEGO Millennium Falcon box seeing as we couldn't bring the one we built while I was on IR as we didn't want to risk breaking it, but instead, he grabs my hand and leads me around to his side of the bed. He opens his bedside table drawer and pulls out a large velvet box, and as he returns to his full height, I recognize the box as the one that held both our wedding bands.

A few weeks back, Carter mentioned getting our rings cleaned. I didn't think anything of it at the time, but now I'm confused about what he's done with them.

Luckily, he doesn't keep me waiting. His eyes sparkle and his lips tilt up in a smile as he opens the box to reveal our wedding bands set in a cushion. They're similar to the platinum engagement band he gave me when he proposed, as I wanted us to match, and I often wear the black engagement band on a chain around my neck.

I look at the bands, then back at Carter, unable to see the difference.

"I don't get it?"

He laughs. "Let's go into the light so you can see."

We walk to the windows, and he holds the box up again, and that's when I see it. Engraved inside one of the bands are the words *I love you*. Inside the other, it says, *I know*.

My throat becomes tight as my eyes burn. I look back at

Carter, and his teeth are digging into his bottom lip, like he's nervous, but he's still grinning widely.

"You Han Solo'd our wedding bands?" I croak.

He nods. "Damn right, I did. I have been saying those words to you for as long as I can remember. It used to be because I loved you as my best friend, but now I say them because I *love* you."

A tear falls down my cheek. I'm quick to wipe it away before taking Carter's face between my hands. "I love you so fucking much, baby."

"I know, baby." He winks.

We both burst into laughter, and we slide each other's rings back on, just like we did one year ago, before pulling each other into a kiss.

I was ten years old when I fell in love with my best friend. Over the years I had to watch as the one I loved shared his life with other people who weren't me, but now…

Now, I finally get to call Carter Lockwood mine.

And if there's one thing I know for certain, it's that we were always meant to be together, in this life and every one after.

The End

To get a spicy Zach and Carter bonus scene, visit my website

https://www.jodioliver.com/bonus-content

About the Author

Jodi Oliver is a British author who writes MM sports romance, happily ever after guaranteed. She loves donuts, dogs and ice hockey, and when she hasn't got her head in a book or hiding in the writing cave, you can find her at an ice hockey game.

She lives in England but dreams of living in the Canadian countryside, with some highland cows and otters.

You can find her on Instagram @JodiOliverAuthor or in her Reader Group 'Jodi Oliver's Sin Bin'

JodiOliver.com

Chicago Thunder

Trade Deadline
(Blaine & Alex)

Off Season
(Ethan & Jacob)

Defensive Zone
(Zach & Carter)

Power Forward - coming early 2025

Acknowledgments

Zach and Carter have been living in my head for years. When I decided to create the Thunderverse, I tried to write their story first, but there was something in the back of my mind that was telling me they needed to wait. That they shouldn't go first, or even second. Then while I was writing Off Season, I knew they were ready to be next. I'm glad I waited because I fell in love with these two even more.

I couldn't have done it without some amazing people.

Rachel, thank you for being the best friend a girl could ask for. For picking me up when I struggled. For being my constant cheerleader and support beacon. I genuinely don't know how I would get through every day without you.

Becca, I'm so happy I have you in my life! Thank you for believing in me and supporting me, and I'm sorry for the endless tears I put you through. Here is to all the exciting things to come!

Emmy and Megan, for being the most wonderful betas and having the patience while I battled with my own migraines.

Leticia and Lori, thank you for polishing up my words and removing the commas I like to scatter like confetti.

The Sin Bin members, thank you for making my reader

group such a fun, incredible space. You make me smile every day, and I promise Elliot is coming!

Finally, thank you to *you*! Thank you from the bottom of my heart for picking up this book and reading Zach and Carter's story, and supporting me on this wild ride.

www.ingramcontent.com/pod-product-compliance
Lightning Source LLC
Chambersburg PA
CBHW051248210726
48287CB00002B/397